In the blink of an eye, Jack had placed the people in his charge in jeopardy.

Now he had to face his darkest hour.

The air was split again with screams of human pain that Jack would never have imagined, even in his worst nightmares. He heard a man, a young man, yelling for help on the other side of the ER. Jack wanted to cover his ears, but even if he could have, he knew he would never forget that scream for the rest of his life. It was so terrifying it sounded inhuman.

But above it all, he heard the high-pitched wail of a young girl's terror that turned his blood to ice.

"That's Aleah!" Jack growled as tears burned his swollen and bruised eyes.

A voice came over the loudspeaker. "Code Blue. Code Blue. Dr. Barzonni to the ER, stat."

Sophie glanced back at Jack with pleading eyes. "I want to help you, but I have to go to her."

Jack reached out his aching arm and motioned her away. "Save her, Sophie. Save her."

D1315343

Dear Reader,

Since I first conjured the inhabitants of Indian Lake, Sophie Mattuchi was a favorite because she was so complicated, intense and an audacious flirt. If you read *Heart's Desire*, book two in the Shores of Indian Lake series, you will remember that Sophie was Maddie Strong's rival for Nate Barzonni. Sophie went so far as to lose eight pounds, cut her hair and bleach it to look more like Maddie. The ploy didn't work, of course, because Nate only had eyes for Maddie. Then in book three, Sophie tried flirting with Nate's brother, Gabe. That didn't work, either.

Sophie's infatuation with being infatuated, combined with her dedication to cardiac nursing, could only ignite fireworks when she meets handsome Jack Carter in the ER on the night of a devastating car accident. An accident caused by a man high on drugs.

The battle against drug addiction is being fought in far too many families. Mine is no exception. The challenges facing parents are agonizing and daunting. Sophie's empathy toward addicts captured me. If you are a parent, I urge you to go to www.notmykid.org and make use of their guidance. Stopping drug addiction before it starts for your children is the wise course.

Sophie's Path also gave me an opportunity to peek back into the lives of some favorite characters in town: Mrs. Beabots, Sarah and Luke Bosworth and of course, Liz and Gabe Barzonni, who are about to give birth to their first child. Boy? Girl?

As always, I'd love to hear from you. Your comments have a strong influence on my upcoming stories. Visit me on Facebook, Twitter @cathlanigan, Pinterest, LinkedIn, Goodreads and my website, www.catherinelanigan.com.

Happy Reading!

Catherine

HEARTWARMING

Sophie's Path

—

Catherine Lanigan

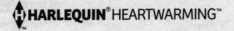

Recycling programs
for this product may
not exist in your area.

ISBN-13: 978-0-373-36798-6

Sophie's Path

Copyright © 2016 by Catherine Lanigan

Printed in U.S.A.

www.Harlequin.com

Catherine Lanigan knew she was born to storytelling at a very young age when she told stories to her younger brothers and sister to entertain them. After years of encouragement from family and high school teachers, Catherine was shocked and brokenhearted when her freshman college creative-writing professor told her that she had "no writing talent whatsoever" and that she would never earn a dime as a writer. He promised her that he would be her crutches and get her through his demanding class with a B grade so as not to destroy her high grade point average too much, *if* Catherine would promise never to write again. Catherine assumed he was the voice of authority and gave in to the bargain.

For fourteen years she did not write until she was encouraged by a television journalist to give her dream a shot. She wrote a six-hundred-page historical romantic spy thriller set against World War I. The journalist sent the manuscript to his agent, who then garnered bids from two publishers. That was nearly forty published novels, nonfiction books and anthologies ago.

Books by Catherine Lanigan

Harlequin Heartwarming

Fear of Falling
Katia's Promise
A Fine Year for Love
Heart's Desire
Love Shadows

MIRA Books

Dangerous Love
Elusive Love

Harlequin Desire

The Texan

Visit the Author Profile page
at Harlequin.com for more titles.

This book is dedicated to my late husband, Jed Nolan, my hero, my best friend, my love.

Acknowledgments

The days and nights of writing this book were difficult and a struggle for me because my husband was dying of leukemia. Much of this manuscript was written in his hospital room and then the hospice room. My heart was breaking and my mind was often distracted, though I continued to write. The gratitude I have for my editor, Claire Caldwell, who was able to take my "compilation of sheets of paper" and be my pathfinder to the core of this story that we both knew was there under too much exposition, is as deep as the ocean. Thank you and bless you, Claire, for being all that you are for me.

And to Victoria Curran and Dianne Moggy for the heartfelt empathy you had and have for me. You have been my champions and I honor and cherish that.

A special hug to Rula Sinara, my Heartwarming blog partner and "sister" of the heart, who answered my midnight texts from Rush Hospital in Chicago. To Kate James, who listened and emailed endlessly to a woman she barely knew, but to whom she extended her friendship and caring. At the time, none of us knew the outcome, but you were all there offering hope.

Always, to Lissy Peace, my agent of over two decades, love and more love.

To ALL my Heartwarming author sisters who sent flowers, cards, phone calls, emails, text messages, each and every one of you saved my sanity and allowed my heart to begin to heal.

God bless you every one.

CHAPTER ONE

JACK WAS AT the bottom of a dank, wet drainage tunnel. He smelled earth, rain and blood. It was dark and he couldn't see even a few inches in front of him. The ringing in his ears drowned out everything else. He felt as if there was something nibbling at his ankles. Rats? He hated rats. Just the thought of them made his stomach lurch. He tried to shake them off but couldn't move his legs. No, not rats. It was pain. Shooting, biting, sharp pain that now went careening up his calves.

His thoughts were confused and morphed into one another, creating a senseless universe. That was it, he reasoned. He'd been catapulted into some black hole. Floating. Spinning. Weightless.

And alone. Utterly, completely alone.

Except for the pain. The pain was his bedfellow. His traveling companion. It overtook his entire body now. His spine felt as if someone had shot it with molten steel. His skull pounded in agony. He couldn't open his eyes for fear that the tiniest beam of light would penetrate him like bullets.

Surely, he was dying.

This was what it was like at the end, he thought. Every cell in his body felt as if it had been shot with electricity strong enough to fry him to ash. No human could endure this kind of torture and live. No human would want to. This was the moment, that sliver of awareness that he was about to give up the ghost. And in his moment of choice, Jack knew it was okay to let go. Except for his sister and brother-in-law, he had no one. No wife. No children. No one would mourn him. He wouldn't be missed.

Then he heard a familiar male voice, though he couldn't place it.

"9-1-1? There's been an accident. Hurry. We're going to lose them!"

Like the high-pitched, irritating buzz of a mosquito, a voice reached into Jack's consciousness. Impossible as that was to accept, he struggled to figure out what it was saying.

"Jack? Can you hear me? Help is coming. Stay with me."

Jack had expected to talk to an angel upon dying, but this was a man's voice. A young man who sounded vaguely like the new recruit he'd hired for his insurance agency, Owen Jacobs. Yes. His mind slowly ground into gear.

"Jack," Owen said. "Can you hear the sirens?

The cops are here. The ambulance, too. It's going to be okay."

Jack didn't hear sirens. It took all his effort to listen to Owen's voice, which he was positive was coming to him from the other end of a tunnel. Jack wanted to answer Owen, but there was so much blood in his mouth, all he could do was choke, cough and spit. His tongue refused to obey his commands.

Now that he was a little more aware, though, his training kicked in. Apparently, even in his last minutes on earth, he was an insurance agent through and through. He wanted to know all the particulars. Where was he? What happened? Why was he paralyzed and in pain? And what was Owen doing here in this tunnel, if that's where they were? He wanted facts. Even if Owen was talking to him, Jack couldn't be sure he'd understood all the words. Each wave of pain smothered reality like a desert haboob that engulfs land, water and all living creatures. Jack's world now contained only himself and the pain. The incessant, unrelenting, excruciating pain.

For some reason he couldn't open his eyes. Something had glued them shut. He forced himself to listen, to make out even the faintest sounds, but Owen's voice had faded and all that was left were the surges of his pounding blood and rapidly beating heart. Mercifully, that one sound told him he was still alive. For the moment.

Just as Jack's mind was beginning to ease away the fuzzy edges of confusion, a searing, debilitating pain shot across his forehead, making him feel as if his eyes had just been scorched out of their sockets.

Everything went black. Jack was floating in the galaxies again.

SOPHIE MATTUCHI HAD a little over an hour before she began her weekend night shift as a cardiac nurse in the ER at Indian Lake Hospital. Sophie had signed on for the extra hours because the ER was shorthanded and because she saw the need. Sophie always saw the need.

Although it was an unusually foggy evening, she pulled on her running shoes, determined to fit in a run around the three-mile running trail that circled the lake. It had been a rainy and cold early June, and before that, she'd felt as if winter would never end after a record four-foot snow pack that stayed until late March. Still, she hadn't missed a single day's run since she'd taken up the sport two years ago to keep her weight under control and her mind off Louise Railton's extra creamy homemade ice creams. The city had installed LED street lights all along the trail that allowed fanatics like Sophie to run in just about any kind of weather.

Sophie had invested in the best running shoes, clothing and gadgets to track her fitness, and she'd downloaded motivational podcasts to listen to while she ran. There was nothing like starting her workdays or evenings with inspiring mantras to help her reinvent her life.

And these days, she was all about reinventing, restructuring, realigning and rebooting Sophie.

Ever since she'd kissed a very reluctant Scott Abbot in first grade, Sophie had been labeled the town flirt. For most of her life, she hadn't minded the moniker at all. She liked boys. A lot. She liked flirting and dating and being around men. She liked living in a man's world and she liked being as good as any man in her job. Sophie thought that men were more interesting than women, or at least she'd been telling herself that since high school because she'd never had many girlfriends. She was too busy dating two, three, four different guys in a single week. Sophie always took it upon herself to explore whatever world it was that her newest guy was into. Baseball, football, track, cars, boating, weight lifting. She didn't care. They liked her because she was "interested" and she loved their attention. The truth was that Sophie learned to be good friends—and often more—with all the guys she knew. They liked holding her hand and stealing kisses on the Tilt-A-Whirl at the county fair.

However, the moment anything started to get serious, Sophie moved on. It had been the only way to handle her life when she was in school. She'd been dead set on obtaining her degree, and nothing and no one could stand in her way.

When she graduated, she'd spent a year at a hospital in Grand Rapids then moved back in with her parents to help them with her aging grandmother. What Sophie thought was going to be a single summer at home while she applied to top hospitals in Chicago and Indianapolis had evolved into an entire year. One year had turned into five. Her biggest surprise had been landing her dream job with Dr. Caldwell and Nate Barzonni.

In all that time, Sophie's modus operandi for dealing with men never changed. She was an expert at getting a man's attention, but once she'd landed him, she threw him back. Catch and release.

Sophie had come to realize that her commitment phobia and the lighthearted, devil-may-care persona she put on for the world to see, was just flat boring. Like a hamster in a cage, she was spinning her wheels and getting nowhere with her life.

The problem was that in a small town where everyone knew everyone's business and had very long memories, her flirtatious ways had caused her to lose many people's respect. And that was unacceptable to her.

Sticking her earbuds in her ears, Sophie smiled to herself. She bent down to press her nose to her knees as she clasped the backs of her thighs. She'd made some real changes over the past year.

Running had become nirvana for her and for the first time she had the body she'd always wanted. These days when she got depressed, she headed for the lake trail instead of a dish of Louise's salted caramel and pecan ice cream. Her favorite store now was the organic farmer's market. She had stamina that she hadn't known before, and her weekend shifts at the ER, which could run as long as eighteen hours, didn't compromise her regular weekday workload helping Dr. Nate Barzonni with heart surgeries.

Despite all these changes, Sophie hadn't yet gotten a handle on love. She had no earthly idea how she'd overcome her bad habits, phobias and insecurities, but this was the year she'd start trying. Her self-help podcasts promised she could make it happen. She had to think differently and then she'd be able to make the right choices. She had to trust in the universe. Believe in the laws of attraction. Be the master of her own fate. Write her own script...

Her cell phone blared with an ambulance siren alert. It could only mean the ER was calling.

Sophie halted her run before it even started. She whipped the cell out of her shorts' pocket. "Mattuchi here."

The excited woman's voice on the other end said, "How fast can you get here? We have a multiple-car accident on its way in from Highway 421. Possible DOA."

"I'm there," Sophie shouted into the phone, already sprinting toward her car.

CHAPTER TWO

JACK CRAWLED OUT of the rabbit hole. Or maybe it was some kind of wartime trench. Lights were flashing like mortars and bombs exploded. But this wasn't war. He'd never been in a war, though he'd seen those kinds of movies. Maybe he was *in* a movie. No. Impossible. This wasn't the drainage tunnel either, because they'd moved him out of that.

But who were "they"?

"Can you hear me, Mr. Carter?" a woman asked in the softest, most melodious caress of a voice he'd ever heard. It came to him like the peals of church bells tumbling through a mountain valley, distant yet beckoning.

It had happened. He'd died. Life was over. *Pfft*. Just like that. And this voice was that of the angel sent from heaven or the beyond to take him to his new life. He was struck by the utter finality of it all.

A thousand regrets fluttered across his heart. Jack never thought of himself as a family man, but the first person he pictured was his sister, Ava.

He'd never see her again. Nor his brother-in-law and business partner, Barry. Would Ava be okay without her big brother Jack to watch out for her? Would Barry be able to handle the company without Jack's guidance? And what about his niece, Kaylee? She wasn't even a year old yet. He'd arranged for a bank account in her name to start her college fund. Ava and Barry were planning to come to Indian Lake for Katia's wedding. Jack had hoped to talk them into moving here. Or had he already done that?

Facts tumbled into Jack's brain like slow-falling snow. No, Ava and Barry still lived in Chicago, but Katia said she missed Ava a great deal and had investigated housing options for them, should they decide to make the move.

Now that Jack believed he was dying, he wished he'd pressed the issue more. He'd missed six months of little Kaylee's life. Suddenly, oddly, that realization was very important to him and the loss filled him with sadness.

He also realized how vital Katia was to him. She was more than his stellar salesperson, manager and second-in-command at the office. She was a dear friend. He loved her like a sister and she took care of him like he was her brother. Katia juggled her own life—right now, she was planning a wedding and a two-week honeymoon in Italy—managed his business, grew their sales and made certain that just about everything in Jack's world ran smoothly. How would he manage without her while she and Austin were on their honeymoon?

But if I'm dead, I won't care. Will I?

His head was a jumble of thoughts and he was having a difficult time sorting out the present from the past. He supposed that was to be expected, considering he was dying. Or was already dead. But how did he get here?

Jack's head felt like it was torn in two. Pain seared through his temples like a sizzling lance.

If he was dead, why was he in such agony? *Think, Jack. Think.*

A minute ago he was driving his car, though he couldn't remember where he was going. Then the squeal of his brakes, the thud of the initial impact with the other car; the grind, crunch and thunder of his car being mangled. And the voices. His voice—cursing. Owen shouting and cursing even louder than Jack. And Aleah's blood-curdling scream. Then soft whimpers. Then nothing.

Aleah. She was the reason he'd insisted on this seminar in Chicago today. Katia had hired Aleah to be an assistant. Sweet kid. Only twenty-one but with the wired kind of energy he could only get from a triple cappuccino at Cupcakes and Coffee. She didn't know a darned thing about insurance, but she was smart and so willing to please. Jack had wanted Aleah and Owen to learn as much as they could about the business as quickly as possible. Proper information and training were key. Jack didn't have time to teach them all he wanted them to know, and this seminar was perfectly timed for his needs.

Needs.

"...needing immediate attention," the angel voice said. "I'm so sorry if I cause you any more pain, Mr. Carter." Her voice brought him back to the present. "I have to clean the glass out of your eyes."

I'm not dying.

Hospital. I'm in a hospital.

She was wiping his mouth with a warm, wet cloth. With light dabs, she sponged at his nose and he realized that the musty smell he'd thought was the drainage tunnel had been the scent of his own blood. He heard, but did not see, the plinking sound of bits of glass as she plucked them away from his face and put them in a hard plastic container.

She leaned her face close to his and he smelled mint mouthwash and a floral perfume.

"Mr. Carter? I know you've been through a trial. The police said they had to use the Jaws of Life to get you and the woman out of the front seat."

Jaws of Life... Was he alive now? He thought

he was dead. Floating in the stars. No. He had to be alive because he felt excruciating pain.

"Aleah," he said, but her name came out like a choke and was indecipherable even to him.

"Mr. Carter, I'm so sorry if I'm hurting you. Am I hurting you?"

The angel's words somersaulted over each other and didn't make a lot of sense, and then Jack realized it wasn't the angel, it was the fact that his brain was working on slow track. But he didn't mind letting her voice wash over him. It took away his fears.

Impossible as it was, he clung to hope.

"I know it's difficult to talk. Just go slow, Mr. Carter. Try to say your name. Can you do that for me?" she urged.

He wanted to please her. He didn't know why, but he thought there might be some kind of judgment about all this. He lifted his tongue. "J-Jack."

"Wonderful," she breathed. "Marvelous." She smoothed the cloth over his right eye and continued to wash it before moving on to his left. "It's looking good. You'll probably need some stiches over your eyebrow and along your hairline. Can you open this eye for me?"

The struggle was like Sisyphus pushing his boulder up a mountain. His eyelid barely lifted and what little he could see swam in front of him like a school of silverfish on one of his snorkel dives in the Caribbean. "I'm—not blind?"

"No." She chuckled softly. "The blood and glass had matted them shut. I'm almost done with the other eye. I'm glad to see that no glass hurt this one." She continued cleaning his left eye then rinsed the cloth. She used what appeared to be a long pair of tweezers to remove a tiny flake of glass from his upper lash. "You have long lashes. Good thing. They helped to capture this little rascal."

She wore medical gloves, but he could feel her warmth as she traced her fingertip over the top of his left eyelid. "I think you should go ahead and open this eye for me now."

Jack couldn't believe the enormity of his task. If he opened his eye and didn't see, what would he do? How would he cope? Would he have to have surgery? What if there was no cure?

"You'll be just fine," she assured him, touching his forearm and holding his hand in hers. "I'm right here." She offered him more comfort and more confidence than he'd thought possible. He realized he was deeply afraid.

He finally managed to get his eye open, and as he looked at her he realized that in some sacred part of him, he'd hoped this was heaven, and that she might be an angel. Yet his slow and beleaguered consciousness affirmed that he was alive. As his eyes focused through swollen and bruised lids, he saw a beautiful stranger with an illuminated smile and dark eyes that promised a universe filled with hope.

"Hello, Jack," she said with that voice he knew would haunt him for the rest of his life, even if he never saw her again.

She had a heart-shaped face; naturally, being an angel of mercy and saving lives, she would be all heart. She wore a white lab coat over maroon scrubs. Her name tag rested over her right side, heart pocket.

S. Mattuchi. RN.

"Nurse Mattuchi?" Jack mumbled, feeling a jagged pain saw through his head.

"You can call me Sophie. The doctor has ordered more tests for you. I've assured him your heart is stellar." She leaned close.

Jack caught a floral scent in her dark hair as she fluffed his pillow and continued talking.

"Hearts are my specialty," she continued. "I'm a cardiac surgical nurse, but I help out in the ER when they need me." She pulled away and added, "I was off duty but came immediately when I got the call about you and your friends."

Friends?

Suddenly, Jack's mind was alert and the jumbled pieces of information in his brain fell into place. He moved his sluggish and swollen tongue.

"Owen and Aleah?" He reached for Sophie's forearm and squeezed it anxiously. "Tell me."

"Owen is just fine. A broken collarbone and a few bruises. Aleah is being examined by the doctor right now, as is the driver of the other car. We were quite worried about you. You were unconscious and I was afraid you'd been blinded."

"What else— I mean…" He closed his eyes and felt a scratch across his eyeballs as if they were filled with sand. Even the most minute movement was so difficult. "Please. Sophie. What else happened?"

"You have whiplash. No broken bones, but your ankle is sprained. No internal injuries. We'll keep you overnight for observation. That concussion is dangerous. The neurosurgeon will be down later to check on you and she'll probably order a CT scan."

"Neurosurgeon?" Jack's fear meter leaped to high alert.

"We have to make sure there are no blood clots or other damage. Best to cover our bases. Yours and ours."

Jack tried to nod and failed. "Good thinking." He paused for a moment. Words were reluctant to move from his brain to his lips. "Your insurance carrier will commend you for your prudence."

Her expression was quizzical. "I wasn't thinking of our liability—I only want what's best for all our patients."

"Don't...take me wrong—" Jack tried to sit up but failed. He slumped back on the pillows. He groaned as he tried to touch his aching head, but when he lifted his arm he saw the IV and several butterfly bandages over a nasty gash in his forearm. A fleeting worry about scarring shot through his mind, but he dismissed it. He'd come razor-close to losing his eyesight. He was thankful that, in all likelihood, he'd walk away from this with some scars on his arm, a badly sprained ankle and a headache.

A beep went off in Sophie's lab coat pocket. Anxiety distorted her pretty features and suddenly her entire demeanor changed. Her motions were brusque, hurried, but exact as she tore a plastic wrapper away from a disposable hypodermic needle. She dabbed gauze with alcohol and cleaned his IV site, then took the IV line, unhooked it and cleaned both ends of the plastic connections before injecting a vial of medication into his IV. "This will help with the pain," she said, glancing into the hallway. She turned back to him. "This is your call button if you need anything. I know you must be thirsty, but we can't let you have anything to eat or drink for a while. If you feel nauseous, you hit that button immediately. Do you understand?"

Jack nodded, disconcerted by her stern tone, and suddenly realized that the soothing melody of her voice had distracted him from what was going on in the rest of the ER. Sophie peered through Jack's privacy curtain, and he heard what sounded like dozens of people all talking at the same time. Orders were being shouted. Someone was rattling off clipped, terse instructions. Rubber-soled shoes and sneakers pounded against the linoleum floor. Wheels of gurneys wobbled and screeched.

Though it sounded like pandemonium to Jack, an outsider, he knew these were professionals. He believed in this hospital and its very qualified staff. After all, it was only a few months ago, thanks to Katia Stanislaus's expertise, that he and his company had landed the insurance contract for the Indian Lake Hospital. He'd met with President Emory Wills himself. Jack also knew cardiac surgeon Nate Barzonni personally. He was an excellent surgeon and could have had his pick of positions at Sloan-Kettering in New York, but being the altruistic man he was, Nate chose to divide his work between the Indian reservations up in Michigan and here in Indian Lake.

It eased Jack's nerves to know that he, Owen and Aleah were in very capable hands.

Still, Jack wanted to talk to somebody who knew what had happened to him and his employees in the fog on Highway 421 tonight. Had he gone off the road? Had he fallen asleep? Was this his fault? What could have caused all this suffering?

Just considering that he could be responsible in the slightest degree was intolerable. Guilt flooded him like a tsunami, taking over his thoughts and causing more agony than his physical pain.

His whole life, he'd tried to do the right thing in every circumstance. From striving to live up to his marine father's demanding and impossible expectations to taking care of his sister and mother after his father's death. He chose insurance as a career to help others protect their lives and their possessions. Jack Carter was a guardian.

In the blink of an eye, he had placed the people in his charge in jeopardy.

Now Jack had to face his darkest hour.

Just then, the air was split again with screams of human pain that Jack would never have imagined, even in his worst nightmares. He heard a man, a young man, yelling for help. Then he screamed again with such agony, Jack thought he must be torn in two. Jack wanted to cover his ears, but even if he could have, he knew he would never forget that scream for the rest of his life. It was so terrifying it sounded inhuman.

But above it all, he heard the high-pitched wail of a young girl's terror that turned his blood to ice.

"That's Aleah!" Jack growled as tears burned his swollen and bruised eyes.

A voice came over the loudspeaker. "Code Blue. Code Blue. Dr. Barzonni to the ER, stat."

Sophie glanced back at Jack with pleading eyes as she burst away from his bedside. She flung back the curtain and said, "I want to help you, but I have to go to her."

Jack reached out his aching arm to Sophie and motioned her away. "Save her, Sophie. Save her."

CHAPTER THREE

SOPHIE RUSHED AROUND the nurse's station to the ER bay on the opposite side. Bart Greyson, an RN with a decade of ER experience, had just gone in there with a stainless steel defibrillator cart.

Bart ran the ER with an iron fist and more stamina than the entire staff combined. He could pull over forty-eight hours on duty with only a half dozen, ten-minute catnaps while sitting at his computer. Bart had brains, insight and skill…and a case of Red Bull in his locker. He was a legend at Indian Lake. No one second-guessed Bart or his orders.

"You're the first of the cardiac team here," Bart said to Sophie as he shoved a medical chart into her hands.

"Dr. Barzonni is on call?" Sophie asked, never taking her eyes from her patient.

"I just got word he's upstairs with an emergency surgery. We've paged Dr. Caldwell. I left a message at the nurse's station, as well. I don't know who will show up," Bart replied with a huff of exhaustion. He stuck his hands on his hips.

"Figures. It's a full moon. It's always an asylum here during a full moon."

Sophie gently lifted Aleah's eyelid and examined her. "I heard her scream but she's unconscious," Sophie observed.

"She was unconscious on arrival and except for that one time, she's been unresponsive."

Sophie turned to the defibrillator. "She's in arrest?"

"No. Arrhythmia. The Code Blue was for the other victim. Dr. Hill had to leave Aleah and see to the John Doe. He was the driver of the other car. The cops are working on getting an ID for us."

Sophie had worked with Dr. Eric Hill nearly every weekend since she'd begun her ER duties six months ago.

Dr. Hill was five years past his internship and residency at Cook County Hospital in Chicago. He'd told Sophie that in those five years, he felt he'd seen everything emergency medicine could throw at a person. He'd come to Indian Lake for a change of pace. Well, he'd gotten it. Unless there was a major accident like this one, most weekends in the ER were run-of-the-mill household accidents—falls or injuries with tools—and relatively minor illnesses where the patients or their parents didn't have medical insurance.

Sophie watched Dr. Hill and three nurses work

on a tall, overweight man in the next bay. He appeared to be in his late thirties. "He's hardly got a scratch."

"Drug overdose. Cops said he had heroin in the car with him and as the paramedics were tending to the three other victims, he shot up."

"How are they bringing him down?"

"Paramedics gave him naloxone on site. Nasal spray was all they had. They didn't get to him right away because he didn't seem injured, just confused. It wasn't until he dropped to his knees and passed out that they noticed the dilated pupils and white patches on his mouth. Once they got him here, we gave him more naloxone by injection. What a mess." Bart shook his head but continued to work.

Sophie scanned Aleah's reed-thin, very still body while two other members of the ER team hurried in to assist. Donna Jessup was one of Sophie's coworkers on Dr. Caldwell's team and worked one weekend a month in the ER. With her was Rob Seymore, a lab technician who quickly began drawing blood for the usual tests.

Aleah's brown hair was matted to her head with glass and blood, much like Jack's had been. She was still in her street clothes, though her blouse had been cut away and twelve electrodes had been placed on her chest.

"Donna, did you run an EKG yet?" Sophie asked.

"We had another cardiac patient just after these accident patients. It's been bedlam, but I'm on it. I'm on it." Donna attached the leads and turned on the EKG machine. She held the printout. "Infarction and atrial fibrillation."

"A-fib?" Sophie circled the gurney and studied the printout. "Did Dr. Hill order an echocardiogram?"

Rob continued, "Yes. He was in the middle of examining her when the other patient started convulsing. And his heart stopped."

Sophie flipped the pages of Aleah's chart as Bart continued.

"Dr. Hill said Aleah's suffered a blunt chest trauma which is quite obvious from the bruising. He ordered the requisite round of tests."

"Did he mention cardiac contusion?"

Bart and Donna shook their heads.

"No, but it's my guess…" Donna winced. "Sorry. It's not my place to—"

"Don't apologize." She held up her hand, though she didn't take her eyes off the chart. "If she's ruptured the cardiac chamber or if there's a disruption of the heart valve that could be the cause of her dysrhythmia."

Sophie assessed more of Aleah's condition. Her skin was growing more pale and gray by the second. The bruises on her chest were turning a deep purple. Sophie pressed lightly on Aleah's ribs. "She's broken nearly every rib on the right side."

"Dr. Hill thinks her lung may be punctured," Bart said. "He ordered thoracentesis." He began inserting the catheter into Aleah's chest while Sophie went around to the other side of the bed.

Sophie stuck the earpieces of her stethoscope into her ears and listened to Aleah's chest. It rattled like a freight train and Aleah's breathing was labored. She was bleeding internally, but until all the tests were run, they wouldn't know the extent of the damage.

In the meantime, they had to get her stabilized. Aleah's chest cavity was filling with blood and fluid, which would be putting pressure on her heart and lungs. Sophie didn't want to guess how much time they had to prevent respiratory arrest or another—this time deadly—heart attack.

First, she needed do a thorough examination. In a trauma case like this, every nanosecond counted.

Sophie glanced at Bart as he continued to work. "She's lost a lot of blood. Transfusion?"

"It just came down from upstairs." He nodded to the stainless steel counter where the IV bag of blood sat. Donna was rushing with her EKG cart out of the bay. "Sophie, can you hook up the plasma for me?"

Immediately, Sophie attached the plasma bag to the IV and regulated the monitor. Then she felt for Aleah's pulse. It was almost imperceptible it was so weak.

Bart finished with the catheter and Sophie turned to him. "Her chart says that she was born in this hospital. She had coronary artery abnormalities at birth." She paused as Bart nodded gravely. "I'll need Dr. Barzonni to confirm, but because of the trauma to the chest wall, blood flow to her heart could be severely diminished."

As she spoke, she saw Nate Barzonni race into the ER. Dr. Hill quickly gave him the specifics about the addict's condition. They both hung over the patient, assessing.

Sophie had worked with Nate for over a year now, and she knew his professional moves better than anyone. Though Nate always showed an implacable expression to his staff and the patient, when he raised his left eyebrow even a fraction, it meant he was concerned. If he dipped his chin to his chest, his brain was analyzing input like a computer. The longer his head remained bowed, the more difficult the case. The minute his head snapped up, Nate had made his diagnosis and decisions on how to proceed.

While Nate's head was still lowered, the attending nurse said, "Blood pressure is ninety over fifty. Pulse is dropping, as well. Fifty. Forty-eight. Doctor, I have no pulse!"

The addict's heart monitor flatlined. The alarms

beeped. Sophie's head shot up. Most people thought those sounds signaled pandemonium, but to her it meant action. All hands on deck. It was the moment when everyone's skills, talents and expertise were paramount. They were like fine-tuned mechanics in a precision Swiss watch. Each cog, each spring was essential to the whole. Except they were not marking time as a clock would. They were racing against time. Trying to beat it to save a life.

"Defibrillator!" Nate shouted. He locked eyes with Sophie and nodded abruptly, with almost a jerk.

Sophie turned to Bart. "I'm going with Dr. Barzonni. You got this?"

"Go!" Bart said and continued his efforts to stabilize her.

As Sophie rushed between the beds, her gaze shot across the room. Jack Carter was sitting ramrod straight in the bed, staring at the action around him. His eyes bore into hers. For a fleeting second she thought she could read his mind.

What about Aleah?

Icy chills shot down her spine. She nearly turned and went back, but Nate needed her. The patient did, too. Once in the bay, she sprang into action. She pulled the paddles out of the defibrillator dock and spread them with lubricating gel. She handed the paddles to Nate. Holding her breath, she stood back as he placed one paddle on the left side of the man's heart. The other he placed to the right over the sternum.

"Clear!" Nate said loudly as the attending nurse and Dr. Hill backed away.

Sophie hit the defibrillator's button and watched the needle on the monitor jump as the electrical shock was discharged into the dying man.

The patient's barrel chest heaved. His back arched as it rose off the gurney with the shock and then flopped back down. He remained still. Nate listened to his heart with the stethoscope. He checked the monitor.

Still flatlined.

Dr. Hill's eyes were filled with defeat. He spun on his heel and rushed over to Aleah.

Sophie knew Dr. Hill was desperate to save all his patients. This loss was going to hit him hard.

"Again!" Nate said and presented the paddles to Sophie for more lubrication gel. He positioned the paddles.

"Clear!"

Sophie's eyes were wide as she depressed the defibrillator's button again. The monitor jumped.

This time the man's body arched only slightly.

"Epinephrine!" Nate barked, holding out his hand for the vial that Sophie knew was the last hope.

Sophie reached over to the stainless steel tray where one of the nurses had already prepared the syringe. She grabbed it and properly placed it in Nate's hand the way she did with all his surgical instruments. They worked well together. She knew it. And she knew he knew it, too.

Nate jammed the long needle straight into the patient's heart and depressed the plunger. Sophie watched as the lifesaving serum left the syringe and hopefully did its job.

She checked the monitor.

Flatlined.

She hit the blood pressure machine hoping it would show even the tiniest indication of life.

Nothing.

Nate put his stethoscope to the man's chest. Sophie knew what he was hoping to find—a blip. An echo. A whisper of life.

Nate straightened. He shook his head.

"I need you in the next bay, Doctor. She's cardiac contusion I believe, with a history of dysfunctional coronary arteries from birth," Sophie said to Nate.

"How old?"

"Twenty-one. Punctured lung. We're doing thoracentesis now. She's A-fib," Sophie explained in soft but professional tones as they walked over to where Aleah clung to life.

Sophie struggled not to glance over at Jack, but noticed he was now sitting on the side of his gur-

ney, legs over the side, hands clenched on the edge
of the bed. He looked like a man ready to bolt.

His eyes were dark with anger, pain and confusion. She saw his mouth move. She realized that
the word he kept saying was "Please."

Bart handed the catheter over to Dr. Hill. They
had now siphoned over a quart of fluid from
Aleah's chest cavity.

"Sophie," Dr. Hill said. "Take over for me. Bart,
get Donna back here."

Bart bolted from the bay.

Sophie went to work while Dr. Hill and Nate
conferred. Nate listened to Aleah's heart.

Sophie depressed the button on Aleah's blood
pressure machine, which squeezed the cuff on her
upper arm. "Ninety-five over sixty." She looked
up at Nate. "She should be improving with the
tube in her chest. Not getting worse."

Sophie needed Nate's brilliance to take the lead
in Aleah's case. The girl's lips were turning blue.
Sophie took her pulse and then her blood pressure once again to be certain. "She's dropping."

Suddenly, the heart monitor flatlined.

"Get me those paddles!" Nate motioned to the
defibrillator at the head of the gurney.

Sophie grabbed the paddles, lubricated them
and handed them to Nate, who placed them on
Aleah's chest.

Just as she'd done only minutes ago, she pressed the button to send the electrical current into Aleah's body.

Sophie felt as if she were falling over a rushing waterfall. The sounds in the room, the alarm of the heart monitor, Dr. Hill's voice and Nate's commands swam together and created an undecipherable cacophony. Her motions were rote.

Sophie could almost feel Aleah's soul leaving her body. She glanced above Aleah's head to see if there were any odd lights in the room. Her grandmother had told her that souls exited the body through the top of the head. Probably an old wives' tale from Italy. But something was happening here. Sophie could feel it.

Nate shocked Aleah's body a second time, but to no avail. Again, he called for the injection of epinephrine and Sophie watched as he rammed it into Aleah's small chest.

Aleah was completely lifeless, but Nate didn't give up. He placed the paddles again and commanded Sophie to hit the button.

The heart monitor was still flatlined.

They'd lost. Death had won. The monitor's long, droning alarm was telling her she hadn't performed her duties correctly.

Dark thoughts filled her mind, putting an acrid taste in her mouth. She couldn't find the strength to beat them back to their cave.

She felt utterly inadequate. She wished she'd continued with school. She should have become a doctor. Maybe with more knowledge she would have known how to save this young woman. Though she was certain that Aleah's chances had been worse than the man in the next bay, and he hadn't made it, either.

Sophie blinked slowly. Time trudged forward as though she was moving through a thick gelatin. She felt weightless and leaden simultaneously. She would have liked to sit right down on the floor and go to sleep.

"Nurse Mattuchi!" Nate shouted.

"Yes, Doctor?" Sophie snapped out of it. Whatever *it* was.

"Are you okay?" He pulled off his latex gloves.

She looked down at Aleah's lifeless body. "She…"

"Never had a chance," Nate said. "I'm surprised she lasted this long. Your assessment was on target. So was Dr. Hill's. I also think she was anorexic."

Sophie's eyes flew to Aleah's body. She understood what Dr. Barzonni was saying. The improper balance of electrolytes alone, in an anorexic person, was enough to bring on a heart attack. Aleah had a congenital heart condition, anorexia and blunt chest trauma. "I thought she was rather thin. It just didn't register."

"This was a massive trauma. She was hit very hard. I'll get more about it from the cops outside. But with her birth defect and the punctured lung…" He shook his head and put his hand on her shoulder. "You did all you could."

"I wonder…" she started.

"No," Nate said and turned to Dr. Hill. "Eric, you and I will have a lot of paperwork. Do you know if either family is here?"

"Just the girl's," Bart interrupted. "We're still searching for the John Doe's family. He was driving without a wallet or any papers. Maybe the cops have an update."

"I'll talk to the police," Dr. Hill said.

"And I'll handle Aleah's family," Nate volunteered.

"We still have Mr. Carter here overnight," Dr. Hill said. "Nurse Mattuchi, you're on duty?"

"Yes, Doctor. I'll see to him."

"I want a CT scan. I want no other—" He swallowed hard. "You know what I mean."

"I do," she replied, softly feeling a flood of empathy for both these highly trained professionals who had lost not one, but two patients in a matter of minutes.

Sophie checked the clock. It had only been twenty-five minutes since all three victims had been brought in. She'd been assigned to Jack Carter first. She'd spent fifteen of those minutes with him. Then five minutes with Aleah before the John Doe flatlined. In the final five minutes, they'd lost both of them.

Time. Sophie had never taken time for granted. She trained hard and worked hard. She spent time with her family and helped them out whenever she could. But this absurd, needless loss of two lives shocked her to her core. Aleah had only been twenty-one. The man was in his late thirties. They both had a lot of life in front of them. They could do anything they wanted to with their time. Laugh. Love. Try to find happiness and joy...

Odd that Sophie would think of happiness at a time like this, but she did. She felt tears fill her eyes as she covered Aleah's body, but not her face, with the sheet. Her parents would want to come in to see her. Sophie would meet with them and try to comfort them. She hoped she would find the right words to say. Good words. Or maybe no words. Maybe they would just ask her to go away.

Sophie wiped the tears off her cheeks with her fingertips. She wasn't just crying for this young woman. She was crying for herself. She believed she'd done all she could as part of the team tonight. These were tears of self-pity. They came from a deep and lonely place inside of her. A place she seldom visited and barely acknowledged. She guessed these tears had been trying to form for a long time, but she'd told herself that crying was for weaklings. She was strong. She was able to handle just about anything, including injury, illness and death.

But happiness? That was really tough.

Sophie's twenties were nearly behind her and she'd done little to grab happiness for herself.

She couldn't afford to wait any longer. Tonight had shown her how lives could be snatched away in an instant. Oh, she'd begun her self-evaluations and internal makeover, but she'd only stuck the spade into the first few inches of her psyche. She had a lot of digging to do before she'd find treasure.

For the first time, though, she thought she knew what she was looking for.

Happiness.

She just hoped she recognized it when she uncovered it.

CHAPTER FOUR

JACK WAITED ON teetering legs for some definitive word about Aleah. He'd heard the commotion. He'd heard the second round of instructions for a defibrillator. He'd heard the second heart monitor announce the dreaded flatline bleep, but he couldn't see around the heads of the doctors and nurses. He watched people going in and racing out. Then suddenly, they all stopped moving and became still.

Aleah was dead.

Jack's mouth had gone dry and his blood had turned cold. It had been a long time since he'd experienced death that was close to him. Not since his father died. He'd mourned him deeply, but his father had battled cancer for over two years. The family had expected him to die. He'd been prepared.

Jack battled the biting tears and thunder in his chest. He'd liked being a mentor to Aleah. She and Owen were only a decade or so younger than he, but right now, he felt ancient.

All his concerns from earlier in the day came

back to him suddenly: his banter with his sister and brother-in-law, his anxiety over the White Sox's loss to the Yankees. Even the ambitions he'd been mulling over after the seminar seemed trivial compared to what he was facing now. He would give everything he had to save his sweet, unsuspecting assistant from death.

He pinched the bridge of his nose. This shouldn't have happened. It was a mistake. Some cruel trick of the universe. And it was hitting Jack hard.

He wished he felt stronger because he wanted to do something. He was so confused, and Jack was seldom confused. He prided himself on his ability to stay focused. Responsible. That's what everyone in his family had called him. He was their rock. He was the leader.

If only he could remember the accident. Maybe he could have prevented it, but the pieces of his memory were as vague as the fog he'd been driving through.

Jack watched as Nate Barzonni shuffled down the hall with a somber face, his hands shoved into the pockets of his surgical scrubs. He moved like a man carrying a cross. Jack knew Nate and Maddie Barzonni both. He was almost a daily customer at Cupcakes and Coffee. Maddie's brew was legendary and her made-to-order cupcakes and icings were his must-have indulgence.

Jack hobbled to the entry of his bay. A sharp pain made a jagged path up his calf.

His ankle hurt more than he'd anticipated. "Nate, please. What happened?" He had so many questions.

Nate barely glanced at him, giving him a dismissive nod. Then Jack saw the raw pain in Nate's eyes. He understood.

"Jack, I'm sorry about your assistant. Real sorry. But I have to see her parents. Is that okay?" Nate choked out the words and shook his head sorrowfully. "I can't…not right now."

"It's okay," Jack replied empathetically.

Nate gave Jack a slight wave and then practically jogged to the ER exit doors.

Jack had never seen Nate like this. How often did a doctor lose a patient? Once a year? Once a month? And Nate had lost two in a matter of minutes. How did a doctor, with years of training and the most up-to-date studies and research, handle something like this? Did they take it personally? Even if there was nothing more they could do, this had to feel like a failure. Did it affect them emotionally?

As far as Jack could tell the rest of the staff went about their work as if nothing had happened. Except for Nate, Jack hadn't seen one iota of remorse from the other doctor or the nurses. He told himself they had work to do. Serious work. But it still stung.

Jack felt hollow. He glanced at the bed and wondered how he'd make it back under his own steam.

"Mr. Carter," Sophie addressed him professionally as she rushed toward him. "What are you doing? You're not supposed to be walking around yet. It's dangerous. You have to stay in bed."

She put her hands on his shoulders, and with more strength and force than he'd thought possible, she led him to the bed and pressed him into it. He sat on the edge, refusing to lie down.

"What happened to Aleah?" he asked.

"Cardiac arrest."

Jack felt as if he'd been punched in the gut. Aleah's heart was young, but that wasn't enough to keep her alive. He lifted his eyes to Sophie.

She was composed and self-assured. Yeah, she was good. He had to give her that.

He felt hollow, yet his insides burned with the unfairness of it all.

He balled his fist. Flexed it. Balled it again.

She bent over and grabbed his ankles, favoring his sprain, and spun his legs up and onto the cot. "We have to get that CT scan. Dr. Hill is concerned…"

Jack pounded the gurney with his fist.

"Concerned? About me? He should have been *concerned*—" Jack nearly spit the word out "—when he had a chance to save Aleah. Maybe you should

have been, too. You left her to go to that monster…
that addict who killed her."

Sophie's jaw dropped. "How did you know he
was an addict?"

Jack jerked his head toward the ER entry doors
where two policemen stood talking to Dr. Hill.
"Cops. They said they have to get a statement from
me."

"Not yet. You have to rest."

"I'm not taking orders from you—"

She placed three fingers over his lips. "Shh.
Don't say something you'll regret," she whispered.

"Regret? I'm not the one with regrets. *You* let
Aleah die," he growled.

Sophie's eyes widened with shock. "That man,
that patient—" She stumbled.

Jack could see her ire rising as she continued.
"He'd gone into cardiac arrest. At that very same
moment, Aleah was holding on. My colleagues
were stabilizing her. My judgment was that we
had a chance to save them both."

"Well, your judgment was incorrect. Your *judgment* was skewed." Now that Jack's anger was ignited, he couldn't stop himself. "Frankly, I don't
know where your priorities are. An addict who
nearly killed all three of us and *did* kill Aleah,
made the choice to drive high. He didn't deserve
your concern, or Dr. Hill's." Jack was so filled
with rage that he felt light-headed. He wasn't sure

if he'd made his point, so he balled his fist again and slammed it against the bed. The plastic beneath him crackled.

Jack felt woozy as he stared at his hand. How practical of hospitals to put plastic under the thin sheets. Plastic. So that the blood wouldn't ooze through when a person bled out. Plastic protected the mattress but did nothing to save the patient. Plastic, like the black bags they used to take bodies to the morgue.

"Plastic," Jack mumbled as he dropped his head back onto the pillow.

"Mr. Carter? Jack? Can you hear me?"

He knew his eyes were rolling around because the room was spinning.

He heard Sophie dash over to the nurse's station.

"Doctor Hill. Stat!" she yelled into the intercom.

Jack hated that his head injury was getting in the way of his tirade. That's exactly what it was, he realized. He was accusing the hospital and its staff of bad practice. He didn't know if it was malpractice, but he blamed them all the same.

Aleah was dead. A terrifying fact that he knew he still hadn't come to grips with.

"Doctor Hill, I think he's in shock," Sophie said, though he couldn't see her anymore. Where did she go? She was just here a minute ago. Now the room was dark. Vacant. Like that drainage tunnel he'd been in before. That was it. He'd gone back to the place where it all started.

Maybe he'd find some answers there. Perhaps even solace.

SOPHIE TOOK JACK'S blood pressure while Dr. Hill examined him.

"He's asleep. I would be out cold myself if I'd been through all that he has tonight. Take him down for the CT scan. He'll wake up once he's there."

Sophie chewed her bottom lip as Dr. Hill straightened. "What?"

"Jack—er, Mr. Carter thinks we were negligent with Aleah. He thinks we should have let the other patient die in order to treat her."

"Good thing Mr. Carter doesn't run this hospital. We used our best judgment. We're not divine. We do the best we can." Dr. Hill touched Sophie's shoulder. "Besides, Mr. Carter here should be singing your praises. If it hadn't been for you getting that glass out of his eyes, he could have been severely impaired."

"He doesn't know that. He thinks I was simply cleaning him up."

Dr. Hill raised his chin and peered at her. "I don't mind setting him straight. Be glad to do it, especially if he's accusing us—"

She put up her hand to interrupt. "Not us. He's questioning *me*."

Dr. Hill squeezed her shoulder gently and smiled. "Don't take it so hard. He's had a very rough night. You know as well as I do that irritability is a sign of concussion. He's confused and has complained to Bart Greyson of both double vision and sensitivity to light. Oh, by the way, I'll order an EEG, as well."

Sophie was surprised because an EEG was only required when the patient had been having seizures. "Yes, Doctor."

"I realize it's overly cautious, but just in case this fellow is more than simply irritable and decides to follow through with a malpractice suit, I want our examination to be as thorough as possible."

Sophie hated how the medical world had been forced to adapt to the tort wars. Extraneous tests were performed as a standard course of action in even the simplest cases. A broken toe, if not properly x-rayed and treated, followed up on, double-checked and documented could cost the hospital hundreds of thousands of dollars in lawsuits. Sophie despised the whole system. The paperwork and extra steps she had to perform for the administration, which, rightfully, was trying to keep the entire hospital safe, took time away from her patients.

Her eyes dropped to Jack. *Patients like Jack.*

When she'd been tending him, she'd felt a pleasant and approachable energy that instantly caused her to like him. He'd looked at her with the anguish and wariness she often saw in patients. She'd sensed she was his link to the world in that moment. It wasn't the first time Sophie had seen that deep pleading, felt the clutch of fingers around her wrist or witnessed a tear slide down a lonely cheek. But there was something else…

When she'd placed her fingers over his lips, she'd intuited his tenderness. She didn't actually know anything about him except his blood type, blood pressure, height and weight, but she believed he was a gentle man.

That was why she'd been quite shocked when he'd turned on her. He was an enigma and that fascinated her.

"You're right, Doctor. It's best to be safe."

"Cover our butts," he replied, moving toward the curtain. "Page me when you're back down from Radiology. And don't let him sleep any more than two hours at a time."

She chuckled. "That won't be a problem. This is a hospital."

BY SATURDAY MORNING, Sophie was wired on too many cups of bitter break-room coffee and a late-night cafeteria meal that didn't sit well. The ER had been calm after the turmoil of the car accident. That alone was a blessing, she thought. Most of the staff went about their paperwork and duties with solemn faces, their thoughts easily readable in their anguished eyes. Sophie wasn't sure how many people died on ER tables typically. She'd only been working in the ER for a little over six months, but in a small town where everyone knew everyone else, or at least their business, death touched them all

Bart, who had just come back on duty, scurried from bay to bay, reviewing Donna and Bob's documentation in patient charts and checking in with the pharmacy about orders he'd placed. Though Bart appeared to have put the tragedies behind him, Sophie suspected his actions were all a cover-up.

She'd spent nearly the entire night with Jack Carter. She took his vitals every hour. Woke him up and forced him to drink water. She helped him to the bathroom and helped him back to bed. Jack shirked off her assistance at first, but when he realized he was dizzy and his legs were still wobbly, he insisted Sophie get him another nurse. Sophie tried to grant his wish, but she was told they were short-staffed. He was stuck with her.

Now Sophie was bringing Jack his dismissal papers, a list of follow-up appointments and home-care instructions, prescription Tylenol for the headaches he complained about and fresh gauze and bandages for his lacerations.

He was sitting up with two pillows behind his back. "Who put me in this gown?" he demanded roughly.

Sophie smiled. "Good morning to you, too."

"Was it you?"

"Yes." She wouldn't let him intimidate her with his sour expression. His dark stubble enhanced his good looks, even though his eyes were still so swollen and bruised he could easily be mistaken for a boxer who'd lost a match. She stopped abruptly.

She thought he was handsome? Where had *that* thought come from?

Don't go there, Sophie.

Jack Carter was her patient. That was all. He was certainly not the type of guy she would have had a fling with in the past. He was very, very different. For one, he despised her right now. And two, it was unethical to date patients. And she was done with flings, anyway.

Jack bristled. "Where'd you put my clothes?"

"In the closet. What's left of them, that is. I didn't have time to send them out to the laundry if that's what you want to know. But I did go down to the gift shop to buy you a T-shirt."

She opened the plastic bag and pulled out a pink breast cancer T-shirt with the looped ribbon logo on the front. "It was all they had. I got a large."

"It's pink." He reached out and snatched it from her hand, his lips twitching. "My mother says I look good in pink."

"I'm sure you do." Sophie smiled. "I'll help you get dressed."

Jack threw his hands up. "No thanks! I think you've seen enough. Who knows what you checked out while I was sleeping."

"Mr. Carter, I'm a nurse. It's my job. I stayed with you most of the night to make sure you didn't slip into a coma."

"Coma?" His eyes widened as much as they could with stitches and swelling. "You guys were afraid I would fall into a coma?"

"We had to take precautions, yes. Several times you, er, fell asleep on us."

"Passed out. I remember," he said, touching his forehead and wincing. He patted the dressings around his eyes then made a face. "I bit my cheeks, as well." He hugged himself, his muscular arms flexing.

Sophie dragged her eyes off his battered face. She was drawn to his vulnerability. She'd always prided herself on her professional yet empathetic care, but something about this man made her heart ache more than usual. She glanced at the papers in her hand. "You'll need plenty of rest once you get home. You should tell your wife—"

"I'm not married," he interrupted.

She looked at him. She knew that. Nate had told Sophie who Jack was. When Sophie had asked him earlier if he wanted her to call Katia, he'd refused. Katia and Austin were out of town for the weekend. No girlfriend had come to see him last night. His emergency contact was his sister, Ava, but she lived in Illinois and Jack told Sophie he'd make his own phone calls when he was up to it. He hadn't asked for anyone but Aleah. Jack had been so confused and out of it, and Sophie knew from experience that victims sometimes couldn't even remember their own names. She had to be sure.

But why, Sophie?

Habit. That's all it was. Her reaction to Jack was habit. She'd been a man magnet for so long, she didn't know how to meet an attractive man on any other basis.

Ugh. She had a real problem.

"Well, someone needs to see you through the next twenty-four hours to make absolutely certain there are no complications from the concussion. You'll need to see Dr. Hill in his regular hours to have the stitches removed. And we suggest that you see an ophthalmologist immediately about your eyes. You were asleep, but we had Dr. Mason come in and give you an exam. He'll see you Monday afternoon. The rest of your instructions are the usual. Hydrate. Eat properly. Get rest and no sports for two weeks."

"What? No sports?"

Was he serious? Sophie cocked her head. "Is there a problem? Are you on a summer baseball league or something?"

"No, but I run. A lot. Every day. I can't live without running."

She put her hands on her hips. "You have a sprained ankle. It won't let you run for at least ten days."

"I can handle that. A week or so. Fine," he harrumphed.

"So," she probed, unable to stop herself. "Where do you run?"

"Around the lake. That's where I live. Running is my life."

She shook her head emphatically. "You'll have to live without it for two weeks. In addition to the sprain, you could risk a second concussion. If you aren't fully healed from this first one, a second could increase the chances of swelling in the brain. Most concussions are not terribly dangerous, but a second one could be fatal."

"Fatal?"

Sophie cringed, realizing the word would remind him of Aleah's death. But since she couldn't take it back, this was as good a time as any to test Dr. Hill's theory that it had been shock and irritability alone that had made Jack accuse Sophie of abandoning Aleah in favor of another—and in his opinion, less deserving—patient.

"A concussion sometimes takes months to heal. Our advice is that you take it easy the next few weeks to a month. Don't push. There will be plenty of time for running in the fall."

Jack's eyes fell away from Sophie's face as he turned his head to the window. She followed his gaze to the fully leafed maple trees outside.

"A month would be torture," he said quietly, as if accepting his defeat. "But I'll try."

"Excellent." She went to the closet and pulled out his ripped but wearable pants, shoes, socks and underwear. His tattered shirt she'd put in a plastic bag.

"Where's my sport jacket?" he asked.

"You didn't come in with it," she replied.

His brows knit together and she could tell it was an effort for him to think and remember. "I put it in the backseat with Owen."

"Mr. Carter, I need to make arrangements for your dismissal. You're not allowed to drive for the next week. Who should I call to come get you?"

Jack's eyelids drooped and he lowered his chin to his chest. "Don't tell me I can't drive. I have to drive. I have to work. I have to go to Aleah's funeral…"

Sophie let Jack take a moment with his thoughts

before interrupting him. He was being forced by the circumstances to take a lot in. She truly felt for trauma victims and their families. One minute their lives were normal and made sense. In the flash of an exploding gas main, a head-on collision, a tornado, a drive-by shooting, an accidental overdose of prescription medication, a drowning... Their lives would never be the same. Jack Carter was still able to walk and talk and function. He hadn't lost a limb. He hadn't lost his eyesight. He hadn't lost his mind. He had to give up running and driving for a short time, but even though he groused, she knew that he'd be just fine. He'd cope. He had to.

But she knew he didn't see it that way. What harangued Jack was that Aleah had died. His young assistant wouldn't be in his office on Monday. He would meet with her family and he would go to the visitation. Then the funeral and burial.

Sophie understood that even though he'd have a full physical recovery, Jack's world would be forever altered.

She placed his shoes on the floor, turning them so he could slip his feet in more easily. Even this simple thing would be hard for the next little while.

It was her way of trying to say she was sorry about Aleah without admitting any guilt. The hospital was not at fault. Dr. Hill and Dr. Barzonni had both told her that no one was.

But Sophie knew that some part of Jack would always believe she had committed the gravest of errors.

He met her eyes as she straightened up. There was no spark, no hint of the flirtation she often found with men. There was only anger and blame.

"If you have no one to take you home, I'll drive you," she said.

"I'll get a cab," he huffed.

She ground her jaw and could feel her heels digging into the linoleum. "I'll drive you home and I will make sure you are inside the door safe and sound."

"Forget it," he said.

"Fine. Then I'll tell the staff you'll be staying here through the rest of the weekend."

"You can't do that!"

"I can do anything I feel I need to do for the well-being of my patient," she retorted.

Jack snorted and punched the bed. "Fine. But I'll dress myself."

"Absolutely," she chimed in. "I wouldn't want to do anything that made you uncomfortable." She went to the curtains and pulled them around the track to give him privacy.

As she walked out, she heard Jack growl, "After this, I hope I never lay eyes on you again."

CHAPTER FIVE

"THIS IS WHERE you live?" Sophie peered through her windshield at the white three-story condo building tucked into a mass of oak, pine and maple trees on the northwest shore of Indian Lake. "I didn't know these were here. Looks like only four units," she mused, thinking how much she'd love to live by the water. Wouldn't everybody? She leaned over the steering wheel to see the second-floor deck. Instead of a typical railing, twisted steel designed to resemble nautical ropes ran between white posts. "When you said the condos on the lake, I thought you meant those ugly brown monstrosities that look like a federal penitentiary. This is absolutely beautiful."

"Thanks. Cate Sullivan found it and worked the deal for me."

"Wow," Sophie gushed, inspecting the private outdoor staircase that led down to the beach, a drive-in first-floor garage. The second story obviously held the main living space and on the third story were the bedrooms. She'd seen these floor plans all over the south end of Lake Michigan. She smiled as she saw a chimney wall, which could only mean a wood-burning fireplace.

She heard the seat belt alarm ping as Jack undid his belt.

"Well, thanks for the ride," he said with a perfunctory nod.

Sophie spun to face him. "What do you think you're doing?"

"Leaving," he replied, his tone so brittle she snapped her head back.

"Not without me."

He glared at her. "I think I can make it on my own."

She gave him a daring look. "Think so? Go for it."

Jack snickered, got out and slammed the door. He stood perfectly still for a long moment and then leaned against the car.

Sophie had already unhooked her seat belt and opened her door in the time it took him to shut his. Before he could say a word, she raced over and wrapped her arm around his waist.

"I've got this," he said.

"I see that."

She walked him up to the garage door and he punched in his security code.

"Am I having a second concussion?" he asked.

"You've barely eaten since the accident. You're

fine. Nothing that chicken parmesan and spaghetti wouldn't cure."

Jack opened the door and wrestled away from Sophie's grasp. "I can make it."

She glanced up the stairs. "Let me be the judge."

Jack clung to the railing, but he managed to take the stairs at an almost normal pace.

Sophie followed him to the first-floor living area. It was completely open. Living, dining, kitchen and a small study co-existed under a high-pitched, beamed ceiling. A massive river rock fireplace filled the left wall. The wall facing the lake was entirely glass, and the view was stunning.

Sophie was struck by the emptiness of the place. There was hardly any furniture. In the study alcove was a desk, chair and computer. A printer and a small television set. There were no sofas, chairs, tables or lamps in the living room and no dining table. Just bar stools. The condo's kitchen was a cook's dream, with a six-burner gas stove, double convection ovens, dishwasher, a double-wide Sub-Zero refrigerator, a six-foot-tall wine cooler with glass doors and yards of granite countertop. However, except for an espresso machine and a commercial-grade juicer, there was nothing on the counters. No knickknacks, no canisters. It was as if he'd just moved in, but she didn't see packing boxes anywhere.

Obviously, Jack put all his energy into his business and his employees. He hadn't done much for himself at all. In that way, they were very much alike.

Jack lumbered over to one of the bar stools and sat down. He rubbed his injured ankle and then put his elbows on the tortoiseshell granite countertop. "So. I'm good. You can leave."

Sophie stuck her hand on her hip. "I'm going as soon as you eat something."

He shook his head. "Will this nightmare never end?"

Sophie went to the stainless steel Sub-Zero refrigerator and opened the door. The shelves were filled with carrots, turnips, kale, spinach, tomatoes, cucumbers, lemons, limes, apricots, peaches and berries. She saw almond milk, coconut milk, protein powder, protein shakes and an entire shelf of vitamins.

"You keep your vitamins in the fridge?"

He slid his arms across the counter and laid his head on them. "Just give me one of my power drinks."

Sophie clucked her tongue as she pulled out a vanilla shake and popped the pull tab. She handed it to him. "There's no garlic in that refrigerator."

"I don't like garlic," he said, taking the drink and chugging it.

"What kind of guy doesn't like garlic? Every Italian dish my grandmother taught me has garlic. It's a food group all its own."

He slammed the can down on the counter. "I don't like Italian food, either."

Sophie cleared her throat. "I can see you'll be okay. Get some rest and don't forget your appointments on Monday." She took her car keys out of her pocket and headed for the staircase.

Just as she reached the newel post, she looked back. He was staring at the counter and not at her. "Jack. I'm sorry about Aleah."

Jack's face contorted with pain, anger and sorrow. "Please, Sophie. Just leave."

She rushed down the stairs and out of the garage. As she started her car, she realized she was crying. Her tears flowed like a dam that had burst. From the moment the accident victims had been brought into the ER, Sophie had checked her emotions. She'd kept her mind on her work and the duties she needed to perform in the moment. She and the other team members lived in a bubble during events like that. There was no past and no future. Only the instant. A tiny fraction of time where souls were suspended between the life on earth and the world after this one. The decisions she made had been critical. And everlasting.

Was Jack right?

Had she made the wrong choice about Aleah? If she'd stayed with her, if they'd done tests or performed the thoracentesis sooner, would that have made a difference? Would they have gained another five or ten minutes that might have allowed the defibrillator to do its job?

Was Nate correct that Aleah was likely anorexic? Were her electrolytes to blame for her heart attack? Was it true that she'd never had a chance in the first place?

Sophie drove out of the wooded glen and back to the road that led to town. She turned left instead of right so she could drive around the lake. The lake helped her collect her thoughts. Often, after a particularly hard day of surgeries, if she couldn't run the lake trails, she would at least drive around it to clear her mind. The water, whether choppy or placid, gray or crystal blue calmed her. But not today.

Today, Sophie didn't feel much like giving thanks or praise. Her heart was as heavy as Jack Carter's. She wondered if one of the reasons he'd urged her to leave so quickly was because he wanted to drown himself in tears just as she was doing.

IT HAD BEEN two weeks since Aleah's death and today was the first day Sophie had felt like stepping beyond the boundaries of the hospital or her apartment.

She sat on a red-leather-and-chrome fifties-style stool at the lunch counter at Lou's Diner, sipping an iced tea while she waited for her lunch. She liked the former train car that had been turned into a retro diner years ago. In the next car over was The LTD, also run by Lou, which served gourmet meals that made Sophie drool just reading the menu. She'd only eaten in The LTD once. That was the night of her graduation, when she'd received her RN. Her father had been healthy then and her mother was electric with pride. Even her Italian grandmother, who spoke little English, agreed to eat in an American restaurant. It had been a hallmark day for the Mattuchi family.

Sophie tried to remember what dreams she'd had for herself then. Mostly, she'd just been happy to be done with finals and evaluations.

However, she must have had some ambition because she'd only worked for a year at Grand Rapids Hospital before she realized she wanted more. She'd decided to specialize in cardiac surgery. She went back to school to get her master's degree in nursing science and then she entered a highly competitive fellowship program to specialize in cardiovascular care. During her placement, she often felt she was only a half-step behind the heart surgeons she worked alongside. Until she returned home to Indian Lake. Once she started working with Nate Barzonni, she realized that there truly were gifted, intuitive talents in every field. Nate was a virtuoso. A genius. He could have written his own ticket to the country's top hospitals, but Nate had decided the fast lane was not for him. He spent nearly as much of his time working at a free clinic on an Indian reservation as he did in the high-tech ablation unit at Indian Lake Hospital.

Still, Sophie supposed that Nate's main reason for setting up shop in Indian Lake was Maddie Strong—now his wife. Sophie grimaced, remembering how she'd literally thrown herself at him when he'd first moved back to town. She had decided that to win Nate Barzonni, she'd attempt a makeover. Granted, her initial thoughts were veering down the right path because she'd needed to make changes. But she should have realized that her tactics had "disaster" written all over them.

Sophie had chopped off her hair and streaked it blond to look as much like Maddie Strong as possible, since Maddie had been Nate's type when they were in high school. She went on a diet and lost eight pounds. She bought new clothes and fell back on her old standby—flirting.

But Nate was a one-woman man and he'd chosen Maddie.

Rightfully so. Maddie was the best woman, a fact that Sophie had known all along.

The following spring, Sophie flung a bit of caution to the wind and—not coyly—made a pass at Nate's brother, Gabe. Gabe was very forthright and told her he just wasn't into her. Little did she know that a few months later he and Liz Crenshaw would be married. Frankly, at the time, she didn't think Gabe knew Liz at all. In fact, Sophie could almost claim that if it hadn't been for the Mattuchi family selling Gabe part of their vineyard, Gabe and Liz might never have gotten together at all. Now, they were expecting their first baby.

Yep, I learned my lesson all right. It was time to get her act together. But in the right way.

A waitress dressed in a blue-and-white-striped uniform with a white pinafore apron delivered a cheeseburger and fries.

It had been over half a year since Sophie had ordered a meal that contained double the calories she now consumed each day. But she hadn't ever been responsible for someone dying on her watch before, either.

Two thousand calories? Who cared? Maybe she'd have apple pie à la mode for dessert.

She was just about to squirt mustard on the burger when she heard a woman's voice say her name.

"Sophie? Is that you?"

Sophie twisted around on the stool. Oh, no. It was Katia Stanislaus. The most gorgeous creature God ever built. Just looking at Katia's svelte figure, dressed in a gray linen sheath dress, matching gray pumps and some exotic designer purse Sophie guessed cost three times her car payment, caused her to clench her teeth. She glanced down at her burger and fries. She could already feel the lead they'd form in her belly. She plopped the bun down and wiped her fingers on the paper napkin.

"Katia! Hi!" Sophie wondered if she sounded cheerful enough.

Katia was several years older than Sophie, but Sophie remembered when Katia was named Indian Lake High School Homecoming Queen. Track Queen. Yearbook Queen, but not Prom Queen. Katia had left town abruptly right before prom. Katia was one of those women who grew more beautiful with the years. Sophie would have liked to blame her own hard work for the fine lines around her eyes that Katia didn't have. But Katia was a steamroller in the insurance business. She'd heard everyone from Maddie to Olivia Melton praise Katia's work ethic.

Katia glided right over to Sophie and sat on the stool next to her. She glanced at Sophie's lunch. "How's the iced tea?"

Sophie smiled wanly. She'd have to add merciful to Katia's attributes. "Good. Not as good as Olivia's raspberry herb tea at the deli."

Katia laughed.

Her voice sounded like tinkling chimes. No wonder Austin McCreary melted when she blew into town last fall. What man could resist her?

Now that Katia was back in Indian Lake, amazingly, she and Sophie had become reacquainted. Actually, if it hadn't been for Katia, Sophie would probably still be apartment-hunting. Katia had been on the verge of vacating Mrs. Beabots's apartment in order to move into Austin's house while they planned the wedding, when Sophie overheard Maddie Barzonni and Sarah Bosworth at Cupcakes and Coffee discussing Mrs. Beabots's soon-to-be-vacant apartment.

Several years ago, right after Sophie moved back to Indian Lake from Grand Rapids, her father had been diagnosed with cancer and Sophie had moved into the family home near the Crenshaw Vineyard on the north of town to help her mother and grandmother. Sophie's salary had also paid off a large portion of her father's surgical and chemotherapy bills. The family had been deeply grateful, but once her father recovered, Sophie couldn't wait to be out on her own again.

Once she'd heard about Mrs. Beabots's apartment, Sophie knew if she didn't snatch the place that afternoon, she'd miss out. Indian Lake was not like any other town in the northern hemisphere. There was little to no new construction, no apartment buildings, very few condos and no place for young people to move to except their parents' basements. Until the town experienced an uptick in new business or manufacturing, residential construction would remain at a standstill.

Sophie was struck by how such an economic situation could affect the younger generations of Indian Lake. Unless they relocated far from home, it was as if they were all stuck in a vat of molasses. Fleetingly, she wondered if this inertia, this lack of "normal" growth into adulthood, had any effect on the rising drug problem in their town.

Katia was still beaming a megawatt smile. "So, do you mind if I sit here, or were you waiting for someone? Knowing you, the next handsome hunk walking through that door doesn't stand a chance."

Sophie winced. Katia wasn't being catty or petty. She probably thought she was being complimentary. The old Sophie would have agreed with her. *Bring 'em on.* That had been Sophie's motto for years. But not anymore. "Uh, I don't think so," Sophie replied, squirting ketchup onto the side of her plate.

Katia eyed her as she signaled the waitress. "I'll have an iced tea and a romaine salad. Dressing on the side."

Katia propped an elbow on the counter and turned to Sophie. A shower of auburn hair fell over her shoulder, acting like a privacy curtain. "It's pretty coincidental that I ran into you today," Katia said. "Jack and I were talking about you only this morning."

Sophie sucked in a breath. "Really? Nothing good, I'm sure."

Katia put her hand on Sophie's shoulder.

Great. It's that bad.

Since the accident, Sophie had been so busy with her job and battling her own demons that she'd almost pushed Jack Carter from her mind. Almost.

"To be honest, Sophie, I'm worried about him. He's taken Aleah's death very hard. Austin and I went to her service with Jack. I'd expected him to need our help to get through the day, but he was…well, I've never seen him like that. He's always been the strong one in his family, you know? None of us had even known her more than a few months. But Jack is acting like she was his sister or daughter or something. I don't have any idea what to say to him."

"There's nothing you can say, Katia," Sophie

reassured her. "Grief is its own timekeeper. Some people move on in a few weeks. Others never quite get there."

Katia examined Sophie's face. "And what about you?"

"What about me?" Sophie parroted with more sarcasm in her voice than she'd intended. She was instantly defensive.

How could Katia really know her when Sophie was in the process of regrouping? Reinventing herself?

"I don't need a medical degree to figure out that those dark smudges under your eyes are not from too much mascara," Katia whispered compassionately.

"Oh, that."

"And that's a lot of comfort food on your plate."

"Yeah, well." Sophie sighed, feeling like the culprit in a sinister caper.

Katia frowned. "Mashed potatoes was my go-to food. That was when I left Indian Lake heartbroken over Austin."

Sophie followed Katia's eyes to the burger. "Hmm. Not very original of me."

"No." Katia leaned back as her salad and iced tea were served. "I'm guessing you're as upset about Aleah as Jack is."

Sophie needed to bob and weave. She didn't

want Katia running back to Jack with some tale of woe that he could use against her. If Sophie told Katia anything that resembled guilt or wrongdoing, Jack could sue her and the hospital. Sophie didn't really know Katia *that* well. And she was in the insurance business, after all. What if Katia's friendliness was an act? What if she'd been sent to spy on Sophie? "You're very observant, Katia."

"I think I can help, Sophie," Katia said, spearing a cherry tomato with her fork. "Spend a day in the city with me?"

"What on earth for?"

"For fun. We'll go to lunch. Window-shop and pretend to buy clothes we can't afford. It's the kind of thing you do to take your mind off your troubles."

Sophie smoothed the hem of her scrubs. "I don't think shopping will help. Besides, I haven't done anything like that since college."

"Then you're overdue. Maybe we can get Mrs. Beabots to go with us."

"Is she up to that?"

"Are you kidding?" Katia's eyes were round as plates. "Just mention shopping to her and watch her reaction. Has she shown you her treasures yet?"

"What treasures?"

"Her closets are a treasure trove. She's got so

much vintage Chanel, it brings tears to my eyes. I'm a discount junkie. Seriously. I drive into Chicago to do most of my shopping since I know where to get all the best deals. I took Maddie and Sarah last weekend. You really need to come with me. We'll have a blast."

"I'm not sure. I've never had the time—" Sophie's voice dropped off as she realized what truth she'd spoken. She didn't have girlfriends because friendships took time and effort. She poured all her concern and caring into her patients. That and the fact that once Sophie turned on her charm, most of her friends' boyfriends couldn't resist her. Sophie wasn't beautiful like Katia. Who was? But she had magnetism, and in the past she'd used it to her full advantage. Right now, Sophie couldn't muster a spark of allure for anyone. "Thanks for the invitation, Katia. But I don't know when I could break free."

Katia nodded. "I understand. Apparently, you've been saving mankind. Admirable. Very admirable. But I still want to take you shopping."

"I'm not that altruistic," Sophie replied as the image of Jack's face flashed across her mind.

Katia sipped her tea. "I think you are. Lots of people do."

"But not Jack Carter." Sophie was fishing for information. That definitely wasn't altruistic, and it wasn't even a good strategy, but Sophie felt the glare of Jack's condemnation each time she did a shift in the ER.

"He'll come around," Katia replied with a reassuring look in her eyes.

CHAPTER SIX

JACK COULDN'T BELIEVE he was nervous about his meeting with Indian Lake Hospital's president, Emory Wills, but the butterflies in his stomach were about to drown in roiling acid. This deal had been over six months in the making. Katia had initiated the conversations with Emory and the hospital board, but as their inquiries and demands grew and their list of needs expanded, Jack felt it imperative that he take the reins in the negotiations. Katia had been present for most of the meetings so far, but a scheduling conflict had caused both Jack and Katia to do some quick shuffling. In the end, they decided that Katia would proceed with an extensive presentation to a group of local farmers that was nearly as important to Jack as the hospital's insurance policy.

Jack shook his head. When Katia had suggested last year that he move his insurance company from Chicago to Indian Lake to save on rent and other Illinois taxes, he'd actually scoffed at her. No more. How could he have known that this small community would be vital and progressive in some ways, while its appearance was that of another era? On the whole, Jack liked Indian Lake more and more by the day.

The receptionist in the hospital's admin wing was clearly above retirement age, and she appeared to handle a bevy of phone calls and issues with seasoned practice. As her hand flew over the phone intercom and dial pad, he noticed a large diamond wedding ring set. It wasn't the kind of thing Jack noticed ordinarily, but for some reason, he'd begun paying more attention to just about everyone and everything since he'd moved to Indian Lake.

Especially since the accident.

This was the first time he'd been back to the hospital since that night. He'd seen his doctors, as prescribed, but in their clinic offices. It was strange, almost eerie for him to be here, thinking about business…or at least *trying* to thing about business. He kept seeing flashes of Aleah's face from that day. Her eagerness during the seminar, asking intelligent questions of the speaker. Later, seeing her laugh and joke with Owen in the car. Then came the pandemonium in the ER as the doctors tried to save her. Sophie's stricken face as she delivered the news that Aleah had died.

Jack told himself he'd never forgive Sophie for not saving Aleah, but already the grooves in that record were wearing deep. If he hadn't pushed

Aleah to go to Chicago… If only he'd signed her up for the webinars online that she could have studied on her own, in her free time…

If only he'd seen the other car coming at them. But he'd been laughing at one of Owen's jokes. He'd glanced in the rearview mirror and in that split second, he'd missed it. He'd missed seeing death driving smack into them.

Jack's head pounded with pain, but he knew it had nothing to do with his concussion. It was stress. He was thinking too much.

Feeling too much.

He should be grateful for the medical care he'd received.

His ankle had healed nicely, and except when he turned a corner a bit too abruptly, he didn't notice it at all. The bruises around his eyes were a memory, but the scar over his eyebrow and those on his arms would take months, maybe years to disappear. It was just as well. They would remind him always of Aleah and what he owed her.

As his memories of the accident whipped up a fresh batch of guilt, Nate Barzonni walked up, accompanied by another man. Jack rose to greet them.

Nate grasped Jack's hand and then squeezed his forearm. "Good to see you, Jack. You're looking well."

"Doing well," Jack replied.

Nate turned to his left and said, "Jack, this is Dr. Roger Caldwell. It's his ablation unit that you'll be insuring for us."

Jack smiled brightly. "Pleasure, Doctor. I'm impressed with your work and with your team."

Dr. Caldwell beamed. "I'm very proud of my group—especially Nate. We were lucky to get him." He smiled at Nate.

Nate gestured toward a group of chairs out of earshot of the receptionist then leaned toward Jack. "As you know, Jack, I worked with Katia to put this proposal together. I want to make sure President Wills doesn't flinch over a single aspect. So, I'll introduce you and give him a little background. That kind of thing."

"I appreciate this, Nate. Katia has told me that Emory has been here since she was in high school and that he has a penchant for only doing business with Indian Lake natives. She would have been giving this presentation, but when he changed the meeting on us, she couldn't be in two places at once."

"I understand," Nate said.

"You can go in now, Dr. Barzonni. Dr. Caldwell." The receptionist looked at Jack with steady green eyes. "And guest."

Jack bit his lower lip to keep from laughing. It was his guess the woman had been in her position for decades. She was as protective as a mother lioness with her cubs. Employees like her were rare these days.

Jack wondered if he could hire her away from the hospital.

They entered the president's office.

Jack had expected something more grand, but then he was used to Chicago hospitals and private clinics. The room was the size of a suburban living room. Big enough for a desk, three side chairs and a small sofa against the far wall. The furnishings were dated. The pictures on the wall reminded Jack of cheap chain motels.

Jack chided himself for mentally criticizing the man's taste—or lack of it. Jack hadn't done much better himself. Katia had decorated the office beautifully, sure, but he had yet to put out his family photographs on his desk. They were still in a box. To say nothing of his condo. The last time he'd bought fresh flowers was at Christmas, which were unexciting cedar sprigs and holly that had lasted nearly till Super Bowl Sunday.

"Jack," Emory Wills said, shaking Jack's hand. "It's good to see you again."

They all sat in the chairs surrounding Emory's desk. Nate spoke first.

"Emory, Roger and I wanted to join this meeting today because we both support Jack's proposal. I'm here to vouch for Jack as a friend as well as a businessman. Though he's new to town,

I met him through my wife and her friends. I believe that Jack and his company truly have the best interests of the hospital in mind."

Jack kept a warm smile on his face as Nate spoke. Ordinarily, Jack was not a suspicious man. He made a habit of taking people at their word. He'd liked Nate since the first time they'd met, but in light of Jack's accident and his experience in the ER, Jack wasn't completely sure if Nate wasn't trying to dodge a bullet for the hospital. Was Nate's effusiveness sincere? Did he really think Jack's company could help Indian Lake Hospital? Or did Nate feel guilty about the way Aleah died? What was his true motivation?

Jack still had questions about Aleah's treatment that he hadn't had the opportunity to discuss with Nate.

The irony of all ironies was that Jack was presenting the hospital with a massive malpractice insurance policy at the very time when he believed he might have cause to file a lawsuit of his own. Still, he couldn't bring suit if Aleah's parents didn't agree. At this point, they'd not returned any of his phone calls. They'd been perfunctorily polite at the funeral and burial, but that was all. It was as if they blamed Jack for the accident. Jack still hadn't received the complete police report, though he'd talked to Detective Trent Davis, the investigating officer that night in the ER. Actually, Jack had placed a call to Detective Davis that very morning requesting a meeting. He hadn't received an answer.

Jack didn't like loose ends. He was the kind of person who would dig through dozens of insurance products to find the best policy for his clients. Even Barry said he took his responsibilities too seriously, but Jack didn't care. He was a serious guy.

The Indian Lake Hospital was Jack and Katia's top pick for clients. Katia had signed Austin McCreary and his new antique car museum six months ago, and that sale had stabilized Jack's company in Indian Lake. Two months back, Jack had put together the package for Katia to present to the hospital, which would cover the buildings themselves. However, the high-tech equipment that Nate and Roger Caldwell used was insured by another provider. Jack had studied their current coverage and discovered that he could save the hospital thousands of dollars a year. Jack was here to discuss a comprehensive equipment insurance policy with Emory. What he had not proposed yet was a new malpractice policy, which would bring the entire hospital into Jack's sphere of responsibility.

The hospital was an enormously important coup for Jack. With a bit of persuasion, Emory might be agreeable to recommending Jack's company to other hospitals and medical clinics throughout the region, possibly the entire state of Indiana.

Jack and Katia had spent over a hundred hours on their presentation for a package that Emory would be negligent, at the very least, to turn down.

"As you know, Emory, my company already covers the building and campus. I've talked to you about the equipment policy, which is what we sent over to you a few weeks ago. So I'm here to address all your concerns."

Emory tapped the file folder that bore the Carter and Associates logo against his desk. "I'm impressed, Jack. As I was with the policy you put together for us last winter for the campus. Your meticulousness is commendable, and I like the fact that you look out for my dollars as much as I do."

"Thank you, sir," Jack replied, feeling the warm glow he always did when a sale was going well. He'd get that hot rush of excitement once he heard Emory's pen scratch his signature on the last page, but not before. Emory's pause was longer than Jack liked. Was he rethinking the proposal already? Just how many objections was he going to raise? Jack's heart was in his throat, pounding out anxiety-riddled thumps. Jack had been too close to the finish line on deals just like this one and walked away empty-handed. Small town.

Big city. The deals were virtually the same. It all came down to a few dollars and cents in the end.

"Jack," Emory said in a tone that put Jack's instincts on alert. The other shoe was about to drop. No deal could be made without bumps. He just hoped it wouldn't be a rut.

"Yes?" Jack waited. He reminded himself to make sure his smile wasn't overly wide.

"There are a couple provisions that I've highlighted here." Emory turned a group of pages toward Jack for him to peruse. "If you'll note, you broke out Dr. Caldwell's lab and surgical unit from the rest of the hospital. Why is that?"

Jack nodded. He had this one. "The ablation unit is brand-new and most of the insurance companies were asking for a very high premium. I was looking for something more..." Jack drew out his pause. "Affordable for you."

"Excellent," Emory replied. "Then the second point is the timing of the first premium. We can't do this."

Jack gulped but hoped no one noticed. "Sir?"

"The board is prepared to switch over from our current carrier at the end of this year but not before. I realize that if we went with you right now, we'd save over twenty grand. However, there were some, er, allegiances from the board—that is to say, one of our members—"

"Is a very old friend of your present insurance agent. I know that, sir," Jack finished for him, hopefully alleviating any embarrassment on Emory's part.

Nate and Roger exhaled with relief. Just as he'd thought. They'd known about this complication. It was a good thing Jack believed in background research. He was prepared for this delay. He didn't like it, but he would have to accept it if he wanted the business.

Jack continued, "I can prepare the paperwork to be executed for a December thirty-first date. How would that be?"

Emory's bushy gray eyebrows shot up as he grinned widely. "That would be just fine, Jack."

Jack picked up his leather briefcase and put it on his lap. "Now that we're agreed on this first order of business, I wonder if I might make another proposal to you, Emory."

Emory glanced at Nate and Roger, then back at Jack. "Do they need to leave?"

"Not at all." Jack withdrew a thick, three-ring binder with his company logo. "Though I don't have access to your current policy, I took the liberty of preparing a proposal for you because I believe that no matter what you are paying now, I can save the hospital more money."

Jack handed the binder to Emory, who flipped open the cover and gasped. "This is malpractice insurance."

"That's correct. It's my guess that your current agent also provides this service for you. All I ask is that you review my product and see for yourself if I can't provide a larger umbrella at a lower cost."

Emory had already been rifling through the pages and checking out the tabs as Jack spoke. He pinned Jack with his eyes. "I will look at it, but that's all I can promise."

"I totally understand, and I'm grateful for the opportunity."

Emory rose from his chair, signaling the end of the meeting. He held out his hand. "I'll be in touch, Jack."

"Thank you, sir," Jack replied before leaving the room with the two doctors.

Sophie stood in the middle of the reception area dressed in her street clothes. It was the first time Jack had seen her since the accident. Her hair had been pulled back that night, but now it just skimmed her shoulders in dark, luminous waves and she'd pinned a piece of it over her right ear with a massive coral and rhinestone barrette. There were coral hoops in her ears that matched her cotton sundress. On her feet were beige espadrilles. She was tanned and her skin glowed.

Jack couldn't take his eyes off her.

Sophie hadn't noticed him at all. She went straight to Nate.

"Dr. Barzonni," she said, handing him a group of faxed papers. "The office just got a call from the reservation clinic. There's been an emergency. Here's the patient's information for you to review. They said you've treated him before."

Nate peeled back the top sheet. "Tom Running Bear." He started speed walking toward the elevators with Sophie right at his side.

"What do you want me to do?"

"Call the clinic. Tell them I'm on my way. I'll call my wife and tell her where I am. Could you call my mother and tell her I won't be coming out to the farm for dinner?"

"Absolutely. What else?"

"My cell?" He patted his pockets.

Sophie handed him an iPhone. "You left it on your desk. I also filled up your Hummer."

"How did you do that?"

"You left your car keys on your desk, too." She sank her hand into her straw purse and flipped the keys to him. "Good luck."

The elevator doors opened and Nate jumped in.

Roger Caldwell said his goodbye to Jack, then he excused himself and took the stairs, telling Jack it was part of his cardio routine.

Sophie turned and spied Jack for the first time. "You, er, look good. I mean, well."

He walked toward her.

"No problem with the ankle, I see." She smiled slightly, but it slid off her face as her eyes met his.

Jack saw trepidation and question in her face. Rightly so. He still wanted answers, but he knew her explanation wouldn't have changed from what she'd delivered to him before.

"Ankle is good." He tapped his head. "So is the noggin'. No more checkups for a couple months, I'm told."

"Good. So, you're fine. Well, I gotta go," she said but didn't move. Her eyes tracked over to the president's door.

Jack thought she'd stopped breathing. Her back went rigid and her eyes were wide. "Why are you here, Jack?"

"Business," he replied icily. "My business."

Not a muscle on Sophie's body flinched. It was as if she'd turned to stone. She didn't blink or breathe. "Business with the president?"

"Yes, and now we're finished for the day," he said, moving around her and pressing the elevator button.

He let his eyes slide to Sophie's sleek, tanned legs. When she pirouetted to face him, her calves flexed just like a ballerina. He wondered if she had taken ballet when she was a little girl. He remembered going to his sister's recitals and making fun of her pink tutu and feather headdresses. He didn't think he'd make fun of Sophie.

"Jack," Sophie said his name just as the elevator arrived and the doors whooshed open.

He got in and shook his head. "Don't."

The door closed, leaving a stunned and enticingly beautiful Sophie on the other side.

Jack stared at the ceiling. Though it was the first time he'd been with Sophie since Aleah's death, he hadn't thought of his assistant at all.

CHAPTER SEVEN

SEEING JACK SHOT Sophie back to the night of Aleah's death in the ER. Since then, she'd learned from the police report that the driver's name was Greg Fulton. He was from Chicago. Never married, though he was from a large family of five brothers. He'd lost his job in the steel mills as an engineer a year and a half ago and had fallen headlong into the drug scene.

Knowing only those few facts about Greg amped up Sophie's empathy.

Sophie believed the hospital should do more to help addicts like Greg. Sophie booked a meeting with Tanya Stewart, the Indian Lake Hospital administrator who headed up four different hospital-related community health projects. Each project had a three-letter acronym and each was impossible to remember without looking at her notes, which exemplified the ineffectiveness of all the hospital's outreach programs.

"Thanks for seeing me," Sophie said, standing as Tanya entered the windowless office in a rush of air, her long paisley-print silk jacket trailing behind her. Tanya plopped into her chair, carrot-red hair bouncing around her face like coils.

"What can I do for you, Nurse Ma…"

"Mattuchi. Sophie Mattuchi."

Tanya shuffled papers and peered at phone memos. She dug her cell phone out of her jacket pocket and glanced at it, acting as if Sophie were an intrusion in her extraordinarily busy day.

"Right." She checked her messages again. Then rolled her eyes. "When I was in Chicago I had two assistants and *they* had secretaries." She shook her head. "There aren't enough hours in the day—or enough of me." She flipped her hand in the air, turning her fingers around like she was whipping cream. "So what is it?"

Clearly, the woman was overwhelmed. Sophie dove in. "I'm here to talk about the hospital's drug addiction program."

"I feel a criticism coming on here," Tanya replied with a bit of a nervous squeak to her voice.

"Well, given the problems Indian Lake is having with drugs and now gangs moving in, I feel there is more we can do."

"More? The hospital offers seven-day drying-out periods. That's almost double the four days the law gives addicts when they're arrested."

"The cops think an addict can go straight after four days? Who are they kidding?"

"That's the law. We do better."

Sophie could tell she was going to need to take a different tack. "That might be true, but in the ER we see an overdose nearly every weekend. The numbers are rising and our programs don't touch the surface. Is there any way that we can hire suitable, licensed professionals to help us?"

Tanya shook her head vigorously. "Our budget is set for the year. We're tightening our belts more every day."

"But there's a need…" Sophie placed her hands on the edge of Tanya's desk, imploring. Sophie had wanted to be convincing and she was losing the battle before she'd drawn a single sword.

Sophie had researched as much as she could about the disease. She remembered a colleague from Butterworth Hospital in Grand Rapids, Phillip Jessup, who now worked at Renewal Rehabilitation Center in Chicago and called him up. Not only had they spent several hours discussing the Indian Lake Hospital's approach to drug addiction, but Phillip had also sent her research papers, surveys and the materials they used in his program at Renewal. Educating the parents, family, close friends and concerned associates of an addict was key to their recovery. Renewal conducted a "family week" several times a year for the families of the addiction patients. The interaction between counselors, doctors and patients' families was crucial.

"My hands are tied," Tanya said.

"But I want to *do* something," Sophie said, hating the whine she heard in her voice.

"I think you should know, Sophie, that this hospital has a very strict policy that its staff members participate in *only* those programs that the hospital supports."

"What if the hospital conducts a seminar for the families of addicts?" she tried. "I could put it together. On my free time."

"No," Tanya rebutted before Sophie could go on. "In the end, I would have to staff up, find funds. Just thinking of the kind of organization it would take gives me a headache. And the hours of work—oy!"

The woman was shutting her down. Sophie pressed harder. "But the family programs are working at other facilities," Sophie countered.

"I'd have to study their reports. Meet with the organizers. That would require months of trips to Chicago and wherever else, phone calls…"

Sophie was getting nowhere with Tanya. The woman folded her arms across her chest and glared at Sophie. "We provide psychiatric evaluations and from those we recommend rehabilitation stays."

"Those evaluations are superficial, Tanya, and you know it. I've seen three of the hospital's addiction patients as an overdose in the ER in the last two months. If someone hadn't called 9-1-1 they'd all be dead."

Tanya shrugged. "When it comes to drug addiction, even the best rehabilitation centers have low success rates. We're a hospital. We treat overdoses and severely addicted patients when they come in with acute problems, or the cops bring them in after an arrest. This is as good as we get."

Molten anger shot through her veins. The hospital was quitting without giving her a chance to try something new. "There are other established organizations with updated, well-researched approaches that work with the families and schools. Drug testing the kids in elementary school has proven massively effective in Phoenix."

"It's not going to happen, Sophie. And let me say this—if you were to try to bring something like this Phoenix organization to town, your support would invalidate our expertise. Our standing in the community would be jeopardized. Your loyalty to us is paramount. Not to mention the liability aspect. Say a client under your care suffered an injury or worse. The hospital would be liable. Lawsuits must be avoided, Sophie," Tanya finished, with a condescending parting of her lips that was meant to be a smile. It was anything but.

Just then, Tanya's phone rang. "Sorry. I have to take this." She put her hand over the mouthpiece. "We'll talk about this another time."

Sophie rose from her chair and just as she was about to walk out, Tanya shoved a white folder toward her. "Here's our employee information about our programs. I'd suggest reading it over." Tanya went back to her call.

Sophie closed the door quietly behind her and bit back her anger.

EARLY MORNING FOG swirled across the placid lake and drifted over the beach and running trail like diaphanous angels' skirts. It was barely five thirty, but for Sophie, who was used to running in the evening, this was part of her personal makeover. She was ready for new routines. Anything that would shake her out of the cocoon she'd woven in the past.

Sophie wondered why it had taken her so long to discover running. It was the perfect prescription for de-stressing after hours in surgery or a long weekend in the ER. It was the one place she could find euphoria these days, which was a sad accounting of her life in general, but if an endorphin-induced runner's high was the only joy she could get right now, she'd take it.

Feeling her gel-cushioned running shoes against the asphalt as she gobbled up yards and then miles of track, she felt a sense of accomplishment. Most days, she ran with her earbuds in place, listening to positive mantras or inspirational quotes that kept her mind focused and off her guilt over Aleah's death. The podcasts helped motivate her to do something about the problem of drug addiction in Indian Lake. If Aleah, Owen and Jack had not been hit by a drug addict, they would not have found their way into her ER that night. Aleah would be alive and Jack wouldn't blame Sophie for anything, nor would Sophie be doubting her own judgment and action.

Changing the past was impossible, but what Sophie could do was find a way to help prevent another tragedy like this one.

Sophie didn't have many hours left in her days after her shifts in surgery or the ER, but she also didn't have many social demands. Though she could only commit a few hours a week, she wanted to use those hours to help the city fight the drug problem.

Clearly, her meeting with Tanya had been a bust. She'd have to think of something else.

Sophie slammed her feet against the pavement as she rounded the north side of the lake. Lost in her thoughts, she hadn't paid attention to how far she'd run and realized Jack Carter's condo was in view. Perched high on the hill above her and surrounded on both sides by tall trees and evergreens, it was no wonder she hadn't seen the place from the trail before. Even now, she had to slow down and crane her neck, squinting through the foliage to see it.

Jack.

She wondered what he was doing at this time in the morning. *Probably stuffing some carrots and turnips into his fancy juicer.*

She had to give him credit for watching his nutrition. She could probably benefit from a healthier diet. She was trying. Organic spinach salad had replaced burgers and fries. The lack of ice cream made life pretty boring, but she'd lost another pound this week. Amazing, considering how depressed she'd been.

Sophie was convinced that the only way for her to get out of this funk was to take action. She'd tried to do that with Tanya and bombed out. Well, she'd have to go around the woman and find another way to bring some of Phillip's successful programs to Indian Lake.

She ticked off the names of doctors and administrators who might help her. Nate Barzonni. Dr. Caldwell. Even President Emory Wills might listen to her. Of course, if she went to the president, his first question would be where she was going to get the money. They would need an endowment.

Sophie hadn't even paid her car off yet. She had little money in savings and her parents certainly didn't have any extra money lying around to donate to a new rehabilitation program.

With sweat pouring off her face, Sophie rounded the turn that headed east and into the rising, already hot summer sun. She spotted a runner coming toward her. He was dressed in tight summer running shorts and a sleeveless black T-shirt that was plastered to his muscular chest and rippling abs. He wore a Cubs baseball cap pulled down low so that she could only glimpse the blue, reflective sunglasses he wore. He was unshaven and his dark hair poked out from beneath the cap.

He pounded the asphalt trail with a vengeance, yet he moved with a fluidity that told her he'd been running for years. The man knew what he was doing. No earbuds. No iPod. She guessed he was the kind of guy whose own thoughts filled his head.

He probably didn't need an inspirational speaker to give him a positive boost for the day. He probably did that kind of thing for others.

His legs moved in such perfect motion that she imagined his feet never actually touched the ground. Weren't all those gods from Greek lore like that? Living just above the earth and not part of the human condition?

His hands were balled into fists as he pumped his arms back and forth. Sophie wondered how many decades it would take her to achieve the same mastery. Maybe he was a physical trainer.

Gym rat. If she'd been in Chicago, she would have assumed he was a model or an actor, but in Indian Lake, he probably worked construction.

As he came closer, she moved over to the right. He looked like a bullet train and she didn't want to get in his way. Though she couldn't see his eyes, there was nothing about his stern expression that suggested he'd even seen her. Whatever his thoughts were, they were intense and all consuming.

He drew nearer and she saw sweat slaking down his temples to his cheeks. Rivulets ran down his cut and chiseled arms. Not that she was taking notes. She didn't do that anymore, she reminded herself.

Still, the guy moved with the grace of a panther. He was the kind she couldn't help being attracted to. Her nerve endings sizzled as if touched with electrodes. She couldn't stop the pounding of blood through her veins that didn't come from exercise. It was automatic. She was being Sophie.

The old Sophie.

It took every ounce of self-control for her not to flash him one of her come-hither smiles. The kind that used to drop men to their knees.

But she didn't.

He raced past her so fast that he created a rush of wind that ruffled her hair.

Sophie continued running a few more feet before she slowed down. She blinked and then turned quickly on her toes.

"It can't be."

Just as the man passed her, Sophie realized it was Jack.

Her eyes fell to his ankle. "No sprain anymore." She took two steps to follow after him and then stopped.

What am I doing?

Jack hadn't acknowledged her with even a glimmer of a smile. He'd whipped by her as if she didn't exist.

Maybe Jack wishes I didn't exist.

Sophie jogged back the way she'd come and watched as Jack continued his run and then raced up the hill where she now knew he lived. He disappeared into the greens and shadows.

Beating back a good measure of anger, she turned around and took up her run once again. "Fine thing. I save the guy's life and he pretends he didn't see me."

Making her way around to the end of the trail where she'd parked her car at Cove Beach, Sophie went to a bench to do her stretches.

She ignored her pedometer and stopwatch. She didn't need to know that her time was off today. She'd been interrupted by Jack. Or maybe she'd interrupted *his* run. This was the first time she'd gone out in the morning. She'd only seen two other people running so early, not counting Jack. As she walked to her car to get her water, several cars pulled into the lot. Six o'clock runs must be more popular, she surmised.

After opening the car and taking out her water bottle, she turned and shielded her eyes and looked toward Jack's condo.

But you run before six. Is that so you'll be undisturbed? Because you can't sleep? Because you like to be alone?

Sophie tipped her bottle to her mouth and drank deeply.

Did you really just not recognize me today, Jack? Or are you still angry?

She tossed the bottle onto the floor of the passenger's side of the car.

"Well, join the club because I'm mad, too," she muttered, slamming the door and going around to the driver's side. "The difference between you and me, Jack, is that I intend to do something about it."

CHAPTER EIGHT

SOPHIE PARKED HER black Chrysler Sebring near the carriage house at the back of Mrs. Beabots's drive and turned off the engine. Gathering up her purse, water bottle and tote bag, she double-checked the interior. Satisfied that it was, as always, immaculately clean, she got out and locked the car.

At the back of the house were two doors. One led into Mrs. Beabots's kitchen, and the other opened onto a staircase that soared to her upstairs apartment.

Sophie had just unlocked her door when she heard a massive crash from Mrs. Beabots's kitchen. Fearing that the octogenarian had fallen, or worse, Sophie pounded her fist on her landlady's door.

"Mrs. Beabots! Are you okay? What's going on?"

In seconds, the door flew open and Mrs. Beabots stood on the threshold, her makeup in place, her silver hair precision-cut and styled in a bob. She wore a summer print dress, a crisp white apron and gold Chanel earrings. She gestured with both arms as if she was swimming. "Come in, Sophie! Heavens. I was afraid I'd wake the dead, but I see you've already been out." Mrs. Beabots cast a critical eye to the ring of sweat around Sophie's forehead and face. "I see you could use some cold lemonade. Or iced tea, perhaps?"

"Thanks. That sounds great."

Mrs. Beabots stepped aside for Sophie to enter. This was the first time Sophie had seen Mrs. Beabots's kitchen. In fact, all she'd ever seen of the house, besides her apartment, was the front parlor, when she'd given Mrs. Beabots the deposit for the apartment the week before Katia moved out.

The ceilings were twelve, if not fourteen feet high and lining the expansive room were the original white cabinets with glass doors. The countertops were white marble, and in the center of the kitchen was an island that at the moment was covered with dozens of pie pans, tart pans, muffin tins and sugar, huge sacks of flour, dozens of eggs and several boxes of butter.

"Are you getting ready for a party?" Sophie asked. "I haven't seen this much baking since my grandmother's ninetieth birthday." She inhaled the alluring scent of baking sugar and butter and her mouth watered. It was all she could do to repeat her mantras, reminding her to stay on her diet.

Mrs. Beabots circled around the island to the refrigerator and pulled out an antique, etched-glass pitcher filled with lemonade, complete with slices of fresh lemon.

"That's too pretty to disrupt," Sophie said. "I can just get some water from the tap."

"Nonsense. I make lemonade every day for the kids."

"Kids?"

"Annie and Timmy next door. They like to come over and sit with me while I work in the kitchen. I'm teaching Annie how to make my sugar pie."

"So, that's what this is? A culinary lesson?"

Mrs. Beabots laughed. "Not today. This is for a friend, dear. I'm making sugar pie tarts. You're welcome to stay and learn or help—" Mrs. Beabots stopped midsentence. "Oh, how silly of me. You're probably on your way to the hospital, aren't you?"

"Actually, not today. I have the day off since I worked all weekend in the ER. We had a light surgery day, so I'm taking it easy."

Mrs. Beabots's blue eyes traveled up and down Sophie's length. "It doesn't look like that to me. I'd say you've been working yourself pretty hard."

Sophie couldn't hold back her grin. "Sorry. I can't help but laugh. This is the new me. I run to de-stress and knock off a few more pounds."

"Hmm. There's nothing wrong with your figure, dear. If you ask me, I've always thought people run to outrun their demons."

Reflexively, Sophie shook her head. "I don't have any demons."

"Really? Then that would make you an anomaly. I have dozens of them myself. Now," she said with a smile as she wiped her hands on her apron and picked up a green milk glass mixing bowl and a French whisk, "how would you like to learn the secret to my sugar pie?"

"I would be honored, especially since Katia told me you don't share recipes."

"Ordinarily, I don't. But I've been coming to some realizations of my own lately," she explained as she opened a carton of eggs and began cracking them into the bowl.

"And that would be?" Sophie set her purse and tote down on a chair and went to the sink to wash her hands.

"That I'm not going to live forever."

Sophie chuckled under her breath. "None of us do."

"I know what you're thinking—that I'm in my eighties and this should have been a consideration before now."

Sophie dried her hands and turned around. "I confess, I was. Sorry."

"No need." Mrs. Beabots lifted a linen cloth

from some pie dough she'd made earlier and began rolling it out. She fluttered a hand in the air, waving off Sophie's thoughts as if they were distracting moths. "Quite honestly, this isn't the first time these thoughts have crossed my mind. And I'm not dwelling on it now. It's just that while I still have the energy and my wits about me, I thought I should be doing more. You know what I mean?"

"Like what?" Sophie asked. "Do you want to travel? See the world? Or a bucket list kind of thing?"

"Heavens, I've seen the world. Or most of it," Mrs. Beabots replied, cutting small circles out of the dough and placing them in the tartlet pans. "Measure out three separate cups of sugar for me in those metal cups, would you, dear?"

"Sure. So, when was this that you traveled and where did you go?" Sophie asked with genuine curiosity. She didn't know much about Mrs. Beabots and her background. In fact, nobody did. The woman was the essence of secrecy. Even Sophie's mother and grandmother had heard little about Raymond Beabots or Emma before they move to Indian Lake in the midsixties, opened the Rose Street Grocery and bought this old Victorian home.

Sophie's curious nature had often gotten her into trouble when she was young. Her mother told her it was the root of her flirtatiousness. She was always curious about the next guy around the next corner. That same investigative bent had served her well in her medical career, and if she hadn't settled on heart ablations, she might have gone into diagnostic medicine. Tracking down clues and symptoms to pinpoint disease.

Mrs. Beabots still hadn't answered, and Sophie realized her curiosity might be getting her into hot water yet again. She stopped measuring. "It's okay. You don't have to tell me."

Mrs. Beabots met Sophie's gaze. "It's just that no one has asked me that in a very long time. Not even one of my girls."

"Your girls?"

"Sarah and her crowd. Oh, they're all grown up now, but since I had no children of my own, I've always been quite close to Sarah. Maddie, too. And Liz."

"And Olivia. Katia, too," Sophie added.

"That's right. My circle is growing. Now I include you." Mrs. Beabots smiled widely.

Sophie blushed. She couldn't remember the last time she'd blushed. Grade school? Possibly. She wasn't the blushing type—never had been. But Mrs. Beabots was an icon, and to be a part of her private world was intriguing and flattering. "I'm honored."

"You're the only one of my girls who has both

parents alive. We support each other the way families should. They help me with little things that have become a major consideration for me now that I don't drive anymore." She frowned. "Getting to the grocery in a rainstorm is a real chore if you don't have a car."

"The winters alone must slow you down."

"Believe me, they do. But I manage. I hope you won't mind if I need to ask for a ride now and then. When you're available, of course."

"I don't mind at all," Sophie said. "I'll check with you whenever I go out. I do that with my mom as it is. She can't always get away from the farm and since I'm in town, I pick things up for her all the time."

"Isn't that wonderful?" Mrs. Beabots sighed. "Such a lovely thing to have family. Frankly, that being the case, you may not have as much time for us and our get-togethers over the holidays and such. But you're always welcome."

"Thank you." Sophie smiled.

"Now, hand me that bowl there."

Sophie did as she was asked. "This looks like you're baking for an army. Is it someone's birthday?"

"Birthday? Oh, no." She smiled. "This is for Eleanor Fieldstone's new project. She's having an open house the day after tomorrow and she prevailed upon me to make something special for her fund-raiser."

"Fieldstone?" Sophie knew she'd heard Eleanor's name lately, but couldn't place it. Had she been a patient? That happened to her a lot. Then it clicked. "Is she the woman who started Recovery Alliance last year?"

"She is. Do you know her?" Mrs. Beabots filled the last of the trays with pie crust.

"I've never met her, but I've heard about her work with drug addicts."

Mrs. Beabots shook her head. "It's a terrible plague in this town, drugs. I was over at the police station the other day—"

"The police station? Why?"

"Oh, Trent Davis is a favorite of mine. Actually, it was his birthday and I baked him a cake. All those boys over there at the station love my cakes."

"Funny, but his name sounds familiar, too."

"I know his mother very well. Trent just made detective. I think it's because of the gangs around here. His mother told me he's helped spearhead two large stings and the police have rounded up over twenty drug dealers."

"I had no idea it was that bad."

"Tip of the iceberg, Trent says." As Mrs. Beabots rattled on, Sophie remembered that Trent was one of the investigating policemen after Jack's accident. He had asked Sophie for a copy of Greg Fulton's medical records, and he'd questioned Jack about the incident, though Sophie hadn't been present for that. Still, she'd gotten the impression that Trent was courteous, professional and thorough.

"Trent will be at the open house. I'll introduce you. He's very handsome." Mrs. Beabots winked.

Sophie shook her head. "That's okay," she said, fending off the obvious attempt at matchmaking. "I believe I've already met him. Besides, I don't have time for romance right now. But I would like to meet Eleanor. I'd like to find out more about her work."

"That would be perfect," Mrs. Beabots said, filling the tartlets with cream and sugar. "I needed someone to drive me there and help with my desserts."

Sophie couldn't help smiling to herself. Mrs. Beabots was as crafty as she was charming.

THE RECOVERY ALLIANCE was located across from the county courthouse in one of the original Main Street buildings from the 1870s. It had been refurbished extensively in the late 1970s, becoming a dress shop, and still had maroon awnings out front with gold key scallop edging. The front door, made of brass and etched glass, was so heavy Sophie had a difficult time juggling the two pans of sugar tarts and her purse as she pulled it open.

The main area, formerly used as the showroom, still had the original warped floorboards, which had been recently sanded, stained and coated. There were no rugs, drapes or decorations, except the crystal chandelier that had once hung in the dress shop.

Along the walls were several old bookshelves, which looked like they'd come from a garage sale or a schoolhouse auction. They were filled with brochures, some tattered paperbacks and stacks of colorful folders. Three round folding tables covered in homemade cloths sat in the middle of the room, while at the far end a long table held a coffee urn, teapot, pitcher of lemonade and trays of sandwiches, fruits and vegetables. Sophie added Mrs. Beabots's tarts to the array.

Half a dozen people were putting out little bouquets of garden flowers, brochures, survey sheets, pens and name tags on the tables.

Just as they finished putting out the desserts, a tall blonde woman in her late fifties wearing a brown summer linen suit walked over to them. She gave Mrs. Beabots a hug.

"The tarts are just beautiful. Thank you so much for this, Mrs. Beabots," she said with a smile. "Frankly, I'm hoping your famous pie will be a draw for people."

"My goodness, Eleanor, your work is getting quite the buzz around town. I don't think you need me or my pie in the least."

"I wish that were the case," Eleanor replied glumly. "I was hoping for two dozen volunteers and these poor five folks have shouldered the entire burden. Courtney, over there, missed a day and a half of work just to get our brochure out on time. She only walked in from the printer's ten minutes ago. That was close."

While Eleanor spoke, Sophie noted that the offices and private rooms in back still seemed to be in makeshift condition. Though the partition walls were up, there were no doors. If they needed privacy, they didn't have it yet.

"Let me introduce my friend, Sophie Mattuchi. This is Eleanor Fieldstone," Mrs. Beabots said. "Sophie lives upstairs in my house now that Katia is getting married. She's a cardiac surgeon's nurse at the hospital."

Sophie held out her hand. "I'm very interested in the work you're doing. From what little I've researched, I believe you're an addictions specialist."

"What is that?" Mrs. Beabots's blue eyes were filled with curiosity.

"I'm board certified in addiction medicine. I worked for years in Chicago, but when my husband became ill, we sold our house and moved here to Indian Lake to slow down a bit. Once he died, I needed a challenge."

"I absolutely agree with that," Mrs. Beabots said firmly. "We all have to have passion. Without it, life isn't worth living."

Sophie cocked her head. "Really? I thought it was love we all needed."

Mrs. Beabots waved her hand as if shooing a fly. "You can love all kinds of people, and be loved, but passion for a cause fills those holes inside you when you realize you want your life to count for something."

Eleanor nodded. "I think Recovery Alliance can make a big difference. Indian Lake needs us. Education is essential to stopping this problem. The police can only do so much and they are called in when there's a crisis. The Alliance's job is to inform and educate parents and kids before they start experimenting with drugs. I want to get to the kids in elementary and middle schools. By the time they hit high school, it's too late."

Mrs. Beabots folded her arms over her chest. "This is so disheartening. *High school* is too late?"

"That's part of the addiction problem today. When children get hooked so young, their brains are still developing and they have no chance to mature like their peers. They don't understand consequences. They can't think the way we do. They are relegated to a life of chasing the next high."

"Is there any hope?" Mrs. Beabots asked.

"Yes, there is. But it takes a great deal of commitment. Most importantly, the parents are the drivers. Too many times I've seen that the child is dedicated to his recovery, but the parent is not." Eleanor shook her head then continued, "The Alliance uses a Twelve Step Program with addicts and our recovery rate is in line with AA. What sets us apart is the education we give to parents and younger kids."

Sophie nodded. "About a month ago I was involved with the treatment of an ER patient, an addict, who died. I've been trying to find something that goes beyond the hospital's emergency care for people with drug problems." Sophie held out her hand. "I want to help you all that I can."

Eleanor squeezed her hand. "Believe me, Sophie, we can use you. This means a lot to me."

"What do you need?"

"Well, your job at the hospital must keep you very busy. How many hours a week can you give me?"

"I can spare a couple nights. One weekend a month, possibly, when I'm not working in the ER." Sophie remembered Tanya's warnings about employee involvement with non-affiliated programs. There were a lot of reasons for her to walk away, but already she could see the positive impact Eleanor's program could have. This was too important for Sophie to pass up.

"I'll take it," Eleanor replied excitedly. "We're desperate to simply get the word out that we exist. I need help on social media. Do you think you could meet with local businesses? We need funding, but we also simply need them to talk about us. Maybe sponsor radio or internet ads."

"I can do that," Sophie said firmly. "Let me put some ideas down on paper. My first thought is Maddie Barzonni's café. I could start there. Maybe the Book Shop and Java Stop for another. What do you think?"

"Terrific. Here's my card. Call me when you're ready to start and I'll get some materials together for you."

Sophie smiled as Eleanor walked away, then she realized Mrs. Beabots was staring at her, dumbfounded.

Sophie swallowed hard. She felt every ounce of Mrs. Beabots's concern. Sophie knew exactly what she'd just done. She'd broken one of the hospital's explicit rules. She was not to align herself with other organizations that conflicted with the hospital's programs. She couldn't let anyone know she was helping Eleanor.

"Mrs. Beabots…"

"You don't even have to ask. As far as I'm concerned, all you did was drop me off."

"You understand, then?"

"Maybe even more than you do. Emory Wills

runs a tight ship over there at the hospital. He's always been like that. Too controlling." Then she winked. "And absolutely no fun. Now, let's have some coffee and see if my tarts are any good."

Sophie filled a Styrofoam cup with coffee for Mrs. Beabots. The black liquid reminded her of all the coffee she'd downed the night Aleah died. Aleah's face haunted her. Flashes of that night came back to her. Jack's pleas for her to save Aleah. The fear in his eyes and the compelling, imploring look he gave her. He was incapable of saving Aleah himself and he'd counted on her to do it.

And I failed.

Sophie watched several groups of people come through the front door of Recovery Alliance. Men, women and kids of every age. Some she'd seen around town at the grocery store, the dry cleaners, even at the hospital. They were her neighbors.

Warmth spread through Sophie, then surged like a fire that had been fanned. It was nearly overwhelming, but somehow reassuring. For the first time in a long time, she felt balanced and whole. With a start, she realized she was feeling exactly what Mrs. Beabots had talked about. Sophie had found her passion.

CHAPTER NINE

SINCE MEETING ELEANOR, Sophie had spent her break hours calling Scott Abbot at the bookstore, Jerry Mason's construction company, Louise Railton and Captain Redbeard. All had agreed to put up posters in their businesses. Scott couldn't have been more cooperative, especially once Sophie told him she'd learned of the Alliance through Mrs. Beabots.

After about a week of doing outreach and learning about the Alliance, Sophie realized how desperately the Alliance needed operating capital and volunteered to make fund-raising phone calls, as well. She'd never asked anyone to donate money before. Sure, she'd sold Girl Scout cookies door-to-door when she was in elementary school, and she'd helped Isabelle Hawks last year with her art booth at the summer festival, but she'd never asked someone to give her money for a cause or charity.

"How difficult can it be?" she asked Eleanor on Tuesday morning. Sophie had an afternoon shift and decided to spend her free hours at the Alliance offices.

Not even an arched brow and a "you've got to be kidding me" glance from Eleanor could daunt her, though. Sophie enthusiastically grabbed the receiver. "I'd better get to it."

Eleanor nodded knowingly. "I'll bring you coffee. And shut the door for privacy."

Sophie's first call was to Austin McCreary. She bumbled her way through her pitch and sounded like a grade schooler asking for a hall pass. Though she didn't have any training or a script to follow, she hoped her passion for helping the people in the next room would shine through. Austin was gracious and donated five thousand dollars.

"This is very generous of you, Austin. We all want to thank you," Sophie said.

"Actually, Sophie, once I get back from my honeymoon, I plan to help Eleanor even more. Aleah's death has really shaken Katia and me up. It's made us look around our little town and see that there's some serious work to be done. Thank you for all the help you're giving Eleanor."

"It's not much, really. Just a few hours here and there. She can't do it all."

"It's like sticking your thumb in the dam, I'm sure," he said. "Good luck."

Austin's donation gave her the confidence to go to Mrs. Beabots, Helen Knowland, Debra La Pointe, Sarah and Luke Bosworth and Gina Barzonni. Not one turned her down.

What surprised Sophie the most was the outpouring of affection toward her for helping the Alliance. She almost felt as if she'd been accepted by them, despite her long-standing reputation. Almost.

SOPHIE STRIPPED THE blue nitrile gloves from her hands and pulled off her surgical gown after the last ablation surgery of the day.

"Good job today, Sophie," Nate Barzonni said, pulling off his mask.

"Thank you, Doctor." Sophie smiled, enjoying the feeling of accomplishment she got each time they completed a surgery. "I'll check on the patient."

Nate stopped her. "I understand you made a phone call to my mother yesterday."

Sophie's mind was still on the ablation. "Your mother?"

"About the Alliance and the donation?"

There was something in Nate's voice she didn't like. That sharp, stern edge she heard only when he was frustrated during a surgery. She remembered her conversation with Tanya and gulped. "Is there a problem?"

"Not with my mother. When she told me what she donated to the Alliance, I thought it kind of her. What concerns me is that it was you who made the call."

"Um, why?" Sophie felt as if she'd fallen into frozen waters. Suddenly, the world had grown cold.

How could she have believed word of Gina's contribution wouldn't get back to her son? True, Sophie still didn't understand how the hospital could frown on anyone who was trying to make a positive difference in people's lives. But Tanya's warning had been serious. Sophie had been so caught up in the work she was doing, and the positive responses, she'd forgotten how small Indian Lake truly was. She'd forgotten to be cautious.

How far would Nate go with this "inside information" about Sophie and the Alliance?

"Sophie, you have to know that Emory Wills dislikes any of his staff working for what he considers the opposition."

"Opposition?" *Did the man think they were at war?*

"The Alliance is not funded or endorsed by the hospital. Their methodology is very different from Indian Lake Hospital…"

"Thank God," she interrupted. "Sorry."

Nate's frown deepened. "I'm serious, Sophie. You're the best cardiac nurse I've worked with. I don't want to lose you."

"You think I'd get fired for just helping Eleanor? I'm not even doing that much." Fear grabbed her by the knees and threatened to take her down.

"I'd say raising money for them to continue is grounds enough. I'm not saying you should stay off the phones or stop putting up posters, but I'd be, well, more discreet."

Sophie's shoulders slumped. She felt deflated. "I see."

He put his hand on her shoulder. "Look, Sophie. It's not just Emory. I know you. You don't do anything in half measures. You're already starting to seem tired. I can see how much you love working in the ER. So do I. But with the Alliance on top of that, you could be in danger of spreading yourself too thin. Don't let that happen."

"I'll be okay," she tried to assure him, but she saw the wariness in his eyes.

"I'm just trying to warn you. That's all. Forewarned is forearmed. Okay? And you and I never had this conversation. What you do on your free time is no concern of mine. By the way, I have an envelope with my own donation in my office. Anonymous. Give it to Eleanor. 'Kay?"

Sophie felt her smile rise from her toes. Her chest inflated. "Thank you, Doctor."

"You bet," he said and winked. She'd escaped the extracurricular police.

JACK PEELED OFF the plastic lid from the cappuccino that Maddie Barzonni had made for him and chuckled. Today she'd drawn a sunflower in the thick foam because he'd told her yesterday that sunflowers were his favorite summer bloom. He shook his head and walked toward Carter and Associates' massive window wall, which overlooked downtown Indian Lake.

That's what he loved about his new home in this small town. Little things. Thoughtful things that friends did for friends. Maddie's café had the best cappuccino Jack had ever tasted, bar none. The best barista Chicago could boast didn't hold a candle to Maddie, and she was teaching young Chloe Knowland to follow in her footsteps. Except when Chloe was running to acting classes, of course.

Jack was amazed by how quickly he'd become attached to so many people in town. Mrs. Beabots was now his client, as well as Sarah and Luke Bosworth. Liz and Gabe Barzonni, too. Maddie had recently bought a policy for her entire franchise of cafés in Chicago.

He passed Aleah's desk and stopped. Her parents had requested all her personal items and Jack had packed them in a box and mailed them himself. He had kept her nameplate. It was identical to the ones they all had. He liked uniformity. He believed clients sensed subconscious impressions. Katia wanted their clients to think of Carter and Associates as family. Jack wanted them to feel protected.

Jack picked up Aleah's brass nameplate and held it.

He wasn't sure if he felt her presence any more strongly by keeping her nameplate. Most bosses would throw it away once they'd hired a new assistant.

But Jack wouldn't do that. He'd keep her nameplate in his desk drawer—not to keep his guilt close, but to remember her as the bright young woman she'd been and hope that he could find another assistant even half as enthusiastic.

Jack's eyes slipped over to Melanie who was taking down an insurance application over the phone. Owen was setting up appointments. Katia was on the phone with a new corporate client.

They didn't need him right this minute, but as soon as they were off their respective calls, they would.

His thoughts about Aleah faded as he sipped his coffee, blowing on the surface. Something outside caught his eye. Rather, some*one*.

Still dressed in her scrubs, Sophie stood at the corner, watching the traffic. She pulled a huge clip from her hair and let her waves tumble down. Sliding her fingers to her temple, she smiled as if relieved.

Pretty smile. Pretty woman. He hummed a few notes of the song.

She adjusted the shoulder strap on her black

purse and the light changed. Sophie stepped off
the curb and greeted an elderly couple as they approached her in the intersection. As she stepped
onto the sidewalk next to his building, another
man greeted her with a hug. They conversed for
a moment and then parted. The man stopped,
shouted something to Sophie. She turned and
blew him a kiss.

Jack cocked his head and lowered his paper
cup. *Boyfriend?*

A phone rang. Jack heard Melanie's voice answer just as another call came in. Owen picked
up. "Carter and Associates. This is Owen."

Jack spun around. *Time to get back to work.
Time to stop thinking about Sophie.*

THE ALLIANCE OFFICE was only a few doors down
from Carter and Associates. It was impossible
for Sophie to walk to the Alliance without thinking about Jack. What he was doing. How he was
feeling. Wondering if she could help him. As-
suage his pain. Relieve his grief. As often as she
chided herself that Jack wasn't her responsibility, the memory of his stricken expression while
sitting on the edge of the hospital bed lingered
in her mind—indelible and haunting. It was the
image that shot her full of guilt and recriminations. Both of which were nonproductive.

Eleanor greeted her as she entered the office.

She looked up from the stack of files she was carrying and smiled, exhaling deeply. Was that relief in her expression?

"Sophie, I didn't expect to see you today. Are you on break?" Eleanor asked as she tilted her head toward her office. "Come with me."

"I have two hours free, so I thought I'd stop by." Sophie followed her and glanced toward the far end of the main room, where a group of people were sitting in a circle talking with Earl Belkowitz, a counselor she'd met on the day of the open house. They'd spoken only briefly, but she'd been impressed with his easy manner and sense of humor.

"Eleanor, I counted fifteen people out there," Sophie said, closing the office door behind her. "Just four days ago, Earl only had six clients."

Eleanor smiled. "Word is getting out about our services, and even I have to admit that the response is growing faster than I'd planned for." She sighed as she plopped the files on her desk, smoothing a clump of hair that had fallen across her brow. She was clearly frazzled. "That group is the second one today. We have requests for daily meetings because for so many, these sessions are their lifeline to sobriety. I love that we're vital, but…"

"It's a lot of work."

"And costs a lot of money, as you well know.

Thank goodness for you, Sophie. You've raised over ten thousand dollars in a short time. I have no idea what I would have done without you."

Sophie reached into her pocket. "I have another check here, from my boss. It's supposed to be anonymous." She handed it over. "Eleanor…I need to talk to you."

Eleanor was reading the check, and her eyes grew wide as she took in the amount. "This is amazing. I could hire that counselor from South Bend I interviewed yesterday…" She stopped cold then lowered herself into her chair. "I can tell you why you're here, Sophie. You don't need to say a word. This is too much for you, isn't it?"

Sophie felt her face crack with emotion. "That's the problem—I love what I'm doing and feel like I'm making a difference."

"Then what is it?"

"There's been…a development. My job may be in question if I continue working with you. Too many people around town know who I am. Too many hospital administrators watching too many of us." Sophie pressed her fingertips to her forehead and closed her eyes. "Honestly, I'm beginning to feel as if I'm on a surveillance camera."

"Now you know how my addicts feel when they have to wear ankle bracelets and report to their probation officers."

"Uh-huh. I empathize and I still want to help."

Eleanor gnawed her bottom lip pensively for a moment. She sat up straighter. "Maybe there's another way."

"Like what?"

"Be an advocate for an addict. A sponsor."

Sophie paused. Fund-raising was making her too visible to the hospital administrators who worried about liability. Perhaps being a sponsor might keep her participation with the Alliance under the hospital radar.

"But aren't sponsors usually former addicts themselves?" Sophie asked.

"Traditionally, yes. Still, we have lots of doctors and psychologists who help out this way. With your experience and medical knowledge you would be the kind of empathetic yet tough-love sponsor I need on the team," Eleanor explained, her blue eyes suddenly glistening with tears she blinked away.

Sophie touched Eleanor's arm. "You have someone in mind for me, don't you?"

"Yes. His name is Jeremy…" Eleanor flipped through the charts and withdrew a brand-new folder containing only a single sheet of paper. It was the standard client information sheet, but Sophie noticed most of the lines were blank. No phone. No address. Little medical history.

"And you want me to take him on?" Sophie asked with a jolt of apprehension. Was she edu-

cated enough for this work? She'd immersed herself in a sea of information; she'd fallen asleep
with reports and personal testimonies and jour-
nals in order to better understand what people
with addictions went through. The cure for addiction to drugs or alcohol was not purely medical or
scientific. It took immense will and fortitude to
fight the insidious lure of narcotics. Addicts were
tough to cure. Many often felt as if they were only
one half step away from falling over the precipice
into oblivion. Back into that dark hole they may
or may not crawl out of again.

"Every case is unique. Jeremy Hawthorne is
originally from Phoenix. Hitchhiked to Indiana
last year. He told me he plays trumpet, or did in
high school, but he sold his instrument to buy
drugs. He's worked odd jobs from town to town.
That's all I know."

Sophie felt her heart grow heavy just listening
to Eleanor.

"I'll try, but I have to ask—why me? I'm not
trained—"

Eleanor cut her off. "Because you have a gift
for helping others that comes from someplace
deep inside you, Sophie," Eleanor said. "I can
see why you chose nursing. You were born to do
it. I'm guessing you've never harmed a soul in
your life. Human or animal."

Sophie struggled not to show the raw emotion

coursing through her. All her life, she had wanted to help. From the stray cats, wounded birds and lost fawns she'd nursed as a child on the farm to the first patient she'd ever tended, Sophie remembered all of them. Maybe not all their names, but their faces. Their eyes. Their deep need for relief and their abounding gratitude when she sutured, bandaged and eased their pain with drugs.

Patients like Jack. He'd held her hand so tightly when he was delusional right after the accident. His concussion had caused him to be disoriented. She'd seen that look in other patients—some when they'd been in hospice, dying. Jack had looked at her like she was the world. Or the next world.

With a shock, Sophie realized she wanted to see that penetrating gaze of surrender, gratitude and hope in Jack's eyes again. She wanted to be a safe harbor for him.

Not once with a man had Sophie ever seen anything but desire or conquest. Men had been pastimes. Not people.

Jack was different. She'd seen what she could be to a man—to Jack—and that wanting tugged on her head and her heart. It didn't weigh her down or threaten to drown her. Instead, it was a tether to a hot air balloon that could take her far away, to worlds she'd never dared dream of.

Jack could take her to a place where she might find her value as a woman to be loved.

As the idea settled on her shoulders like a gossamer shawl, Sophie shivered. She shook off the foreign feeling.

What was she thinking? Talk about delusional. In a minute, she'd be the one Eleanor thought was the addict. Thinking nonsense. Daydreaming of impossibilities. Acting like Alice in Wonderland. She needed to stay on track. Sophie was all about helping others. Not herself.

"You're right. I'm at my best when I'm helping. When can I meet Jeremy?"

Eleanor smiled widely and rose to give Sophie a hug. "Is tomorrow too soon?"

CHAPTER TEN

SOPHIE FIDGETED UNCOMFORTABLY as she sat in a booth at the crumbling, seventy-year-old Road House Café on the outskirts of town. She'd lived in Indian Lake almost her whole life and had never been to the place. She remembered her mother describing the inedible food and her father grumbling that the building wasn't safe. Her grandmother told her the ramshackle café had been on the edge of demolition in the 1930s. It still stood. The screen door had banged when she walked in and Sophie had feared the clapboard walls would disintegrate from the vibration. There was an old Coca-Cola cooler outside the front door that still held bottles of soft drinks and beer. Freezing water swirled around them.

Inside, half the bar stools were gone completely. Three aging bikers stood at the bar talking and drinking coffee from thick china coffee mugs.

There were about a dozen booths along a wall of greasy, dirty windows for patrons to see across the farmland. Sophie wondered why the owner didn't just pull down the blinds if no one was going to wash the glass. Though from the look of the wood floor with clumps of dirt kicked under the stools and the torn Naugahyde covering on the seats, no one here was too concerned about appearances or improvements.

The Road House Café had been Jeremy's choice of a place to meet. She'd suggested Lou's Diner, which was close to the hospital, or even the Indian Lake Deli, but he'd nearly hung up the phone.

"Forget it," he'd grumbled arrogantly.

She hadn't even met him face-to-face and he was brushing her off. Discarding any chance for recovery. Refusing help.

Maybe that was the problem. He didn't want to feel like a charity case. She'd have to watch that she didn't demean him in any way.

She rubbed her arms as she propped her elbows on the tabletop. The silver flecks in the gray, white and pink-veined Formica had faded and the surface felt sticky. She pulled a thin paper napkin from the metal dispenser, stuck the end in her glass of water and wiped the surface under her elbows.

A roar of motorcycle engines filled the late afternoon air, turning Sophie's attention away from the collage of antique ice-cream posters, which she was certain were not cherished collectibles but simply tacked up over the years from vendors passing through. Eventually, they probably covered rot, holes and broken paneling.

Eight guys, ranging from midtwenties to midseventies, parked their bikes out front, taking up all the room next to her car. Most wore leather vests, no shirts, boots with studs and stainless steel chains hanging from their necks, wrists and waistbands. Two were bald. The rest wore long hair tied with leather or bandanas. They were trying to seem rough. They succeeded.

Last off one of the bikes and seated behind the biggest, burliest and ugliest of the bunch was a thin young man, wearing torn jeans, a worn and stained black sweatshirt with the hood pulled up. He had a backpack with a fading Giants logo emblazoned across it.

Sophie guessed this was Jeremy as the younger man hung back, assessing the diner as if unsure about entering.

Even from this distance, she saw eyes filled with despair. There was no life in his face. Not even the ghost of a smile. She couldn't help wondering if he'd ever smiled.

Who had this boy been before the drugs? Something told her that was exactly what she had to find out in order to help him. Backward in order to move forward.

He was still hesitating, looking at the bikes as if he longed to jump on one and ride away. But to where? His addiction would go with him wherever he went.

On instinct, Sophie rose, left the booth and circled around the group of bikers who, ordinarily, would have intimidated her. She almost didn't see them, she was so concentrated on Jeremy.

She glanced out the window. He'd pulled his hoodie farther over his face and turned his back on the diner.

She went to the door and pushed the screen open. "Jeremy?"

He looked up, dark hollow eyes peering out from deep inside his hood.

Silence.

"Jeremy. It's me, Sophie. Don't leave."

"You're pretty." He stood still, not shifting an inch. Still judging her, but not seeking an escape route, either.

"Thank you," she replied, stepping out onto the rickety porch. She inched forward as if she were approaching a wild animal in a trap. He was terrified. And in pain.

Sophie guessed that he'd agreed to meet her because the ugly truth was that he had no place else to go.

She gestured toward the array of motorcycles. "Friends of yours?"

He shook his head. "I hitched."

"Are they your dealers?"

Jeremy nearly smiled. Nearly. "No. They said they were accountants from Chicago. They come to Indiana on the weekends and pretend they have a second life. Stupid, huh? What's wrong with their first life?"

"You're right. In the end, we all have only one life, but there's nothing wrong with wearing costumes and experiencing all kinds of adventures."

"I like adventure. Thrills. That's my problem."

She walked closer. "No, Jeremy. You like drugs. There's no adventure in drugs. Just imprisonment."

Sophie spotted an old picnic table under a spreading oak tree. A tire hung from a rope tied to a low limb. She hadn't seen a swing like that in years. Not since she'd been a kid herself and played with the Johnson kids at their farm down the road. She'd been lucky. She'd had a normal upbringing.

The older she got, the more she realized how lucky she was to have grown up with two loving parents, a roof over her head, food to eat and an education.

"Let's sit over there at the picnic table. Unless you'd rather go inside. I'll buy you lunch."

"Maybe later. I'm not hungry."

She eyed him carefully. She would guess he hadn't eaten in days. "Suit yourself." She walked toward the table, letting him follow. She didn't want him to think she didn't trust him. That's what this was right now—a dance of trust.

She sat down at the end and motioned to the space beside her.

He sauntered, barely picking up his feet. His sneakers looked like he'd walked from Arizona. She knew he had access to newer, cleaner clothes through donations from several agencies in Indian Lake, including Recovery Alliance. He had not availed himself of those services. She wondered why.

He stared at her but didn't start the conversation. His frame was even thinner than she'd earlier suspected. She guessed he was still using.

Sophie realized she had one shot with this guy and if she blew it, she'd never see him again. She had to be careful and effective.

"I'm surprised you agreed to meet me." She gestured at his sweatshirt. "You don't take charity from anyone, do you? Otherwise, you'd have better clothes and you'd be eating more."

"I eat," he snipped.

"Yeah?" She reached over and yanked his hood down.

His blond hair was patchy with short clumps that stuck up in unwashed stacks.

"I'm a nurse, Jeremy. Your skin is pasty under all that dust and dirt. Your eyes show early signs of liver failure, probably from too much alcohol.

Your teeth are cracked and several are missing. That tells me that you've done a lot of crystal meth. There's not much you can say or do that will fool me. If that's what you're all about, then this meeting is over."

She started to rise and he grabbed the edge of her sleeve.

"You're right," Jeremy said. "Please, sit down."

Sophie sat. And waited. It was his turn.

He kicked the ground, then stuck his hands in his sweatshirt pocket. "That's the part I hate the most about being me. My life."

"What's that?"

"The lying. I've been doing it since I was a kid. Born to it, I guess."

"I don't believe that. You learned it. But why?"

He shrugged his bony shoulders. "Trying to get attention from my parents, I guess. They were always too busy. They both worked. Professionals. Dad was an architect. Mom was an attorney. He was chasing down clients or dreaming up some new skyscraper that would rock the world with his genius. Mom worked eighty hours a week trying to make partner. There was no time for me," he said morosely.

Sophie winced. Though she didn't have a husband or child, she was doing just what Jeremy complained about. She overscheduled, overpromised, overinvolved herself. She wanted to help

him, but clearly, he needed attention. A lot of it.
Could she truly be valuable to him?

"Do you have brothers or sisters?" she asked.

"No, just me." He heaved a sigh. "That's a good
thing. They didn't have the chance to mess with
another kid's life," he spat out.

"You're very angry with them, aren't you?"

"I shouldn't be. You know, they spent over four
hundred grand on rehab for me."

Sophie's eyes widened in surprise. "I didn't
know. I thought you were in this all alone."

"I am now. They finally threw up their hands
after fourteen stints in treatment. But I kept using.
I learned more about drugs, how to buy them,
use them, how to cheat on my drug tests. Even if
you're on parole, you can time it so that your officer will never catch you. It's all a game."

"The chasing?"

"Yeah. The chasing is a game."

"But in the end, you're the one who loses.
You've already lost your family. They're all the
way in Arizona and here you are in this little town
in Indiana talking to a total stranger. Is that how
you see your life? Constantly moving?"

He shook his head and his hair moved stiffly.
"My life? Every shrink and counselor I've talked
to in every rehab center has preached to me about
how I need to value my life. Well, I don't. Miss
Mattuchi…"

"Sophie," she corrected.

"Sophie. I only wanted to see you because I liked the sound of your voice on the phone."

"Really? That's it?"

"It was enough," he replied with a faint smile creeping across his face. He put his hands on his knees and stared at them. "Look, Sophie, I don't expect anything. I don't care about anything. I went to the Recovery Alliance because I was walking through town and saw the sign. I was curious. Usually, places like that have free snacks. You know, tea, coffee and cookies. When I got there that day, there was so much food. It reminded me of one of my mom's parties for clients."

Sophie nodded. That must have been the day of the open house. "I was there that day."

"I waited till all the normal people had left."

"You consider me 'normal'?"

"Yeah. You know. Not a user. Like my parents."

She folded her arms. "I don't know your parents and I've never been married or had kids. So don't compare me to them. That's not fair. Lumping me in with everyone else you're angry with. Tell me, Jeremy, what did you expect from our meeting today aside from staring at my...*pretty* face?"

His eyes drifted to the horizon as if there was something there.

"I hung out with Eleanor a long time. She arranged for a place for me to stay with the Salvation Army. They feed me, too. She convinced me to join one of her counseling groups. It was actually pretty good."

"Why's that?"

"It was just me and the counselor. Henry was his name. Volunteer. Didn't take notes or make me feel more ashamed than I already do."

"And do you feel ashamed?"

"I do. I'm sorry I hurt my mom and dad."

"But you're still mad at them."

He nodded. "They wanted everything in the world, but not me."

"So you felt abandoned."

He jerked his head toward her and their eyes locked. She could see he'd just had a revelation. "I...never thought of it that way."

She continued, "Like an orphan. You felt no different than a baby who'd been tossed in the trash. And that's what you're doing with your life. Staying on the move. Going from drug house to shelters to the next drug house. So you live the life of an orphan. No family to report to or be responsible for. And you believe no one wants to find you. But there's something wrong with your scenario."

"Wrong with it? It's all wrong. I'm as messed up as anyone can get."

"Maybe. Maybe not," she countered. "I'm betting your parents do want to know where you are. What you're doing."

He waved his hand, as if to deflect her comment. "So, what's in it for you? You get your rocks off saving people? Is that it?"

"Actually, yes."

"Figures I'd get the Nurse Nancy type." He paused. "Why exactly do you think I'm worth saving, Sophie?"

She studied the razor-sharp planes of his face. There was a trace of innocence, like a small child in need, and yet his eyes were filled with the look of someone who'd seen too much. He roamed the earth with one foot on solid ground and the other stuck in a narcotic dream. His alienation and loneliness struck the deepest part of her heart. No one should ever feel that alone.

She sensed he was reaching out for help. The fact that he'd lingered in Indian Lake since the open house told her something. Perhaps Eleanor's easy and caring ways had won him over. Maybe it was the slow pace of the town. It could be one of a dozen things, but the point was he was there with her now.

"All human life is valuable, Jeremy."

"Cut the platitudes. I'm as worthless as they come," he ground out. He leaned forward, hunching his shoulders, and as he did, something in his backpack moved.

"What was that?" Sophie asked, pointing to the jostling canvas bag.

Jeremy shucked the shoulder straps off and pulled the backpack around to his lap. "This is part of the reason I wanted to meet with you today. You sounded nice on the phone. Really nice. Considerate. Like you were a kind person. A person who would help me."

She nodded. "That's my hope. Yes." She stared at the backpack.

"I have a big favor," Jeremy said, unzipping the bag.

An ink-black furry head popped out of the opening. Two small black eyes peered at Sophie and blinked.

She snapped her head back in surprise. "That's a...puppy!"

"A Yorkie-Poo, actually. Frenchie is a full-grown dog. Two years old and six pounds of love." Finally, Jeremy smiled. He pulled the tiny, curly-haired dog from his backpack. Frenchie immediately jumped onto Sophie's lap and scrambled up to her face to lick her cheek.

"I knew it!" Jeremy exclaimed. "She does like you. A lot. She's got a natural instinct for people."

Sophie held Frenchie with both hands but didn't try to make her stop licking. Sophie giggled at her tickling tongue. "She doesn't do this with everybody?"

"Not at all. I haven't seen her do that with anyone in Indian Lake. Not even Eleanor," he said, zipping his bag up again.

Sophie cuddled Frenchie to her chest. "She's adorable. Where'd you get her?"

"In the town where I lived before I came here, I scooped poop for a kennel. I liked being around dogs. The dogs loved me." He reached over and stroked Frenchie's back. His eyes misted over. "Frenchie was abandoned. Her parents never came back for her. It happens in kennels. Vets, too, my boss told me. Anyway, when I left there, they gave her to me because we'd bonded so much."

Sophie held Frenchie up and peered into her black eyes. Her little head cocked to the right and left, assessing Sophie. "She's lucky to have you."

"No, Sophie, she's not."

"What?" Sophie stared at Jeremy, taking in his downcast eyes and somber expression.

"I can't keep Frenchie. I've already seen what it's like for her when I use. I forget to feed her. Walk her. Bathe her. Even pet her. I'm afraid I'll freak out someday and really hurt her. I love her too much for that to happen. I have to give her up."

"Jeremy...she could be enough to make you want to stay straight." Sophie didn't believe anyone was a lost cause. She had to give him hope.

He shook his head vigorously. "No. No, I know

myself too well by now. I'm not kidding anyone anymore. Will you take Frenchie or not?"

"Me?" She shook her head. "There's no way. I work long hours, even on weekends sometimes. Plus I volunteer for Eleanor. I'd never be home to walk her or care for her. Frankly, I don't think I'd be any better for her than you."

Sophie started to hand Frenchie back.

Jeremy recoiled. "No. I'm not good for her. You have to believe me. Please, Sophie. If you can't be her mom, find someone who will. She deserves a real home. She's the sweetest, smartest little dog ever. Tell me you'll help me."

Frenchie blinked up at her. The little dog had already found a place in Sophie's heart. "I have no idea what to say or do. I'm new to being a sponsor. I don't know what the rules are or how we're supposed to react to this kind of thing…"

"You mean I'm your first gig?"

She nodded with a half smile.

"I figured you were like all the other do-gooder former addicts, trying to erase their own sins."

"I'm not an addict. I've never done drugs or even been drunk. Eleanor took a chance on me because I want to help people like you who are having trouble coping with their disease."

He worried his bottom lip as he listened to her. "So you don't think I'm a loser?"

"No. I think you're lost."

Tears welled in his eyes and he pinched the bridge of his nose. "I am lost." He jerked his head up to meet her eyes. "I've failed at every program imaginable. There's no hope for me."

Shifting Frenchie into the crook of one arm, Sophie said, "I think there is. As long as one person on earth believes in you, then there's hope. She stood. "Besides. You just need to find a new addiction to replace your old addiction. We could start with garlic."

"With…what?"

"I'm an excellent cook. Maybe once we get you some new clothes and a haircut, you could come out to my parents' farm. On Sundays my mother and grandmother put out a spread that you won't believe."

"You would take me to meet your family?"

"Sure. Why not? You and Frenchie both might like them."

He stood up next to her and said, "I wasn't thinking about me liking them. What would they say about you bringing home an addict? Won't they be afraid?"

She kissed the top of Frenchie's head, already feeling bonded to the little dog—and to Jeremy. "Nah. They know I could take you in less than sixty seconds if it came to that."

Jeremy smiled, cracked teeth showing between his thin lips. "That was a joke, right?"

She raised an eyebrow. "Want to try me?" Holding Frenchie, she waved him forward. "Now, c'mon. Let's get something to eat. What do you feel like? Grilled cheese and tomato soup? Hamburger? Chili?"

"Pancakes and bacon," he said. "They're my favorite."

Sophie helped Jeremy put Frenchie into the backpack before they went inside to avoid any disapproval from the owner. She hooked her arm in his. "Pancakes and bacon it is."

Sophie led him inside, where the accountant bikers were eating. Sophie ordered a large stack and two rashers of bacon for him. She sipped coffee while Jeremy ate.

He talked about his childhood. She noticed that most of his recollections and memories were negative. She took mental notes to research the possibility that Jeremy could have clinical depression. It was possible he was a manic-depressive. She remembered reading that bipolar disorder and alcoholism or drug abuse often occurred in tandem.

If doctors could diagnose and treat his underlying conditions, perhaps his addictions could be abated.

Just as Jeremy finished his last bite, he asked, "So, Sophie, can Frenchie stay with you?"

"For the time being—yes. I have to think about it."

By the time they left, Jeremy was comfortable enough with Sophie to accept a ride back to town. She drove him to the shelter at the Salvation Army.

Afterward, she went into the Goodwill a few blocks away and bought him some jeans, shoes, tees and sweatshirts. At the Walmart she bought new underwear and socks. She drove back to the shelter and left the bags with the administrator. She gave the man her card and a gift certificate for Jeremy to get his hair cut at the salon next to the Walmart.

As she drove back to her apartment, Frenchie sat in her lap and stared out the window intensely, watching all the cars. She was obviously mesmerized by the traffic lights and neon signs. Frenchie was one observant pup.

Sophie didn't know what to do with Frenchie. She didn't have all that many friends in Indian Lake. Katia and Austin weren't even married yet and they were planning a long honeymoon. Mrs. Beabots had her hands full, often babysitting Sarah's kids next door. Nate and Maddie might be a fit, but both of them were out of the house all day, just as she was. No, it had to be someone who could take Frenchie to work.

Sophie turned onto Maple Boulevard from Main Street and glanced at Jack's insurance office building.

Jack! His house could use a bit of life. Since

Jack owned his business, he could easily take Frenchie to the office.

Sophie reached over and petted Frenchie's head. The pup preened under her touch. Sophie smiled.

By taking Frenchie and promising to keep her safe, she'd made a difference in Jeremy's life. Tomorrow, she'd go see Jack. She could only pray she would make a difference for him, too.

CHAPTER ELEVEN

ONE DAY WITH Frenchie had taught Sophie that she needed to talk to Jack—and soon. Leaving Frenchie alone in her apartment while Sophie got called to work for an emergency upset the little dog so much that Mrs. Beabots had to come upstairs and comfort her. Then Katia arrived to pick up Mrs. Beabots for a hairdresser's appointment and they had to leave Frenchie alone again for another hour and a half. As far as they could tell, Frenchie barked and whimpered at the front door until their return.

"What are you going to do?" Mrs. Beabots asked that night after Sophie came home from the hospital. "You're the most overscheduled woman in Indian Lake and I can't promise to be home all the time for her, either." She touched Frenchie's head. "So sweet."

"I have a plan."

"I hope so."

"I thought I'd ask Jack Carter to take her."

Mrs. Beabot's sky blue eyes flew open. "Jack? But he works all day, as well."

Sophie smiled. "But he's the boss. He can make the office dog friendly."

Mrs. Beabots grinned. "That is a plan, my dear."

"Still, it's not going to be easy. He despises me. He'll never forgive me for Aleah's death."

"Oh, he will. I've met Jack several times, both with my business and at parties and gatherings. He's a fair man. Be patient."

Patience. Sophie looked at little Frenchie. Even if Jack felt guilty about Aleah now, as time wore on, Sophie hoped he would realize her death was not his fault.

Or mine.

She shivered slightly. She'd been over the incident a hundred—no, two hundred—times, and she couldn't categorically state that she'd made the right decision. Her choice to care for Greg Fulton had been technically and medically right. Accurate to the nth degree. But it had resulted in Aleah's death. What was right about that?

Was it her fault? Or was Aleah's time up? Was she meant to die no matter what, or was Sophie so arrogant as to believe, like many doctors did, that medicine was the ultimate decision maker? That their actions were the sole arbiters between life and death? Sophie was afraid she'd be asking herself those questions forever.

Sophie had a twofold purpose for meeting with Jack. The first was Frenchie. Sophie was convinced the little dog would help Jack mend his broken heart. Frenchie needed affection, and after witnessing Jack's reaction to Aleah's death, Sophie believed he had a lot of love to give. Secondly, she needed to talk to him about insurance for the Alliance. Sophie hoped Frenchie would turn down the temperature on Jack's anger toward her. If Frenchie could help her smooth things over with him personally, maybe he'd be open to providing the umbrella policy they needed.

But deep down, it pained her to think that Jack, a person she held in high esteem, could think so negatively about her. She wanted to be his hero.

AMBUSH.

It was the only way to deal with Jack, who'd refused to take her calls. Sophie had to pull out all the stops. *For Frenchie's sake*, she thought, as she chose a pretty blue-and-white summer dress and a pair of white pumps, letting her thick hair down around her shoulders. The less she looked like a nurse who might remind him of that night in the ER, the better.

As she glossed her lips with a sheen of pink, she wondered if it was possible for Jack to think of her as anyone but a person who brought him pain. The fact that she even cared about his opinion startled her.

Frenchie was sitting on the bath mat, staring up at her with a perky glint in her eye.

"So, little girl, are you ready to meet your new daddy?"

Frenchie barked.

SOPHIE SAT IN one of the red-and-white upholstered French chairs in Jack's office, taking in the view of the courthouse and the traffic below as she stroked Frenchie's head.

Just a few doors down was the Alliance. She pictured Eleanor working with one of her volunteer therapists or holding a meeting with clients. Sophie marveled at how easily someone like Jack could take no notice of what was going on less than a block away. If it weren't for Greg Fulton and the terrible accident he'd caused, Jack might never have glimpsed the suffering drugs had created in this community. And now here she was, hoping to bring him even closer to the situation.

Sophie knew that Jack alone wasn't the answer, but if there were a million Jacks across the country, a million Eleanors educating parents, teachers, doctors and addicts, it would all make a difference, wouldn't it?

Sophie was the tiniest cog in this monstrous wheel, but each effort she made was important. She had to believe that. She did believe that.

Melanie walked up to Sophie. "He's finishing

up an important phone call right now, so it'll be a few minutes. Can I get you another cup of coffee?"

Sophie glanced at the china cup and saucer she held. She wondered if that was one of Katia's ideas. No Styrofoam. No paper. Not a mug. It reminded her of her mother's house. Family. And it gave her comfort. She smiled at Melanie. "I'm fine, thanks. But it's good coffee."

"I like it, too. Katia talked Maddie Barzonni into sharing her beans with us."

"Maddie should sell them by the pound," Sophie offered.

"She does, but only in Chicago." Melanie leaned in conspiratorially. "Maddie doesn't want to take business away from Scott Abbot. He sells his beans, too, you know."

Sophie was again struck by the closeness between Katia, Maddie and other people in town. For so long, Sophie had been caught up in her world of surgery, her father's cancer and helping her mother and grandmother. That and too many unimportant dates with men whose names she often couldn't remember.

In less than a year, she'd started seeing just about everything in a new light. Her town, her friends, her job...even her family. She'd always cherished them, but they were vastly more important to her now than they had been.

Maybe I'm growing up. Finally.

"What about this little one?" Melanie asked, reaching out to pet Frenchie's head. "Can I get her some water?"

"I brought a dish and a bottle for her." Sophie smiled. "She should be fine. Thanks for asking."

Melanie sighed. "She's adorable. What my kids wouldn't do for a dog like her." She straightened up. "But my husband is allergic."

"What a shame."

"You're telling me." Melanie laughed.

Just then Jack stepped out of his office and spotted them across the room. Today he wore a dark navy suit, white shirt, navy tie with white dots and black dress shoes. Though he glared at her as he approached, she couldn't help thinking she'd never seen a more handsome man in her life.

"Sophie," he said, his voice hovering just above a growl. "What are you doing here?" He shot Melanie an accusing gaze.

"She doesn't have an appointment," Melanie began.

He pointed at Frenchie. "Who's your friend?" His voice softened.

Sophie took it as a sign. She stood instantly. "Please, Jack. Don't blame Melanie, it's not her fault. If you have another appointment, I understand. I wanted to talk to you about something in private, if I may."

He consulted his watch. "I have fifteen minutes but that's all. If you tell me what this is about we could schedule—"

"I'll take the fifteen minutes," Sophie interjected quickly, switching Frenchie to her left arm. She wasn't about to give him a chance to dismiss her and never call back. Plus, she was afraid she might not have the courage to face him again.

Jack ground his jaw. "Fine. Let's go into my office." He stood back and politely gestured toward it.

Sophie smiled at him, but when he shot back with a look so cold it could flash freeze small animals, she shielded Frenchie with her hand and wiped the expression off her face. She marched through the door like it was the principal's office in elementary school.

He sat behind his desk, folded his hands in his lap and stared at her.

Sophie gingerly took a seat. Jack was impeccable. Not a dark hair out of place. Gold cuff links on his shirt. This imposing man couldn't have been further from the vulnerable patient she'd treated less than six weeks ago. Still, there were signs that there was more beneath this stern, fastidious appearance. Sophie noticed several paintings on the walls by Isabelle Hawks. Sophie recognized her fairy and water sprite paintings from working a booth with her at the Summer Festival. Beneath each piece was a tiny price sticker. Jack was helping Isabelle sell her art.

"Nice paintings," she said, trying to break the silence.

"Fourteen minutes, Sophie. Not a second longer."

Sophie felt a rumble of fear in her stomach. She forced a pleasant smile. "Jack, I'm here to change your life."

"You already did that, remember?" he said icily, but Sophie felt his broken heart through the cold splinters.

She'd been dead-on. Frenchie was just what Jack needed.

"A friend of mine entrusted this precious little Yorkie-Poo to me, hoping I'd find her a home." Sophie pinned Jack with her eyes. "That would be you, Jack. Your home needs Frenchie."

Jack nearly spat. "You're out of your mind!"

"I'm not. Frenchie is homeless. You have all that space, that gorgeous view and no one to share it with. Frenchie isn't a bother at all," Sophie cooed as she peered into Frenchie's upturned face and ink-black eyes. Sophie smiled at the dog.

At that moment Frenchie bounded out of Sophie's lap and scampered over to Jack. She tapped his shoe, then backed away, sizing him up. With a wiggle of her short tail, she bent her back legs and sprang smack dab onto Jack's lap.

"What?"

Before Jack could say another word, Frenchie had skipped up Jack's middle to his shoulder and rested her tiny legs on his chest so she could lick his face.

"She likes you!" Sophie exclaimed with delight. "Oh, Jack. She doesn't do that for just anybody."

"What about you?"

"Okay. Me. But that's all," Sophie admitted.

Frenchie kept licking, and Jack gently put his hands around her.

"She's awfully thin."

"I know."

Jack laughed. "It tickles." He laughed again.

Sophie felt her heart open, expand and welcome the sound of Jack's laughter.

Jack grew serious. "You're sure everything's all right?"

"I'm fine," Sophie answered before realizing Jack had no idea what had just happened to her. What *had* happened? Something. Everything. But the moment had been so elusive, she wasn't sure. What she did know was that Jack was falling in love—with Frenchie.

"No, the dog. I mean, has she been eating?"

"She's a Yorkie-Poo and only supposed to weigh six or seven pounds. But I also think she's a bit on the slight side."

"Well," he said with a tinge of accusation just as Frenchie leaped up and licked his bottom lip.

Lucky girl, Sophie thought.

"What I meant was, have you checked her out?"

"Checked?"

"Like with the vet? Has she had her shots? Been wormed? All these things are important."

"And you know this because…"

"I had dogs when I was growing up. My sister has a golden retriever. Older than Sarah's Beau."

"I haven't had time to get an appointment," Sophie replied. "She's only been with me a couple of days."

Jack held Frenchie up in the air and wiggled his nose against hers. "She's the cutest thing I've ever seen." He frowned and shoved her toward Sophie. "But I can't take her. I work all the time. I wouldn't want to leave her alone."

"Who said anything about leaving her alone?" Sophie moved to the edge of her chair and rested her right hand on his desk. She took a deep breath for courage. "You could bring her to work."

"Here?" He shook his head vigorously. "No way."

"Why not? You're the boss. You make the rules."

"I'd have to ask the landlord."

"Sharon? I already called her. There's no stipulation against dogs. Just a pet deposit. I'll pay it." Sophie smiled brightly at Jack.

"I can't take the responsibility."

Sophie's eyes rounded. "I never thought I'd hear those words from you." She guffawed. "Boy, I wish I had that one on tape. You take on all kinds of responsibility."

Jack pulled Frenchie back to his chest and started scratching her behind her ears. Frenchie preened. Tilted her head to the side so that Jack could rub the right side of her neck. "You can't just go around making assumptions about people and their lives, Sophie. You should have thought this through."

"I did, Jack." She moved even closer and lowered her voice. "You see, Frenchie has no one but us. She's a rescue to begin with. One of the clients of the Alliance gave her to me…"

"You mean an addict?"

Sophie was undeterred. "He needs help, Jack. Yes. He has a disease, but he's a smart guy and knows he can't care for Frenchie the way she should be. She needs you. She needs love. Just look at you. You can't take your hands off her."

Jack looked down. He'd cradled Frenchie in his left arm like a newborn and had been scratching her throat. The little dog was nearly asleep.

Silence.

"Jack," Sophie continued. "Please don't take your anger out on little Frenchie. She's an angel, but I can't leave her all day and night when I'm in surgery or the ER. You could bring her to work with you. She doesn't like being alone. I bought a little seat for her to ride in the car."

"You had her two days and you bought a car seat?"

Sophie's smile was soft. "I didn't want her to get hurt when I drove her to the store. I want her to be safe."

Jack sighed. "And you'll give me the car seat?"

"Sure."

"Well, *I'm* not sure," he replied.

"Tell you what," Sophie suggested. "Let's walk her down to Grandy's Groomers and have her checked out. We can get an appointment at the vet for shots and a checkup. Then we can go to the pet store to buy whatever else she needs. I'll pay."

Frenchie stretched in Jack's arms, sticking her paws straight out and touching the side of Jack's chest, next to his heart.

"Deal."

CHAPTER TWELVE

GRANDY'S GROOMERS WAS next door to Maddie Barzonni's café. Sarah had told Jack that she took Beau to Grandy's on Friday afternoons. Beau was a big golden retriever with a penchant for digging. Jack was certain Frenchie wouldn't need grooming more than once a month.

Grandy suspected Frenchie was about two years old. She was underfed, but after inspection, Grandy pronounced her healthy. Still, she agreed she should be checked out by a veterinarian to make sure she didn't have worms or any other conditions. Grandy recommended a vet and gave Jack the number, then Jack set an appointment for a grooming on Monday. Even without a bath and haircut, Jack pronounced Frenchie terminally cute.

Afterward, Jack, Sophie and Frenchie drove straight to the pet store.

"I'll get the cart," Jack said as Sophie carried Frenchie into the store.

"Hey, would you look at this? The dogs can wander freely. No leashes," Jack said. Sophie set

Frenchie down and a wirehaired terrier sidled up to her for a sniff. Frenchie barked and hid behind Jack's legs.

"Okay. In the cart you go," Jack declared. Sophie laughed.

That tinkling laugh. He wished she wouldn't do that. It made it harder for him to keep his emotions straight. He'd been very angry with her up until a few hours ago.

Now he was confused with elation, guilt, joy and anxiety. He couldn't help wondering if Aleah would have liked to have a little dog like Frenchie. He swallowed bitterly. She was so young and her life had ended so needlessly.

"She needs a leash," Sophie said, interrupting his grim thoughts.

"Yes," he replied quickly.

"And a collar," Sophie said. Frenchie put her paws on the rail as if she'd often been in shopping carts.

Jack wondered what Frenchie's life had been like before she'd come into his. "What's the name of your…friend…who gave Frenchie to you?"

"Jeremy."

"Did he have her since she was a puppy?"

"No. All he told me was that he met her while he was a kennel tech in another town."

"Kennel tech?"

"He scooped poop." Sophie smiled again, somehow making the fluorescent lighting fade.

How'd she do that?

"I wonder if I could get him a part-time job at Grandy's," Sophie mused while squeezing a stuffed hamburger and bun toy.

"Don't business owners have rules about, er, well…" he began nervously.

"You mean hiring drug users," she finished for him.

"Yeah. All my employees have to pass a drug test in order to be hired. That's a huge barrier. Even the idea of it could upset him, make him feel ashamed. Who knows how he'd react."

"You're right, Jack. I should find something else. Like a handyman kind of thing."

Jack took a deep breath but couldn't hold back his concern. "Sophie, even a seemingly simple repair could turn into something dangerous if Jeremy…well, you know. He could mis-wire something. Hurt himself with tools or fall from a ladder."

"I understand your point, Jack, but if we don't give addicts a chance to become functional again, they lose all hope. Then they never recover."

"Aleah never got a chance to recover from her injuries," he said, sadness choking him.

Sophie's eyes were filled with understanding

and compassion. The longer she held his gaze, the more his heart hurt.

"I don't know," he said quietly, desperate to change the subject. Obliterate his memories of Aleah.

"I understand." She cleared her throat and forced a smile. "Let's go down this aisle."

They pulled up to the leashes. Sophie picked up a collar with rhinestones and held it in front of Frenchie's face. Frenchie barked.

Jack groaned. "Oh, no. She likes bling."

"I'd say so."

Jack grabbed a leash that was mostly leather with a sprinkling of rhinestones. "I suppose this goes with the collar? I can't help thinking how I'm gonna look running with her along the trail at the lake."

"You'll live." Sophie smiled softly. "Besides, she's a tiny dog. You can't run her like she's a Rottweiler. You'll need a pouch."

"Huh?"

"You know, like a sling—to carry her. She can walk with you, but she won't be able to keep up with your runs. Plus, when it's hot, her paws will burn. And if it's cold, you'll have to watch her paws, as well."

"She needs boots?"

"Don't laugh," Sophie warned. "Those are in the next aisle."

Jack took out the list Grandy had given him that specified the kind of food and treats he would need. He added a bed, blanket and pillow to the cart, all in pink and gray plaid—because he liked the pattern, not because it was feminine. He bought several toys, including a stuffed teddy bear bigger than Frenchie, which the little pup immediately claimed possession of by clamping her teeth around the bear's ear.

As they were checking out, Sophie whipped out her credit card, but he grabbed her wrist before she could pay. "Put it away. She's my dog now."

"Thanks, Jack," Sophie replied, gratitude filling her face.

Jack smiled fleetingly, dipped his head and felt a bit like the king of the world.

ON THE WAY back to the office, Frenchie fell asleep in her car seat.

"Jack, can I talk to you about something else?"

"You have a pet alligator you want me to adopt?" he joked.

Sophie laughed lightly, but her expression was serious. "I need your help for the Recovery Alliance."

Jack stiffened. "Me? What do you need me for?"

"Eleanor has barely opened the doors and the response and need are way more than she anticipated. I was going over some specifics with her, and it seems she hasn't confirmed an umbrella liability policy for the building or the volunteers."

Jack whipped around to face Sophie. "You're not serious."

"I am."

"But that's one of the first things any new business owner should settle before day one—"

Sophie held up her hand to interrupt. "I know. She knows. Eleanor said she had trouble getting insurance companies to agree to provide her with a policy because of the high-risk factor. It was more expense than she'd planned. Then things happened so quickly after the open house. Volunteers signed up. Clients flooded in. She was so busy taking care of the clients that insurance fell lower and lower on her priority list."

She paused, and Jack waited for her to continue.

"Jack, would you be willing to give Eleanor an insurance policy?"

"For free?" His tone was shrill. If he drew up a policy for the Alliance, he would be their provider of record. It was true that it was a higher-risk policy, but that wasn't the real problem. He would be entangled with Sophie on a business level, which would mean seeing her more. A lot more. And he just couldn't face that.

Suddenly, she was no longer the woman who'd just given him a dog or whose company he'd enjoyed at Grandy's Groomers and the pet store. She was the dark shadow that had suffused his life since the night of the accident. He'd dealt with his grief carefully, cautiously, as if he'd been wearing protective gloves. As long as he could blame Sophie for the bad judgment, the wasted minutes that might have saved Aleah's life, then he didn't feel the other pain. The pain of knowing it had been his fault.

Being this close to Sophie was dangerous.

He couldn't give Frenchie back; he was too committed already. But he didn't have to see Sophie anymore, either.

"Sorry. I can't," he said finally.

Sophie shot him a sidelong glance. "Can't or won't?"

"Won't."

"At least you're honest," she replied, folding her arms over her chest. "Thanks for that."

"Thanks?"

"Yeah. I know where I stand with you."

He pulled into a space near his office. He kept the car in idle. "Good. Then we understand each other." He nodded toward her door. "You can be assured I'll take good care of Frenchie."

Sophie grabbed the handle, but turned to face him. Her eyes glistened. Tears?

"Jack, I truly appreciate what you're doing for little Frenchie." She pushed the door open. "It's a grand gesture. I shouldn't have asked about the insurance policy. Maybe we can scrounge up the money to pay for it. Would you be willing to give us a quote?"

"A quote?" He hadn't figured she'd persist. Apparently, she didn't understand that he was trying to dodge her. Completely. He made the mistake of pausing just a fraction too long on those honey-brown eyes and long black lashes. He memorized her high cheekbones and her soft, full lips. Then she spoke again and killed his reservations.

"Jack, be a hero here. Please?"

He dropped his chin. He was toast. "I'll think about it."

She placed her hand on his forearm. He could feel that same warmth he'd felt when he was her patient. Healing hands. Loving hands.

"Thanks, Jack."

Then, she did the unforgivable. The unforget-table. She leaned forward and kissed him on the cheek. Her lips barely skimmed it, but his pulse skyrocketed. His heart slammed against his chest. For. No. Reason.

Before he could respond, she was out of the car, the door was shut and she was dashing down the sidewalk, where she appeared to vanish into thin air.

Jack stared at the emptiness she left in her wake.

Frenchie barked, startling him. He turned around. She was yawning.

"Time to go to your new home, girl," he said, and reached to the backseat to scratch her head.

Jack decided to take the rest of the day off and get Frenchie settled at home. He drove away with the eerie sensation that for the second time in a matter of weeks, his life had altered drastically. Both times, Sophie was there.

CHAPTER THIRTEEN

AFTER ATTENDING SUNDAY Mass with her parents and sharing brunch with them, Sophie drove back to town, her car loaded down with bundles of summer roses and sunflowers from her grandmother's garden. She'd taken special care to select a variety of colors for Mrs. Beabots. The deep yellow of Lemon Queen was one of Sophie's favorites, and mixed with the wine-red of Chianti, the white and pale-yellow blooms of Italian White and a few gold and russet firecrackers, the bouquet was sure to bring a smile to her landlady's face.

Sophie parked her car and gathered the bouquets from the backseat. Her mother had tied the stems with twine and wrapped wet paper towels and aluminum foil around the bottoms to keep them from the least bit of droop.

Sophie rapped on the back kitchen door.

"Come in, Sophie," Mrs. Beabots called. "I saw you drive up."

Sophie walked in holding the flowers in front of her face. "Just for you," she said.

Mrs. Beabots was dressed in an elegant navy-and-white summer knit suit, white-and-navy low pumps with a wide navy bow at the toe and a dozen gold chains and strings of pearls. Sophie wondered not for the first time how Mrs. Beabots had amassed such an extravagant wardrobe.

"They're beautiful," Mrs. Beabots exclaimed, reaching for the bouquet.

"So are you. What's the occasion?"

Mrs. Beabots put the flowers on the butcher block and retrieved a cut crystal vase that Sophie guessed was at least fifty years old.

"I'm glad you asked because this is one of those times I need to prevail upon you for help," the older woman explained as she filled the vase with water.

"Help? Sure. What can I do?"

"I'm going to Austin McCreary's showing today at the museum. He's bought a new Rolls Royce and I'm dying to see it."

Sophie slapped her cheek. "Oh, my gosh! Is that today? Katia mentioned it to me when I saw her at the post office a couple weeks ago. I thought it was on the twenty-seventh."

Mrs. Beabots stopped midmotion and glanced at Sophie over her shoulder. "It is the twenty-seventh."

"Oh," Sophie replied sheepishly. "I guess I've been busy."

Mrs. Beabots put the vase on the butcher block

and untied the twine. "Looks to me like you've been more than just busy." She stuck the longest stemmed Lemon Queen into the vase first, as the center pole. "I've never been accused of being a busybody, but I can't help but notice that you've been coming home later and later at night. And what happened to your Wednesdays off when you would sit in the garden to read? You're gone all the time now."

"I guess I am."

Mrs. Beabots finished arranging the flowers. "Stunning. Your grandmother grows the best."

"She does. My mother and I planted the rose garden. I have roses, too, if you'd like them. I'll run out to the car and get them—"

"Sophie!" Mrs. Beabots said sharply. "You're very good at evasion, aren't you?"

"Excuse me?"

"You didn't answer my question, though actually, you don't have to. If you have a new young man in your life, I understand."

Sophie shook her head. "It's not a guy. Far from it. Thank goodness. It's the work I've been doing for Eleanor."

Mrs. Beabots's brows knitted together. "I thought you were giving her a couple hours a week. From what I've seen, you're working a second job."

"Not quite. It's just that there's so much to be done."

"It's important to have a passion, but they can be like black holes if you're not careful. They can suck you in and suck you dry. Just don't let it take over your life so much that you ruin your health."

Sophie chuckled. "And I thought *I* was the nurse."

"All right then. That's settled. I won't worry anymore. Now, since you're dressed appropriately, what do you say we go see about this new Silver Cloud of Austin's?"

"Absolutely. But first, I need to put my roses in water and I need to get more tape."

"Tape?"

"For the Alliance posters Katia promised I could put up in the museum."

Mrs. Beabots rolled her eyes. "Sophie, you need to dial it back or you're going to lose your balance."

Sophie turned and headed quickly for the back door. "I'll be fine. Promise."

As Sophie stepped outside she realized that her landlady was as much of a mother hen as her grandmother and mother. She wondered what she'd done to be so lucky.

JACK WAS LATE to Austin McCreary's event at the car museum and had to park at the far end of the expansive lot. He was surprised at the number of people attending, but then free food and wine were always a draw. For Jack, the antique 1957 Silver Cloud Rolls Royce was all the enticement he needed. Jack had always loved cars, and kept a stack of *Car and Driver* magazines at his office. As a kid, he had the largest Hot Wheels collection in his neighborhood. His first car had been a red 1965 Mustang convertible that he'd paid for with money he'd earned from two jobs, along with a loan his father had cosigned. Jack had loved that car until he had to sell it to help pay for his college tuition. That had been a black day in his life, but he got over it.

Jack didn't envy many people, but he certainly would have liked to have just one of Austin McCreary's exceptional antique automobiles.

Along with the event, this was his first chance to inspect the repairs to the museum. A tornado ripped through it last March. Since Jack's company carried the insurance for the building, Katia had kept him informed about the reconstruction and had shown him photos, but he hadn't managed to see it in person yet.

The landscaping and downed trees had been replaced, and new mulch covered the uprooted giant oak, whose loss Katia had personally mourned. A hedge of blue blooming hydrangeas lined the far right side of the building and clusters of pink and purple impatiens filled the front beds in front of boxwood hedges.

The building was a replica of the Hermitage. Andrew Jackson had blended Federal, Palladian and Greek Revival architecture for the original home—now a museum—in Nashville, a place Jack had visited with his family in elementary school. Jack respected Austin's vision in building such an elegant museum for his antique car collection, started by his father.

As Jack gazed up at the museum, he reflected that when he'd arrived in Indian Lake, he hadn't thought much about the townsfolk or his part in the community. At that time, Indian Lake was a solution to a problem he had with his company's expenses. He'd needed to make quick decisions or he and his brother-in-law were going to have to close. Katia had come up with the idea of leaving Chicago's high rent and taxes and basing their operations in Indiana. Jack had been desperate. Perhaps even rash. But he'd made a decision.

Now, he had to stick with that decision. He and the company had made it through their first six months and landed some important clients. Jack had begun to dig his heels into life in Indian Lake. He'd joined the Rotary and Lions Clubs, as well as the Chamber of Commerce, and met a lot of people. He'd also attended every fund-raiser and community function he could to get his name out to the public. But still, his only real friends here were Austin and Katia.

He'd been so busy with work, he hadn't had time to bond with anyone else. Now that it was summer, he should be thinking about buying a little bass boat and fishing on Sunday afternoons. Or playing golf like he used to do with his dad and his sister. But with Ava and Barry still in Chicago and no one to really spend time with here, those activities didn't hold the same appeal.

The brightest spot in his life right now was Frenchie. Thanks to Sophie. *Sophie*...

He still hadn't given her an answer about the umbrella policy for the Alliance. He'd tried not to think about it—and failed. Since the night of Aleah's death, many thoughts of Sophie had been black and disturbing. Now, they'd softened into a soft cushion he longed to fall into. Sometimes. Other times he was simply confused.

Jack walked into the museum and was greeted by a familiar-looking young woman in her early twenties, dressed in an 1820s costume and powdered wig. She handed him a program. "Hi, Mr. Carter," she said with a bright smile.

As soon as she spoke, he recognized her voice. "Chloe? From Cupcakes and Coffee?"

"That's right," she said. "The program is about to start. It's upstairs on the second floor. You can take the elevator over there." She pointed, then pulled at the white silk skirt and asked, "You like the costume? It's period-appropriate for the museum. It was Katia's idea."

"I should have guessed." He smiled. "She's got everyone volunteering, huh?"

"There's four of us from my acting class here. Debra La Pointe, our acting coach, suggested we help out, and in return we get to advertise for our first play next month. *A Midsummer Night's Dream.* I'm playing Titania." She reached behind her to a small table. "Here's the flyer. Maybe you can bring a friend? We need bodies." She grinned.

"Paying customers," Jack corrected. "I truly understand. I'll make a point of being there."

"Great." Chloe nodded toward the elevator. "You better get going. Austin's doing a real unveiling."

"Thanks." Jack tipped the program to his temple in a little salute and headed upstairs.

When the elevator doors opened, Jack saw a large crowd that had to be well over a hundred and fifty people. Austin stood on a riser in the middle of the rotunda area, and next to him was a lump covered in a white drape that Jack assumed was the star of the show, the Silver Cloud.

Spotting the bar, Jack walked over and asked for a glass of Pinot Grigio. The bartender, dressed in a Regency-era livery costume, poured the wine into a stemmed glass.

Jack moved on to a long table with hors d'oeuvres,

a summer floral centerpiece, two silver candelabras and several piles of printed information about the museum, the cars and the McCreary family. He popped a bite in his mouth just as Austin began to speak.

Austin welcomed everyone and introduced his fiancée, Katia. As the crowd applauded, Jack scanned the room for familiar faces. He noticed several new clients, Melanie and her family, and Owen, who appeared so intent on seeing the Silver Cloud he didn't take his eyes off the white drape, even when Jack tried to wave.

He peered at the stained glass ceiling in the rotunda and sipped his wine. As he turned, admiring the space, he spotted two posters on either side of the elevator doors, which he'd missed on his way in.

The Recovery Alliance.

Jack nearly choked on his wine.

He didn't know why, but the Alliance was a trigger for him, bringing back the night of the accident. In a split second, his head filled with terrible sounds: glass shattering, metal splitting, Owen's moans, Aleah screaming. The feeling that his life was out of control.

And it was.

Since the night of the crash, Jack's world had changed so drastically, it was as if he'd moved into another dimension. He still felt he owed

Aleah something. He couldn't give life back to her, but he felt impotent and insignificant in his efforts to make amends.

He shook his head and the posters came back into focus. There was only one person who could have hung them.

Sophie.

Quite frankly, Jack didn't understand her. He was suspicious. Why did she keep showing up in his life? Trying to help him? Was she trying to off-load her own guilt? Was she seeking forgiveness from him because she knew in her heart of hearts that she truly was to blame? And why this sudden interest of hers in the Recovery Alliance? What did she have to gain? Atonement?

As far as Jack was concerned, Greg Fulton should have gone to the hospital and undergone medical treatment for his addiction. Emory Wills had a full program in place that was supposed to cure people. If Greg had sought help, he would still be alive and so would Aleah. But regardless of what the hospital offered, Jack hadn't done enough research to put his stamp of approval on anything connected with the Alliance.

Suddenly, he heard a clamoring of applause, whistles and whoops. Undoubtedly, Austin had unveiled the Rolls. And he'd missed it.

His eyes glued to the posters, Jack's mind went black. All he could think about was the injustice and heartbreak of losing Aleah. While everyone was occupied with Austin and his new car, Jack walked up to the posters and ripped them off the wall. Then he shoved them in a nearby garbage can amongst empty wine bottles and napkins.

"What do you think you're doing?"

Jack spun around and found Sophie throwing him a poisonous look.

"Those are mine," she ground out angrily. "You have no right to take them down, much less throw them in the trash."

"You're right. I got carried away." Why did he feel so foolish?

Sophie stomped over to the garbage can and pulled the posters out. One of them was wet, but the other was unmarred. "I'll put them back up."

Jack's anger felt like a bomb in his head about to explode. He didn't understand why he was reacting so violently. Posttraumatic stress from the accident?

He had to diffuse it and quickly. "Sophie," he began, his head throbbing. There was no answer for his torment. He had to push her out of his life. Her presence was just too much for him to take. He couldn't figure out his overwhelming need to run from her and at the same time give her the deepest, most soulful goodbye kiss he could muster. He was losing it.

"I've given your proposal a lot of thought. I

won't help you with the umbrella policy. I've been working with Emory since I moved here. I owe him personally. However, I won't say anything to anyone about your participation in this—" he pointed to the posters "—agency."

"That's big of you," she spat out, hoisting the posters under her arm. "You know what, Jack? You do what your conscience tells you. I hope you can continue to sleep at night because I certainly can't. If we don't do something about the drugs in this town, you and everyone else better get used to more overdoses, more car crashes and more innocent people like Aleah dying, because that's what's going to happen."

Jack's face burned. Who was she to lecture him when she was partly to blame for Aleah? "You think a few posters, some radio ads and pat-on-the-back, feel-good counseling sessions are going to stop drugs? National programs and agencies with millions of dollars behind them haven't made a dent in decades. In fact, it's getting worse. And you, one woman, think you can make a difference? Get real."

Sophie moved so close to Jack their noses almost touched. He could see fire in her eyes and the blood vessels in her temple twitched. He'd never felt such animosity in his life. She ground her jaw and he could see her sifting curses out of her language as she spoke.

"I feel sorry for you, Jack. You see a problem and instead of trying to fix it, you wave it off to some other official or accept the status quo. You don't seek the questions that haven't been asked, the ones that just might give us the answers we need. I'm not like that. I'm going to keep searching until I find an approach that works. If I have to collaborate with the cops, I will. Or the courts, I will. But, I swear to God, I will make a difference. And I'm not stopping until I do. Maybe it's only a few posters today, but tomorrow or the next day, I might be the one who saves a life."

Sophie backed away and headed toward the crowd.

Jack watched after her and saw that Mrs. Beabots was waiting for her nearby—and had clearly heard their entire conversation.

Sophie stopped dead in her tracks and spun to face him. "One more thing. You can be angry and blame me forever, but none of it will bring Aleah back."

Sophie marched over to Mrs. Beabots, who took her arm as they moved into the crowd and disappeared.

Jack lifted his wineglass to his lips and realized his hand was shaking. Sophie had hit her mark. He went to the bar and put his glass down.

He walked out of the museum without ever having seen the Silver Cloud.

CHAPTER FOURTEEN

SOPHIE SLIPPED INTO the break room at the ablation center without detection. She went to her locker and took out her work sneakers that never left the hospital, a pair of clean socks and a fresh set of surgical scrubs before going to the bathroom to change. She wound her hair into a coil and clipped it to the top of her head then pulled a surgical cap over it.

She checked her watch. Ten minutes to spare. Carefully hanging her dress clothes up in the locker, she shut the door and moved quickly down the hall to the operating suite.

Nate was in the computer room going over the patient's angioplasty photographs, which were mounted on a large screen. There were six computers in there that would map and chart the ablation Nate would perform this morning.

"Good morning, Doctor," Sophie said brightly as she walked in and closed the door behind her.

Nate glanced over his shoulder. "Ah, you're here. What? No cafeteria coffee this morning?"

Sophie had been at a breakfast meeting with

Art Bellerus, the head of the largest law firm in town, asking for a donation for the Alliance. She'd easily consumed four cups of coffee during her pitch and Art's probing follow-up questions. She often brought Nate a cup of coffee, but it had slipped her mind today. Not that he needed it since his wife never let him leave home without the best cappuccino on the planet. "You can't possibly be missing hospital swill."

"I'm not. But I've noticed you don't hit the cafeteria in the mornings anymore. What's up?"

"Uh…" Sophie trolled for excuses. "I'm going green. Tea, that is. Trying to cut back on caffeine. It's part of my personal overhaul program. Since I started running, I find I don't need so much coffee." She'd have to account for that big fat lie when she died. She was practically living on caffeine these days. She was spending too many hours after work at the Alliance offices with Eleanor or talking to Jeremy on the phone, he in a phone booth, she under the covers in bed, late at night or early in the morning when he was struggling with depression or trying desperately not to use. This was the third breakfast meeting she'd had in a week, which cut into her early morning running time.

Sophie was being anything but healthy. She refused to believe she was obsessed with her work at the Alliance, but the signs were practically neon with warnings.

"I know what you mean. Maddie's cut my caffeine in half. I can't go cold turkey, though. Frankly, I don't see that much advantage in it." Nate pointed at the screen. "See this area here, near the aorta?"

"I do," Sophie replied, moving in for a closer look.

"That's our area of concentration today. There's a cluster of cells over here on the right ventricle, as well. If we ablate all these, I think we can eliminate the patient's arrhythmia."

"Seems textbook to me," she said.

Nate peered at the screen. "Wait. What about this area here? See this spot?"

"I do, now that you point it out."

"Mark that on his chart. I want to go in there and check it out."

"Yes, Doctor," Sophie replied as Nate rose and left the room.

Sophie sat at the screen and made her own notes as she always did prior to any of their procedures. Just then, the cell in her pocket rang. This phone was for hospital use only and was only connected to other stations and units within the building. Every nurse, tech, doctor and assistant had one. "This is Sophie."

The admitting nurse in the ablation unit reported that the patient was being brought down from his room after being prepped for the procedure.

"I'll be right there."

Sophie stood and went directly to the operating room.

The anesthesiologist had just administered a mild sedative since the procedure was expected to last less than two hours. For longer procedures, the patient would be put under completely.

The operation began with Sophie preparing the catheter for Nate to use. Just as Nate reached for the catheter, Sophie dropped it. Fortunately, her quick reflexes snapped into action and she grabbed the hand piece before it hit the floor, which would have contaminated the unit.

Nate frowned, but remained silent as he took the catheter from her hand.

"Sorry," Sophie whispered behind her surgical mask.

Nate ignored her and went to work.

Beads of sweat sprang up on Sophie's forehead. She'd never had to mop her own brow during a procedure, but today she did. And Nate noticed that, too. So did the other nurse in the room.

Nate guided the ablation catheter into the blood vessels around the heart and performed his initial study to locate where the erroneous signals were taking place. He noted these out loud to Sophie so she could track them on the computer. Once pinpointed, Nate was able to destroy the tissue so that it could not continue to send the wrong electrical impulses to the heart, which caused the arrhythmias.

They were an hour and twelve minutes into the procedure when Nate said to Sophie, "Remind me where that last spot was that we talked about this morning."

"Spot?"

He glanced at her and then back at his work. "Yes. When we were in the computer room. I told you to mark it in his chart. I want to check that out."

Sophie had forgotten about the extra area on the left ventricle that Nate had seen. She had not put the information in the computer, but thankfully, she remembered it now. "It's at the top of the left ventricle. Although most of his misfirings are from the right, this spot is at about eleven o'clock."

Sophie immediately entered the information into the patient's computerized chart, which was in the surgery room, then returned to the patient's side. She consulted the screen Nate was staring at. She pointed to the place they'd noticed earlier. "On this screen you can't see it at all," she said as she watched the catheter move toward the area.

"No, wait. There it is," Nate said. "I see it. It's

faint. And you're right. It was easier to see on the other computers."

"Maybe we should switch these screens," Sophie offered.

Nate's blue eyes locked on hers. "That's a brilliant idea. Maybe this one is losing its juice."

"I'll write up a requisition for a new one. This is too important," she stated and prepared for the withdrawal of the catheter.

When the procedure was over and the patient was safely in recovery, Sophie went to the break room and grabbed a high-protein bar.

She propped her elbow on the table and cradled her forehead in her hand. She was so tired she could barely chew. She heard the back door open and close, which meant that one of the staff members was going out for lunch or coming in.

"Sophie? Is that you?" a woman's voice asked.

"Uh-huh," she replied without looking up, taking another bite of the sawdust-tasting bar.

Maddie walked over and placed a silver insulated bag on the table. "A granola bar? Is that how you're staying so thin these days?"

"Me? Thin? You have the wrong Sophie," she replied quickly and then cranked her head to see Maddie. "Oh, hi."

"I brought Nate some lunch from the deli. He didn't get much dinner last night because I was in Chicago till after nine."

"Do you still have to oversee those new cafés?"

"I want them done right. They have my name on them."

"I would have thought owning a franchise would be a breeze. Sign the contract and sit back. Take life easy."

Maddie shrugged off her sweater and put it on the back of a folding chair. "I've come to understand that there's nothing easy about life at all."

"I totally agree," Sophie said, leaning back. She smiled at Maddie.

Maddie stared at her in surprise. "Are you all right? You look like you haven't slept in weeks. Or maybe you're coming down with something."

"I'm fine. Nothing that one of your cappuccinos wouldn't fix," Sophie said with a flippancy she didn't feel. Right now she felt she was over a hundred years old and weighed a ton. If she gave in to sleep, she was afraid she'd never wake up.

Maddie's green eyes narrowed. "I'm not buying it. You worked all weekend in the ER again, didn't you?"

"Uh-huh."

Maddie reached across the table and touched Sophie's forearm. "Listen to me. I may not be the doctor or the nurse, but you need to cut back on your workload. I know what I'm talking about. Last fall, I got so strung out before our wedding, I thought I was going to keel over. Thank goodness we had a honeymoon. That's also when I realized I could make two trips to Chicago every month, but not four or six. These extra hours are taking a toll, Sophie."

Sophie wondered what Maddie would say if she knew the truth about how many extra hours she'd been putting in, taking calls from Jeremy and still trying to raise money for the Alliance when she could.

But she had to admit that Maddie was right.

Today, Sophie had bungled her job twice and Nate had caught her on both counts. She was sure she'd be the topic of conversation when Maddie and Nate were alone.

Whether she liked it or not, choices were going to be made for Sophie if she kept this up. She couldn't risk being outed about the Alliance. What she could do was confess to working too many weekend hours.

"Thanks, Maddie. Maybe I should cut back on my shifts in the ER. I've been doing it for seven months or so now. I guess it's more work than I realized."

"It doesn't have to be forever, Sophie. Just till you get caught up on rest. Reevaluate your priorities."

Sophie struggled to give Maddie a smile. Priorities. That was the problem. Sophie had too many that all should be number one. Her job.

The ER. Jeremy. Eleanor. Oh, and there was that little thing—her own health.

Wisdom told Sophie to take care of herself. Guilt nagged her to push harder for the Alliance. Commitment to those who needed her shouted for her to stay with the ER. From within this din came the sound of Jack's voice.

Sophie had been hearing Jack's recriminations even in her dreams, but she'd also heard his pleas and the words of gratitude he'd given her before Aleah's death.

Her idea to give Frenchie to Jack had been a good one. Not just for the dog and, obviously, for Jeremy, but as a peace offering to Jack. Frenchie had already brought out his softer side. When she'd watched Jack pet and talk to Frenchie, Sophie's heart melted. Remembering their confrontation at the car museum, her emotions flipped over. She would have loved to douse him with ice water. Wake him up.

Her rant should have opened his eyes.

If he could only see that the differences between them were pointless and counterproductive.

Still, she couldn't stay angry with Jack for long. In fact, she felt an unfamiliar closeness to him. He was more than the ordinary challenge a guy presented to her. For once in her life, a man's respect and allegiance to her and her dreams was important. She wished there were no obstacles between them. No grief. No animosity.

Sophie couldn't help wondering what kind of relationship, if any, they would have had if Aleah had lived. Would they be friends? Perhaps even more than friends? In such a small town, it was likely they would have crossed paths some other way. But would they have gotten to know one another as they had now?

A dozen images of Jack's face, broken, bloody and now healed crossed her mind. Would he ever truly forgive her? And why would it mean so much to her if he did?

Maddie was right. She needed to give her "priorities" a great deal of thought. And she needed to start with Jack.

CHAPTER FIFTEEN

JACK STOOD ON the deck of his condo and watched the sky fill with striations of pink, lavender, amber and orange as the sun dropped to the horizon. He'd just finished his second run of the day. He wasn't sure if it was the long summer hours calling him out to the trail or if it was the knowledge that once winter hit, his only option was his treadmill. He didn't want to consider the third reason for his urge to run, which was that no matter how much he accomplished during the day, he couldn't get Sophie out of his mind.

Running till the sweat poured from his body in sheets should have done the trick, but it didn't.

Twenty, no thirty, times a day he heard Sophie's voice telling him that no matter what he did or thought, no matter how guilty he felt, Aleah was never coming back.

Sophie had nailed him. Dead to rights.

He did feel guilty about Aleah. If he hadn't insisted she attend the seminar in Chicago, *none* of this would have happened.

Mainly, though, Jack was guilty of trying to

find people to blame to ease his own conscience. He wanted to blame Greg Fulton, the addict who hit them. Blame the drugs. Blame the legal system. Blame the hospital. Blame Sophie for doing her job.

"Sometimes, Jack, you can be the biggest jerk."

He peeled off his sweat-soaked shirt and draped a towel around his neck. "Stupid, too."

He glanced down at his feet, where Frenchie was watching the view with him. Mercifully, she made no sign of agreeing with him.

"C'mon, girl. Time for your supper."

Jack went to the kitchen and put a half cup of dry dog food mixed with two tablespoons of cottage cheese in Frenchie's bowl. The vet had told him about the cottage cheese, which would help her put on weight. Frenchie scarfed down the food in seconds and slurped up some water before prancing over to her pink plaid bed and settling down.

"Good girl. I have to take a shower."

Frenchie ignored him and closed her eyes, secure in her trust of Jack to do just as he said.

Jack let the water run until it was ice cold. He shampooed his hair, scrubbed himself with a long-handled brush and rinsed off the salt, soap and sweat.

After toweling dry, he put on a clean shirt and

jeans. As he combed his wet hair, he looked at his reflection.

"So, Sir Idiot, while Nurse Nightingale is out there in the world trying to save humanity, you need to find a way to dig your way out of this hole you've created."

He put down the comb on the granite counter. *I should donate the policy. Or I could give her a donation.* He leaned forward and shook his head. "Or you could stick to your guns and steer clear of her altogether."

His stomach rumbled, and he couldn't help but chuckle. No man could think on an empty stomach.

Jack went to his refrigerator and surveyed the contents. Sophie's words came back to him—again. *She's right. There's no garlic in here.* He opened the freezer. *Nothing fun in here at all.*

He snatched up his car keys and took the stairs to the garage.

IT WAS AFTER sundown when Sophie walked into The Louise House. Even this close to nine o'clock, the ninety-degree heat meant Louise Railton's ice-cream shop was packed to capacity.

Sophie carried an Alliance poster under her arm as she circumvented the line and went up to Louise. "Hey, Louise. Is it all right if I put this in the bathroom like we talked about?"

"Sure, honey." Louise smiled as she scooped up a triple cone for a young boy whose eyes were as big as his face. "Once I get these folks taken care of, you come back. I want you to try my new pineapple-coconut-caramel ice cream. Or are you on that stupid diet again?"

"Tonight, not a problem," Sophie replied. Finding the bathroom empty, she taped the poster to the back of the door just as Louise had instructed her on the telephone that morning.

As Sophie turned around she spied herself in the full-length mirror. At first she didn't believe her own reflection. Sure, she'd missed some lunches and breakfasts lately, but she was getting really thin. She'd hit her ideal weight, but she didn't feel as good as she had months ago when she was eating organic veggies and running the trail on a consistent basis. There was something to be said about balance in life. She'd been so busy she hadn't even paid attention to her own body. Her work had become her passion, and she was making some good changes, but she knew she couldn't keep up this pace forever. She'd liked the strong body and endless energy she'd had. Was all this passion worth losing herself for?

Maddie was right. I have to rethink my priorities.

Sophie stepped out of the bathroom and got in line behind the last couple, who ordered single-scoop cones. Once they paid and sat down at one of the antique tables that Louise had covered in aqua-and-white-striped canvas, Sophie asked Louise for her ice cream in a dish.

"Sure, honey. Whipped cream?"

"No. Yes. No." Sophie laughed. "No whipped cream. I want to taste just the flavors." She paid Louise and then looked around the room.

"I love nights like this," Louise whispered. "Every seat taken."

"I guess I'll have to eat standing up."

"There's a fella back in the corner at a table for two. He's all alone. Maybe he'll share," Louise said, handing Sophie her change. Then she pointed to the back right of the shop.

Sophie's smile slid off her face.

"Jack."

"You know him?" Louise asked. "He's new in town, right? He's only been in here once before. Cute."

"I know him."

"Good. Then go visit," Louise urged as a family of four came in the front door. "Hiya, folks! Want to try my new pineapple-coconut-caramel?"

Sophie left Louise to her sales pitch and wended her way to the back table where Jack sat dipping his spoon into a deep dish of what looked like peppermint ice cream mounded with hot fudge.

"I never pegged you for the ice-cream type," she said.

When Jack lifted his head, Sophie could have sworn she saw a flash of light in his eyes. Was he actually happy to see her? Why?

"It's my vice."

"Mine, too," she admitted. "Louise said this is the only available chair in the shop. You can ask her."

"I believe you."

"So, do you mind if I join you?"

Jack jumped to his feet so fast he knocked the table. He pulled out the little black wrought iron chair for her. "Please. Sit."

"Thanks," she said and placed her dish on the table. She smiled at him as she sat down. He did the same.

"How's Frenchie?" She was just making conversation but was surprised that she truly was interested in the little dog's impact on Jack's life.

"Terrific. Amazingly, she has monopolized every room in the condo. Because she loves the deck as much as I do, I'm getting bids from contractors to put up some kind of screen or mesh so she can't accidentally fall through the railing."

Sophie's eyes widened. "But she's been all right so far?"

"Absolutely. When I'm home, most of the time she's right on my feet. Literally. Except after she eats. She naps. At night she sleeps with me. Curled next to my neck."

Sophie's eyes fell to the hard muscles in his neck as they rounded into his shoulders. Frenchie had claimed the exact spot she would have chosen to rest her own head.

Smart dog.

Sophie tore her eyes away and busied herself by tasting Louise's latest concoction. "Oh, my goodness, this is her best yet."

"No way. This was pretty darn good," Jack said. "Peppermint with hot fudge on top. I love this at Christmas. My mom gets vanilla ice cream, I crack the candy canes and fold them in. Then I make the fudge."

"I never would have guessed. You and a kitchen just don't seem to jibe in my mind."

"Christmas makes gourmets out of many of us," he countered. "You'd be surprised what talents I have."

"I'm sure I would." She stuck her spoon in her ice cream. "Still, this is so refreshing. Here, try it," she said and shoved the dish toward him. Jack dipped his spoon and tasted.

He closed his eyes. "Sublime. Practically a health food."

Sophie laughed. She was surprised how good it felt to actually laugh and smile. Why was she tingling all over? And how long had it been since she'd felt even mildly flirtatious?

She took another bite of the ice cream. Just looking at Jack, his T-shirt stretched over his well-defined chest and his biceps bulging out of the short sleeves, made her heart race. She needed a mantra to knock back the attraction.

She watched his lips wrap around another spoonful of ice cream. She couldn't help wondering what it would be like to kiss him.

She mentally erased the image. *Get back on track, Sophie. He's not that into you.*

"You come here a lot then?" he asked, wiping his alluring mouth with a napkin.

Sophie averted her gaze. "I do. Or rather, I did. Louise is a friend. She's closed in the winter so we all take advantage during the summer and fall. Wait till you taste her pumpkin-gingersnap ice cream. Seriously, I wait all year for it. It's my grandmother's favorite."

"Your whole family is addicted to ice cream, then?" Jack cringed. "Sorry. Bad choice of words. I didn't mean to bring any of that up."

"It's okay," she said. "Frankly, I was here to give Louise an All—a poster. The ice cream was an afterthought."

"Oh."

"She doesn't have much money so her donation was small, but the poster will be seen by a lot of people this summer. I'm also hoping to put up some new ones targeted for elementary kids. This place is busy after school every day during the fall."

Jack played with his ice cream. "These are all good ideas, Sophie. Are they yours?"

"Some. A lot. I keep doing my research to see what's worked in other cities."

"And do they work? Really?"

Sophie took a huge hunk of pineapple and chewed the icy piece. "That's a tough question. Are you asking me to round up statistics for you, Jack?"

He shook his head and put down his spoon. "No. Actually, I don't even want to talk about it."

"Fine."

Silence.

She studied him. He was still staring at her. "What do you want to talk about?"

"I saw you running. On the trail. I thought you only ran in the evenings."

"These days, I catch it whenever I can. You?"

"I ran twice today."

"Holy cow, I'd be exhausted," she exclaimed. "Once a day is enough for me. But then I'm a beginner. I love it, though."

"Me, too."

He toyed with his spoon but didn't eat. Her curiosity had always caused her problems, and sometimes had ended relationships before they began. Still, she had to know. "Were you watching for me, Jack? Is that why you saw me?"

"No. Not really. I just thought you ran in the evening."

"Because you saw me in the morning—running. That's how you knew. And you saw me in the evening."

"Yes."

Sophie didn't know whether to be flattered or to escape. "Why were you watching me?" she blurted out like a three-year-old. Always probing.

"I like the way you run," he said matter-of-factly. "I watch a lot of people run, but you're a natural. I'm surprised you've only just taken it up."

She swallowed a spoonful of ice cream. That was honest and more complimentary than she'd imagined. Despite his easy manner, she kept waiting for his wicked tongue to slice her to ribbons. "That's a nice thing to say, Jack."

"Yeah. Imagine that. A compliment coming from me."

"I didn't mean it like that," she countered.

"I know you didn't. But I would have deserved it if you had," he said. "Anyway, I'd better go before I say anything else."

He rose, picked up their empty dishes and dropped them off at the dishwasher window. He didn't look back. Didn't wave to Sophie as he went out the door.

Sophie raked her fingers through her hair then stared down at the tabletop. "What just happened?" she murmured.

She was in a conundrum. Jack was obviously doing his best to be friendly, but try as they might, they couldn't stay away from the subject that ripped them apart.

Death was always an emotional issue, and even more so when blame and guilt came into play. Neither of them had moved on, dealt with the pain or had been able to come at the problem from a healthy point of view.

Sophie was aware of what she was doing. She was anesthetizing herself with work. By volunteering for the Alliance, she assuaged her guilt. Slowly, she was able to erase the image of Aleah's pained face from her memory. Sophie knew that given time, months or maybe years, she would forget the contours of Aleah's face, the sound of her voice and the anguish she felt remembering the young woman and her final moments.

If Sophie could go in a room and scream until her throat was raw, perhaps that would help. Wailing. Some of the other nurses had said it helped them during grief. Sophie wasn't so sure. She was ready to try it.

Lurking in the back of her mind was the worry

that one day there would be another victim on her table. Another addict she couldn't save. Another innocent victim staring down death because of drugs. How would she control her emotions in the future when she was doing so poorly now?

Her grandmother told her to give her sorrow to the angels. Sophie had tried, but so far, it hadn't worked.

And what of Jack? How was he dealing with his pain? He'd said he'd run twice today. Was that his way of staunching his agony? Did he exhaust himself through exercise?

And what was that about seeing her on the trail?

She'd seen him that one time while she was running, but she'd been so certain he hadn't recognized her. He certainly hadn't acknowledged her. Yet he was studying her "style"—presumably from his condo deck.

Easy thing to do. Natural. Even if he hadn't been waiting for her to go by, she would have been easy to spot. Maddie and Nate had often seen her running the trail from their living room window, Nate had said.

Not for a minute did Sophie think Jack was the stalker type. No, Jack was no threat to anyone.

Except himself.

For that she felt pity for him—again.

Sophie's coping mechanisms might not be perfect, but at least she was helping others in the process. If she could make a difference in people's lives, she just might help herself.

If she was truly a generous person, then her desire, her passion, to help others ought to extend even to Jack. Shouldn't it?

She scoffed at her idea. There wasn't a chance in the world he'd accept help from her. He'd deemed her the enemy. He'd drawn the line in the sand. Even though he'd come close to crossing over tonight, he'd gone back to his isolation. Back to his box of rules. Back inside his shell.

Someone had to help bring him out—to save him.

It would never be her.

CHAPTER SIXTEEN

SOPHIE WAS GLAD now that she'd decided to walk to The Louise House from Mrs. Beabots's rather than drive. She needed the time to put her thoughts together. Try as she might, everything in her life seemed just as big a jumble as it had yesterday. And the day before.

"Sophie, there you are," Mrs. Beabots called from her front porch.

"Hi, Sophie," two more female voices chimed.

In the soft glow of yellow mosquito-repelling lightbulbs sat Katia, Sarah and Mrs. Beabots in white wicker chairs. All were waving and smiling at her as if she was a long-lost friend.

It was truly odd, if not downright suspicious, Sophie thought, that for years hardly anyone in Indian Lake had made overtures to be her friend. Yet since she'd moved into town and rented this apartment from Mrs. Beabots, she was curiously being included, when before she felt like a pariah. Maybe that was a little harsh. After all, Sophie *had* gone after Nate Barzonni. Then there was that pass she'd made at his brother, Gabe, when he'd come to buy her parents' vineyard. She couldn't blame Maddie, Liz and their friends for keeping their distance.

But lately, they'd been kinder to her, more welcoming, which had to mean they had forgiven, dismissed or chosen to forget Sophie's earlier behavior. Sophie couldn't say if they were better than she, but they were certainly wiser.

Wisdom. Hmm. Something else to add to her goals.

Sophie stopped on the sidewalk and smiled back at the women on the porch. Katia and Sarah smiled with genuine delight as they waved her up. Incredible. She'd spent so much time flirting with men that she'd never considered building or nurturing friendships. She was achingly guilty of objectifying men like notches on a gun belt. Trophies.

And where had it gotten her? She was still alone.

Then there was tonight with Jack. He'd made several friendly overtures. She didn't understand it. He was foe. Wasn't he?

She'd always run from anything long lasting with the men she dated, but she realized she actually did care about Jack's opinion of her. She wanted him to see her in the best light.

But why?

"Sophie, where have you been?" Mrs. Beabots

asked, sounding far too much like Sophie's grandmother.

"I was at The Louise House. She's got a new pineapple ice cream that's to die for."

"Mmm. Bring us any?" Sarah asked, laughing.

"Sorry. I try not to have it around. Next time I go, I'll call and see if you want some," Sophie offered.

"I'm just kidding. We try to watch the sweets with kids around."

Sophie climbed the porch steps. "I thought kids and sugar were synonymous."

Mrs. Beabots snapped her fingers and smiled. "That's why I like you, Sophie. So down-to-earth. Kids aren't kids without treats."

Sarah frowned. "Frankly, I agree with you both. My mom made pies and cakes for me all the time. I didn't turn out so bad. Luke insists the kids eat healthy."

Katia shrugged. "As long as the kids are active and brush their teeth, what's the harm? I say we start a blog on this."

"What's a blog?" Mrs. Beabots asked.

Sarah rolled her eyes. "Katia! Don't even think it. Too much work." She held up her palms. "Wait, I take it back. I'm with Mrs. Beabots on this. I've never heard of a blog."

Their lighthearted, friendly banter cheered Sophie up. It had been forever since she'd simply joked around with anyone. No wonder she worried all the time. There was no space left in her head for fun or friendship building.

Sophie climbed the steps and sat in the last empty wicker chair.

"Would you like some of my special mint tea?" Mrs. Beabots asked. "Actually, there's no tea in it. Just mint from the garden, boiling water, bourbon and sugar. It's good for the digestion," she said conspiratorially, leaning over and picking up an antique rose-patterned teapot.

Sophie's eyes widened. This was fun and unexpected. Katia was right. Mrs. Beabots was full of surprises. "I'd love it," Sophie replied. "Thank you," she said, taking a delicate cup and saucer from her hostess.

"Sophie," Katia began. "We were admiring the sunflowers you gave Mrs. Beabots. She said you grew them in your garden at home."

"My grandmother's sunflowers are—"

"Legendary," Mrs. Beabots interjected. "Don't be shy, dear. I told the girls here that your grandmother sells them to florists."

"That's true," Sophie confirmed. "The roses are mine and my mother's. We planted only the varieties that have that wonderful perfume and then we give them good doses of manure to keep them fragrant."

"Well," Katia said. "I love them all. I've never

seen so many colors of sunflowers." Katia stared down at her teacup and tapped the scrolled gold handle. "Sophie, I'd like to ask a huge favor."

Sarah interrupted, *"Enormous* favor, Katia." She looked at Sophie with mirth in her eyes. "Bigger than enormous."

Sophie frowned. She should have known they wouldn't have been this friendly to her without a motive. People always had an angle.

Katia put her hand on Sophie's knee. "Forget it. It's too much."

"Wow. What is it?"

"The thing is, I hired Olivia and her mother, Julia, to handle my wedding. And they're doing a great job, but, I hate to say this, my wishes have increased—not that I'm bridezilla. It's just that the flowers are driving them crazy because the florists in Chicago can't get the sunflowers I want. Sophie," Katia said pleadingly, "I wondered if I could buy all the flowers for my wedding from you. Er, from your grandmother."

Sophie put her teacup down without taking a sip. "That's it? That's the huge favor?"

Katia's shoulders deflated and she turned a contrite face to Sophie. "It's just that those flowers are exactly what I'd always dreamed about having for my wedding. I didn't think they existed except in some old Judy Garland movie. You know? And when I saw that bouquet you gave Mrs. Beabots, my jaw dropped."

"It did," Sarah agreed.

"It did," Mrs. Beabots echoed.

Katia rushed on. "But I don't want to do anything that would cause you a smidge of consternation. I want to be your friend, Sophie. We all do."

"We do," Sarah chimed.

"I *am*," Mrs. Beabots said soundly, folding her hands in her lap for emphasis.

Sophie smiled, though she felt like crying. Her positive-thinking podcasts emphasized the idea that once she changed her thinking, she would attract everything into her life that she wanted. She'd wanted friends. Real ones. She'd wanted more meaning, even passion—and she'd found it.

Sophie wasn't the demonstrative type. She didn't hug and gush over sentimental moments. Until now.

"I don't understand. You—" she gazed from Katia to Mrs. Beabots to Sarah "—barely know the real me."

"I wouldn't say that," Mrs. Beabots replied. "It could be, young lady, that we know you better than you know yourself." She winked.

Katia searched Sophie's face. "All three of us knew each other a little bit in high school. Sarah is younger and was just a kid to me. Then I moved away. You were younger, as well. There were a lot things rumored about me back then. The same might have been true of you." Katia glanced at Sarah. "Sarah, not so much, but you know what I'm saying. Those girls are only slices of the women we've become. We got better. We can all see what you're trying to do for this town, Sophie, and it's admirable. And I can appreciate the guts it took to talk to Jack like you did. You were really brave to do that. I'm not sure I could have done the same in your situation, and I've known Jack for years."

Sophie stared at the painted porch floor. "Sometimes I wonder if I'll ever get through to him."

"Keep trying," Katia said firmly.

Sophie had never shared personal feelings with anyone other than her mother. This conversation was groundbreaking, in her book. If she'd been more comfortable with these women, she might have told them she'd seen Jack only an hour ago. Maybe Katia had insight into his feelings, even his condemnations about her. Perhaps he'd confided in her about his anger against Sophie. Maybe Katia knew the best way to make amends to Jack. Apologies certainly hadn't worked. Nor had reasoning with him. Yet Jack had been friendly with her tonight. Sophie was massively confused.

This wasn't the time for intimacies with Katia. Maybe there never would be such a time unless

Sophie allowed others into her personal life—her dreams. It terrified her to even think about it.

To make it worse, the minute Katia had brought up Jack's name, Sophie's heart had skipped a beat. Her breath had caught in her lungs. It was only for a second, but it had happened. What was that all about? She hadn't been running. All she'd done was think about Jack.

In the past when she'd gone after a guy, she'd felt a rush of adrenaline like she imagined a climber might feel when he reached a mountain peak. It was all about the conquest.

Her reaction to Jack was completely different. She empathized with his sorrow, sensed, more deeply than she was willing to admit, his guilt about Aleah and she craved his friendship and respect. These women wanted to be Sophie's friend. They'd told her they admired her. She realized she did want friendship from them. To be part of their warm and caring group.

Earlier, she'd wondered if Jack had wanted to be friends. But her feelings for Jack included attraction, guilt, disappointment and respect. Actually, there wasn't an emotion she couldn't attach to the man. She was slowly coming to realize that Jack had taken a foothold in her mind, if not her heart.

Her heart? What was she thinking? That wasn't possible. Not for "love 'em and leave 'em" Sophie.

There was a great deal of comfort in her bolt-and-run tactics. Suddenly, she was out of her comfort zone—way out. Yet, there it was. She did want more than friendship from Jack. And she didn't like that one bit.

When she'd been with Jack tonight, she'd gotten the feeling, for a few moments at least, that he wanted something more from her, too. But what exactly?

Katia picked up her designer purse and pulled out a cream satin-covered box that had an opening down the center. It was tied with a thick black ribbon and clipped with two antique rhinestone brooches. "This is for you."

"It's so elegant," Sophie replied, staring at the gorgeous box but not taking it.

"Go ahead. It won't bite." Katia chuckled.

"What is it?"

Sarah couldn't contain her excitement any longer. Her knees were jumping with nervous energy. "Oh, for Pete's sake, it's her wedding invitation. She's hand delivering every one of them!"

Mrs. Beabots beamed at Sophie. "Isn't it exciting? We got ours earlier this evening. I thought you were upstairs. That's why I made the mint tea. To celebrate."

"Invitation?" Sophie didn't want to appear stupid, but people, brides especially, did *not* invite Sophie Mattuchi to their weddings. Her reputation cast a long shadow of doubt and fear that she was the black widow who'd weave a spell and kidnap the groom.

Sophie blinked several times to dispel the image in her head. Clearly, she was on a new playing field and these rules were beyond her comprehension. She inhaled and let her face show her pleasure. "It's for your wedding. Of course." Sophie took the box. "It's so beautiful I don't want to open it."

"I've never seen anything like it," Sarah added.

Katia grinned at Mrs. Beabots. "I had help. Just pull back on the brooches."

Sophie opened the invitation to reveal gold parchment, with black French Script. Sophie skimmed the invitation, but her eyes latched on to the words *our family and friends*. It took her a moment to move past the fact that she was being included in Katia's special day. Sophie felt a rush of warmth that went straight to her heart and tugged at the door there that had never been opened. Her eyes stung and her throat constricted with emotions she hadn't experienced since she was a little girl—and even then it was only with her mother and grandmother.

Sophie tried to keep a grip on her composure. She forced herself to read the rest of the invitation, then she looked at Katia.

"This is only a month away."

"I know. It's getting here faster than I'd thought.

We just picked out our rings today. There's so much to do."

"I don't know what to say."

"Sophie, our wedding is very small and it's being held at home. I only want my friends there. Please say you'll come."

Sophie rose and put her arms around Katia. "Thank you. I'd be honored."

As Sophie sat back down, she carefully closed the invitation. "I'll keep this all my life." And she meant it.

"Me, too," Sarah said.

"And, Katia," Sophie began, "I think my grandmother would love to help you with your wedding flowers. She's a romantic, and when you explain how you've dreamed of flowers like hers, she'll be thrilled."

"Do you mean it, Sophie? Because if it will cause any trouble, or jeopardize—"

Sophie waved her hand to stop Katia's words. "Nonsense. Besides the romance, she loves to make a profit. I'll take you out to the farm tomorrow night after work, if that's okay."

Katia's eyes gleamed with delight. "Perfect!" Then she frowned. "Uh, I forgot. I have a late appointment at the office. Can you pick me up there?"

"Sure," Sophie replied without thinking.

"Great. Then it's not far for you from the hospital, either. It's a date!" Katia clasped her hands together. "Oh, my gosh! I think I'm truly going to have my dream wedding."

Sophie forced a smile as the others chatted about the other arrangements. She was lost in her own thoughts.

Would Jack be at the office when she came to pick up Katia? And if so, would his mood be as sour as it was when he left her at The Louise House tonight? Or would she sense forgiveness from him as she had earlier?

If she were to take Katia's advice, she should keep trying to break through the wall of ice around Jack. Something told Sophie he was the one guy who was worth it.

CHAPTER SEVENTEEN

JACK'S DESK WAS a blizzard of files, reports and contact sheets that he and Katia had compiled since his first negotiations with Emory Wills at the Indian Lake Hospital months ago.

Until Frenchie came along, this company was all he cared about, and now that he'd been in Indian Lake for eight months, he was itching to take the business to the next level.

Katia rapped on his door, then breezed in. Cheerily, she plunked a mega-sized latte on his desk with the new Italian-looking logo from Cupcakes and Coffee. "Ah, my favorite rocket fuel. I think we'll need it today," he said, taking a deep drink.

"Not yet," she replied.

Katia handed him what appeared to be a jewelry box, all satin and rhinestone clasps. "What's this?"

"My invitation."

"This cost some bucks."

"Killjoy. I only had twenty-five made because there're so few people coming to the wedding."

He smiled at her. "Well, then, thank you. I'm

honored." He started to hand it back. "You can save this one and give it to someone else. I already marked the day on my calendar."

Katia raised an eyebrow. "You were that sure you'd be invited?"

Flashing her a sidelong glance he said, "I'm walking you down the aisle or stairs. Remember?"

"I was just kidding! Keep the invitation. To remember my day."

"It's so—" he studied the elegant box "—you."

She smirked. "That was the idea." She lowered her eyes to his desk. "So, what's all this?"

Jack exhaled and crossed his arms behind his head. "This, Katia, is our future. At least a decade of it, I would wager."

Katia picked up one of the folders. "This is the policy I sold to Emory Wills."

"Exactly, which in twenty-four months will be obsolete."

"What?" She jolted back in her chair. "I researched that policy…"

Jack held up his hands. "Things are changing for the hospital. That's what I want to talk to you about. I've been in touch with several other hospitals in the Benedictine Hospital Network."

"Good, because I know how much you want their business, as well. What's been their response?"

"Positive. But here's the news. They just put

in a bid to acquire Indian Lake Hospital, which would take Indian Lake out of the independent world and into a conglomerate. Which means we would most likely lose the contract we already have and we'd have to start dealing with the powers-that-be at Benedictine, who are based in Indianapolis."

"No wonder you look anxious. So, when do you leave for Indy?"

"You're quick." He placed his hands on the desk. "Tomorrow."

Katia crossed her legs and folded her arms. "What can I do?"

"We both have to kick into a higher gear."

"And I'm leaving on my honeymoon in a month."

"Yep. So I've decided to bring Owen up to speed immediately. Can you give him a crash course in all this so he can take the lead while you're gone? You're going to hate this while you're staring dreamily into Austin's eyes in Venice, but I need you to keep your cell phone on and check your email while you're away."

She nodded. "That's okay. Austin has to stay in touch with his office every day, as well. We're adults-in-charge, Jack. We understand that at our level of responsibility, total escape is not possible. I'll be happy for half a day, each day, of privacy."

"That's big of you. I'd be wanting all day and

all night. You've burst my honeymoon dream bubble."

Katia stared at him unblinkingly. "You? Have a honeymoon dream? I don't believe it."

"Hey, I can have fantasies."

"Yeah, sure. I just didn't think you did."

Jack knew his grin was impish. "Then you don't know me that well."

"Does anybody?"

"What's that supposed to mean?"

Katia shrugged. "I was like you—before Austin. All work and no play. You have an excuse, though. This is your company. Well, yours and Barry's. You feel like you're Barry's life insurance policy. He told me that he and his family are your sole beneficiaries. He's your brother-in-law, Jack. That I understand. But he's not your life."

"You're wrong."

"Nope. You don't have a life." Katia delivered the words with so much assurance and truth Jack felt she'd thrown a javelin through his stomach.

He jerked back. He felt a burn in his heart. She was right and he hated it. He didn't have a life. No wife. No kids. Only Frenchie—and she was a new addition.

He rubbed his forehead, feeling slightly disoriented.

"I shouldn't have said that," Katia whispered. "But you're my friend, Jack. You're like the brother

I never had. I love you and I care about what you do for all of us and for yourself."

Jack read the affection and empathy on her face. Katia was like family to him. She was one of the reasons he wanted his company to grow. She'd put so much of herself into his business, he could never repay her. And he realized she was doing what a real friend did—she was telling him what he needed to hear whether he liked it or not. Katia had always been diplomatic, but she didn't sugarcoat.

When he needed to give her hard news, she didn't like the truth sugarcoated, either.

"Tell you what, Katia. I'll put some thought into my personal life. But not yet. Not today. In order for us to save what we have and build a larger clientele, we have to be aggressive with the hospital."

Katia made no secret of her exasperation with him and sighed heavily. "Okay. Talk to me about Emory."

"Have you heard talk about a new hospital?"

Surprise filled her eyes. "No way. Who told you that?"

"I heard it at the Rotary meeting from three key people. Two were city councilmen. Benedictine has already sent surveyors here to check out the vacant property on the other side of the railroad station. This means Emory has to scramble to keep his job and then be accepted as the finest administrator, if Benedictine moves in."

Katia speared him with a stony look. "That means he'll be trying to make Indian Lake's bottom line as solvent as possible. We should be in good standing on that point. He couldn't possibly get a better package than ours."

"It also means he won't expand anything right now. I was hoping for that deal."

She shook her head vigorously. "Not necessarily. What if you presented him with something even more competitive? Something that would make even Benedictine sit up and take notice?"

"Possible. Doable." He rolled a pen up and down his desktop. His mind filled with different scenarios. "I think Emory will cut every expense he can. Starting with staff. Anyone not pulling their weight, he'll fire."

"Usual corporate procedure. Which I hate," she said with a biting tone. "I can see why you have to go to Indianapolis."

Jack folded his hands in his lap, as he always did when he made a decision. He didn't know why. Perhaps it was his form of praying he'd chosen the right course. "I also realize I have to keep Emory happy with us. If these rumors are true, we need to be prepared to deal with Benedictine. If they aren't, then Emory is still our guy."

"Can you ask Emory about this?"

Jack shook his head. "I doubt he'd tell me the truth or that he's allowed to. I'm just a vendor."

"So, we're going on speculation."

"I'm afraid so," Jack groaned.

Just then Jack's intercom phone rang. Melanie announced that Katia's appointment had arrived. "You'd better go."

She nodded and headed for the door. Then she looked back at him over her shoulder. "I'll do all I can to help, Jack. You know that."

"I do, and thanks."

"Oh, by the way, Sophie is meeting me here today after my appointment. I hope you don't mind."

"Sophie?" Jack's head bobbed up from his papers like he'd just broken through the ocean's surface after a deep dive. "Why? What does she want?"

"It's what I want from her. She's helping me with my wedding flowers. We're driving out to her parents' farm tonight to pick out sunflowers."

"Oh."

Katia tapped the door with her left hand. "See you later."

He stared after her, still thinking about Sophie. *Wedding flowers. And was that a diamond ring Katia was wearing today?*

Big rock.

Jack dropped his head into his hands. What was

the matter with him lately? It wasn't so long ago that he'd face a situation like Emory Wills and the Indian Lake Hospital and all he'd see were dollar signs and signed contracts.

This time he was concerned about employee cutbacks.

Many of those employees—doctors like Nate Barzonni, nurses, janitors and techs—were his clients now. They were people with mouths to feed. Mortgages to pay. Their families would suffer.

And if he lost Emory's business, his own company would suffer, too.

Jack wasn't thrilled about this diplomatic nightmare, but it was a game he had to initiate if he had any hope of staying afloat. And if he was ever going to sell a corporate plan to Benedictine, he needed Emory's recommendation and support to solidify the deal if and when Benedictine acquired Indian Lake Hospital.

Jack took the lid off the latte Katia had brought him. Maddie had made a little animal face out of a half-melted marshmallow for him. It made him smile. It was his first smile of the day.

He picked up his files and went back to work.

JACK HAD WRITTEN a lengthy email to Tom Hardy, the CEO of Benedictine Hospital Network in Indianapolis, outlining the benefits of his insurance packages and requesting an interview. He reached for his latte and realized it was stone cold. He hit Send and decided to warm the coffee in the break room microwave.

As he stepped into the reception area, he realized with a start that Melanie and Owen's desks were vacant, their computers shut down.

"Hey! Where is everybody?"

He glanced at the clock above Melanie's desk. How could it be six already?

"Hi, Jack."

Jack froze. He'd recognize that voice anywhere. The angel's voice. Or so he'd thought when he believed he was dying.

He spun around. "Sophie."

She was wearing a silky yellow skirt with tiny polka dots and a short-sleeved cotton sweater the color of goldenrods. Her dark, thick hair tumbled onto her shoulders and glistened in the light of the setting sun coming through the French windows. She stood slowly and he noticed that her espadrilles were tied with yellow ribbons. No stockings, just smooth olive skin. She looked like one of those Italian beauties he'd seen in travel brochures walking along a Sicilian beach.

She took his breath away.

"Melanie said it was okay if I waited for Katia out here. She's in her office with a client and asked not to be disturbed."

"Her office?" Jack couldn't tear his eyes from Sophie's. He was mesmerized. "Oh, right. Her office. We just got it finished last week. Luke Bosworth did the work. He's very good."

"He is." She smiled.

The light in her face was more brilliant than the sun's amber rays.

"You know Luke?"

"Not well. Just that he's Sarah's husband. He did the build-out of the apartment in Mrs. Beabots's house. My apartment, that is."

He kept staring. Filling his eyes. He barely heard her.

"My apartment? You know? Where Katia lived before she and Austin... Jack, are you okay?"

"Huh? Oh. Fine. Fine. Hey, would you like some iced tea? Coffee? Lemonade? It's just that powder stuff. It's not really my thing—I make my own from fresh lemons."

"So do I." She smiled again.

His heart did some radical gymnastics that he'd never be able to describe to a doctor.

Sophie was still talking. "I make mine with filtered water and it's so much better. Mrs. Beabots puts mint in hers. Actually, she puts her homegrown mint in just about anything. I should bring you some."

What was she talking about? He saw her lips moving, but this vision *couldn't* be Sophie. He was angry with Sophie. He and Sophie were on opposite sides of a blistering disagreement about how Aleah had died. Who was responsible. He wouldn't give in. Ever. He owed that to Aleah.

Didn't he?

"Iced tea would be great," she said. "It's been a long day. We had three difficult ablations back-to-back."

"Is that unusual?" he managed to say.

"Pretty much. These were all over three hours each. I wasn't sure I'd get here in time for Katia. But we started earlier than we'd planned. Thank goodness," she rambled.

He pointed to the break room. "I'll get some tea for you. Katia shouldn't be much longer."

"That's very kind of you, Jack. No sugar."

He smiled. "Somehow, I knew that."

"Really? I've never liked sugar in my tea, even though I like—"

"Ice cream," he finished for her.

"Yeah," she replied. "How's Frenchie?"

"Er. Fine. She's asleep in her bed. In my office." He really had to concentrate. He was getting tea. No sugar. "You wanna see her?"

"Yeah. I'd love to."

"Feel free," he said, waving toward his office.

Sophie followed him. Light footsteps. Barely hitting the floor. Didn't angels do that? Float? Not walk.

Jack turned and went to the break room. He filled a glass with ice cubes then poured the tea from an antique pitcher Katia had brought from home. Katia was relentless with making the office feel homey. Cozy. Inviting.

Fleetingly, he wondered if Sophie liked antiques. Or was she the modern type—all hard surfaces and antibacterial sprays?

He put his latte in the microwave before finding a napkin and straw for Sophie.

He heard her cooing as she talked to Frenchie. Then he heard her return to the reception area. Funny, it warmed him in some odd way to know that she and *his* dog were so…loving.

When he stepped out of the break room she was sitting. Gazing out the window.

The light on her face made her look like a Renaissance master's painting. He tripped on the carpet.

"Oops!" He spilled the top fourth of tea on the floor.

Jack handed her the glass and then bent down and used the napkin to sop up the tea.

"Here, let me help, Jack," Sophie said, touching his shoulder.

He could feel her warm hand through his shirt. He remembered that hand as she'd cleaned his wounds. Wiped his brow. Held his hand in the

ER. He hadn't known who she was. He was nothing to her then. A number. A victim. A patient.

But she'd treated him as if he were the only human in the world worthy of her time and care. It had been her voice he'd clung to when trying to find consciousness in the sea of pain.

He should thank her. Deep down, he was grateful. He owed her. She'd been patient with him since the accident, even if they disagreed. But his guilt would always keep them apart.

Still, she had been good to him. Great, even.

He put his hand on her knee. "Sophie—"

"Hey, Sophie! You're here!" Katia exclaimed. She turned to say her goodbyes to a man and woman who disappeared down the stairs, then headed toward the waiting area. "Jack? What are you doing?"

"Tea. I spilled the tea," he muttered getting to his feet.

Katia's smile was suffused with curiosity. "Okay. Need any more help?"

"No." He gave the carpet one more dab. "I think I got it."

Katia clasped her hands together. "I just need to get my purse and we can go, Sophie."

"That's great," she said as Katia went back to her office.

Sophie looked at Jack. "Do you have a paper cup I could put the tea in to take with me? I don't want to waste it, though I wouldn't mind stealing this pretty glass."

"Uh, sure. I'll get it for you."

She stood. They were very close.

She smelled like roses and freesia and vanilla. Orchids. Rare, precious flowers. His blood pounded in his ears.

"I don't mind doing the pouring, Jack. And I saw where the break room was. I know you have work to do."

"Yes. Work."

He watched her walk to the back of the office, her skirt swinging ever-so-slightly, the muscles in her calves moving rhythmically. He liked her walk even more than he liked the sight of her running. Her hair swayed in a curtain and he marveled at how natural she looked. She was all woman.

He continued to watch, turning to the window, after Katia and Sophie said goodbye to him and left. They got into Austin's 1958 Mercedes convertible, white with a dark-brown leather interior. Jack remembered signing the insurance policy on it. It was one of the few Austin paid for road usage. He'd wanted Katia to have a "fun" car.

As they drove north, Katia's auburn hair blowing in the wind and Sophie's thick, dark brown waves lifting off her shoulders, Jack felt weak in the knees. Katia was bonding with Sophie. They were becoming friends.

Jack wanted to become Sophie's friend, as well.

With the recent disclosures Jack had heard about Benedictine and the Indian Lake Hospital, he now understood why Emory was making such a fuss about his rules and policies. He was seeking every loophole and excuse to fire employees. And he was doing it to save his own butt.

Jack wondered if Sophie knew how thin the ice was under her feet.

CHAPTER EIGHTEEN

SOPHIE SAT IN Dr. Caldwell's office, looking out at the church spires of Indian Lake. He was talking to one of his surgeons on the phone, though she wasn't paying attention to their conversation. She'd been summoned to his office and all she could think about was why.

Sophie was well aware that her performance had been slipping over the past weeks, and before news of it could get to the top echelons of the hospital, Doctor Caldwell had stepped in.

She hadn't felt this remorseful since third grade, when she'd been caught stealing Andrea Wilson's mittens. Sophie had hated the cheap, plain black mittens her mother had bought her at a discount store. Andrea was an only child of wealthy-enough parents that she had a different pair of mittens for each of her four winter coats: a pink parka, a purple wool coat, a long red coat with a black velvet collar and cuffs and a white rabbit fur jacket with a hood.

When Sister Mary Rose asked Sophie why she'd taken the mittens, Sophie hadn't understood the nun's reasoning. To her mind, Andrea had plenty. Why shouldn't she share her things for a while? Sophie didn't want the mittens forever. Just through the rest of the winter.

When Sophie's mother found out about the incident, she forbade her from eating any sweets for two months. Sophie often wondered if that long-ago punishment was the reason she craved sugar when she was depressed or feeling angry, sad or guilty.

"Sophie, you know that Doctor Barzonni and I value you very much. That's why it distresses me that we have to have this conversation."

Sophie put up her hand and shook her head. "You don't have to say any more. I know exactly what's wrong. And I will correct it."

"Really?" He raised his eyebrows and sat back. "Then enlighten me because I haven't the foggiest."

"I've been working too many volunteer hours. Believe me, Doctor Caldwell, it's not my job here. I'm not stressed in the least."

"Well, that's good to hear. I was afraid we were too much and that we would lose you."

"On the contrary, I intend to stay on staff with you and Doctor Barzonni until I retire—if you're both here that long."

He swiped his face and chuckled. "Let's hope

so!" Then he looked at her with probing eyes. "So it's the ER?"

She nodded. "I do need to cut back. I don't want to cut it out, but just dial it back a bit. I, er, have a few other things I've been volunteering to do and I realize now that it's too much."

He sighed heavily. "That's a relief, Sophie. Quite frankly, Dr. Barzonni and I were afraid that your father's cancer was back."

"Oh, no. It's nothing personal. My family is fine. There are no other, um, significant situations taking my mind off work. I'm well aware that I need to refocus."

"Good."

"I've already said this to Dr. Barzonni, but would you reassure him for me that there won't be any more slipups? In or out of the ablation unit."

Dr. Caldwell smiled and extended his hand. "Consider it done. I'm glad we had this discussion, Sophie. I hope I wasn't prying about your father…"

"No, no. He's doing just fine. Great, actually. He's hired more harvest help than ever before and we're expecting a great year. He's quite happy. So is my mother."

"That's all good news," Dr. Caldwell replied. "Give them my regards."

"I will." Sophie hoped her relief wasn't too obvious as she took her leave.

Sophie went to the elevator bank and pressed the button with shaking fingers. She'd been tenser than she realized. Understandable. Acceptable. If she'd lost her job, she would have flushed away all her years of education, study and hard work to get to the position she now cherished. Sure she could get work at another hospital in another county. A nearby state. But she didn't want to. Not for a minute. Even when she was in Grand Rapids, she missed her family too much. Sophie liked Indian Lake. Parts of it she loved. Despite her reputation and the way too many women still looked at her with skepticism, even disdain, she'd made a good name for herself in the ablation unit. She was part of a real team. Dr. Caldwell was actually protecting her. Warning her. Obviously, he and Nate respected her.

And that meant the world to Sophie.

Her work with Dr. Caldwell, Nate and her coworkers was the gold in her life. This meeting had opened her eyes and helped her chart her course of action.

Bullet One, dodged.

Now for Bullet Two. She had to find a way to help Jeremy be less dependent on her. She needed to find him a job.

CHAPTER NINETEEN

COILS OF FOG drifted off the placid lake and floated across the running trail where Jack pounded the asphalt, pleased that his ankle had healed quickly and well. It couldn't be that he'd had top-notch nursing care. It couldn't be that before the ER doctor had had a chance to examine him, Sophie had realized his ankle was badly sprained and had splinted it, elevated it and wrapped it in ice.

No, Jack knew that his fast-healing body was due to his morning concoctions of fruits, vegetables, aloe vera juice, whey powder and almond milk. That had to be it. He was responsible for curing himself and he was proud of it.

Because of the fog, Jack didn't push himself. It would be just his luck that when he'd finally gotten to the point where he could take the stairs two at a time again, he'd trip over some stupid tree branch he couldn't see.

"Which should be going away by now," he groaned. He looked to the east, expecting to see the sunrise, but all he saw was a milky glow in the distance. What the heck? It was summer; it was supposed to be hot. Instead, the last few days had dropped into the upper sixties and it felt more like September than July. At this rate, he was going to have to start wearing a headlamp each time he came out. Maybe one of those light bars like Barry had had on his Jeep back in high school. Jack, Ava and Barry had all had a lot of fun in that Jeep back then. Blasting Foreigner tunes and Bon Jovi. Driving up and down Lakeshore Drive up to Oak Street Beach. Cubs baseball games. Soldier Stadium in the fall. Eating too much pizza at Gino's, with the graffiti-covered black walls and concrete floors.

Jack felt his insides turn sour. He used to do a lot of fun things. But they'd been kids. Kids did idiotic, crazy stuff. Adults were responsible.

He was being very adult. And not having any fun in the process. Was that the cause of his dour moods lately? Or was it that his life just…wasn't a life?

Man. Lately, he couldn't seem to shake that thought.

It wasn't just fun, either. There was no love in his life. Except Frenchie, he supposed, but when it came to people, he was alone. Sure, he'd thought about finding the right somebody, but he'd never fallen when he should have. Never zinged. Never been entranced.

Shaking off his moodiness, Jack rounded the

north side of the lake, careful of his footing as he passed the Lodges. No tourists out and about this early, which was surprising for summer. He'd figured the kids would have been aching for the first dive off the floating raft. Maybe the gloomy morning kept everyone inside. It was probably more appealing to moms, dads and kids to pull those covers over their heads and sleep in till nine.

Yeah. Only running fanatics came out at five in the morning.

Like me.

Or Sophie.

He nearly stumbled thinking about her. The angel. The Good Samaritan. The talented nurse. The pretty farmer's daughter. The one woman who made him clench his jaw and see red.

Why would he be so fascinated, so drawn to the one woman he could never forgive?

What kind of self-sabotaging behavior was that?

He couldn't get her out of his mind. Whether she was dressed up—like she was last night at his office—or wearing no makeup, scrubs and sneakers, she was beautiful. Inside and out.

But she had screwed up—big time. Her decision not to stay with Aleah was unforgiveable.

Jack couldn't forgive himself for being the driver. For taking Aleah to Chicago in the first place. But there was a deeper guilt he'd been reluctant to face.

Jack had been falling for Sophie ever since her angel voice brought him back to reality in the hospital. While he'd been basking in her tender care, she'd been wasting precious minutes that should have been spent saving Aleah. He'd needed Sophie, but had he kept her at his side too long? Jack had been pointing the finger at Sophie, but how culpable was he? He tried to see the situation from her point of view. Sophie wanted to save all her patients that night. Jack still believed Greg Fulton was in the wrong. Getting behind the wheel when he was high was unconscionable. But it was Sophie's duty to help everyone who came through the ER doors.

Jack was well aware of the increasing drug problems all over the country. Clearly, Indian Lake was not immune. He'd heard the reports from the City Council, the concern about the situation at the Rotary Meetings and especially in the hospital halls. No one knew what to do.

Jack felt even guiltier because he didn't know how to help. Deep down, that was what gnawed away at him. Jack fixed things. He made the world safer. And here was something he had no idea how to fix.

Feeling guilt grip his heart, he put more energy into his strides. He could pound away his pain. He'd done it before.

Jack's mind drifted and, with the sound of his

shoes hitting the trail, he remembered a day long ago when he'd heard a similar sound.

He and his sister, Ava, had been racing each other home from school. Laughing. Goofing off. Suddenly, they'd heard what sounded like a bomb dropping several blocks away.

Within seconds the air was filled with siren screams.

One, two, then three police cars had shot past them. The entourage turned off the main street onto the street where they lived. Though it was daylight, the cars' bright lights ricocheted off the picture windows of the houses and aluminum garage sidings.

"Come on!" Jack had yelled to his sister, who was as curious and as much a daredevil as he was back then. "Let's see what's going on!"

They took off running, their sneakers slapping the sidewalk.

The police cars flashed blue-and-red lights, but their sirens were silent.

They had pulled up to Jack's house.

Both kids stopped dead in their tracks.

Smashed into the monster oak tree in their front yard was their uncle Marty's car with their uncle in it, draped over the steering wheel.

The front end of the car was halfway up the tree trunk, the hood pleated and busted open.

"He came around that corner at fifty miles an

hour," the older of two cops was saying as Jack and Ava walked slowly toward the wreck. "It was like he was trying to hit that tree."

Jack was dazed as he looked from Uncle Marty's bloodied head to the front porch where his mother stood, dressed in jeans and a pretty peach-colored blouse, her hands covering her mouth. She was stark white.

Their mother spotted them and burst into tears. "Ava! Jack! Come here. Now."

Ava instantly obeyed, but Jack hung back.

He wanted to see. To investigate. To learn. What had happened to his uncle Marty?

Jack walked up to the policeman. "Is he alive?"

The man was gentle, but firm. "You need to stay back, son. This is nothing for you to see."

"That's my uncle Marty." Jack pointed.

Another policeman had opened the driver's door and was reaching inside. He put his fingers on Uncle Marty's neck. The cop shook his head.

Just then the ambulance arrived. Two paramedics raced toward the wreckage while another two took out a stretcher.

A fire truck pulled up, then another fire truck and a fourth police car. The place was like a scene out of a Mel Gibson movie. Though in shock, Jack couldn't tear his eyes off the drama. He knew his

uncle was dead. He wasn't waiting for a final pro-
nouncement. But there were still questions.

Like…why?

The neighbors had scrambled out of their houses.
Mrs. James came over to hug Jack's mother. The
Albertson kids, all four of them preschoolers,
watched from the driveway until their mother made
them go inside. Other neighbors just ogled. They
made Jack feel ashamed, as if he'd done something wrong.

The firemen used a hook and chain to pull
the car down off the tree. Then they pried Uncle
Marty out from behind the wheel, placed him on
a stretcher, covered him with a gray wool blanket
and wheeled him away.

Until then, everything had seemed to be happening in slow motion, but now the world went
into fast-forward. Suddenly, Jack registered that
half the vehicles had left and his mother was still
on the porch, clutching Ava to her side and talking to one of the cops.

Jack went to his mother. She simply held out
her arm, reeled him in and hugged him close. Jack
put his arm around her waist and rested his head
against her hip. His head bobbed up and down
with her sobs.

He hugged her tighter.

"Did you know he'd been drinking today?" the

cop asked, writing down details in a spiral pad like the one Jack used at school to write notes to Sherry Cramer, the pretty girl who sat in front of him.

"He's an alcoholic," his mother explained. "He's been sober for years. Since my kids were born. But Marty lost his job last month. And with no wife or kids of his own, he was despondent. The doctor put him on antidepressants, but I guess he didn't mention his drinking. I think he was mixing. He and I got into a big fight yesterday about it. I warned him that if he didn't stop, I wouldn't let him see the kids." She burst into a fresh round of tears. "This is all my fault. I should never have pushed him. They told me at Al-Anon to protect my family first. I never dreamed he'd do anything like this."

"Mrs. Carter, your brother would have done this or something similar even if you hadn't said a thing," the policeman said. "I've seen it too many times. Don't blame yourself. This was his decision."

She swiped her nose on the sleeve of her pretty blouse. "So it was suicide?"

"Yes, ma'am. That's how we see it. Listen, I know it's not much, but you need to take comfort in the fact that he didn't hurt anyone else."

"But you think this was premeditated?"

"I do. He knew exactly how fast to come around

that corner so he would hit that tree. Plus, he wasn't wearing a seat belt and the air bags had been disengaged."

"Oh, my God," she sobbed and pulled Jack in closer.

"We're going for now, Mrs. Carter. When your husband gets home, would you ask him to call me? Here's my card. Just in case he has anything else to add to the investigation."

She nodded. "My husband is on the road. Iowa. He's supposed to be home tonight. He sells insurance."

"Tough business."

"We do okay. For the kids, you know."

The cop smiled and touched first Jack's head and then Ava's. "You kids take care of your mom."

"Yes, sir," Jack had said. Ava kept crying and sniffling.

Jack remained on the porch and watched a tow truck haul the mangled car away. The policemen drove off in silence. Except for the deep ruts that Uncle Marty's car had made in the grass and the scar on the tree trunk, there was no sign of what had happened. Life on the street returned to normal.

Jack had almost forgotten about that day so long ago. He'd only been about eight at the time. It was amazing how well the mind could repress memories that caused pain. Or illumination.

Was his trauma from the accident and Aleah's death linked to his own past? Did his feelings about his uncle Marty and the senseless waste of his life color his attitude toward Sophie and what she was doing?

Jack was more confused than ever.

Sweat ran from the top of his head down his temples and to the back of his neck, soaking his T-shirt. Obviously, he'd needed this run to rid himself of impurities. Flush out the toxins, including terrible memories and maddening thoughts of Sophie.

AFTER HIS RUN, Jack cleaned up, grabbed Frenchie and headed to work. As soon as he pulled out of his driveway, though, he realized he was nearly out of gas. He stopped at the gas station on Indian Lake Drive, which skirted the south end of the lake and led into town on the overpass that ended at Main Street. Jack filled up the car while Frenchie watched him through the window, which was open a crack. He made silly faces at her and she cocked her head and barked at him. He couldn't help laughing. She was too much fun to tease.

Jack decided to go inside the mini-mart and buy a bag of chewy treats for Frenchie before going to the office. He grabbed a bottle of water as well, then went to stand in line. An elderly woman paid for her gasoline and bought a coffee and a pack of cigarettes. In front of him was a young man in a hoodie, which was odd since it was so hot outside. The guy was thin. Very thin. He had a wrapped sandwich and an energy drink in his hands.

The elderly woman left and the guy was next. He put his purchases and a wad of one-dollar bills on the counter.

"You're a dollar six short," the gray-haired cashier told him.

"What?"

"You need more money. One dollar and six cents. That includes the tax."

"This is all I have."

"Yeah? Then put something back. It's not enough," the clerk barked.

"I, uh—"

Jack stepped forward. "I'll pay the dollar six for him," Jack said.

The guy turned around and smiled at Jack. "You didn't need to do that."

Jack took in the guy's cracked teeth and a face that was old before his time. He shoved the money onto the counter.

"No worries," Jack said. "Enjoy."

"Thanks, man." The guy seemed to retreat into his hoodie as he gathered his food and shuffled out the door.

Jack paid for the treats then went outside. And stopped dead in his tracks.

The thin guy in the hoodie had walked over to his car and was tapping on the windshield. "Hi, Frenchie! Do you remember me? Boy, is this a nice car or what? And you have a car seat? You're doing great, girl. Just what I wanted for you."

Jack approached his car slowly, taking in every word. Stunned, he asked, "You know my dog?"

The man pointed. "That's Frenchie. I would know her anywhere. You must be Sophie's friend."

Jack's mouth fell open slightly, but he managed to hold his surprise in check. "You're…Jeremy. Right?"

"Yeah. Sophie told me she'd found a really nice person to care for Frenchie. I'm glad it was you." He glanced at the sandwich in his hand. When he raised his head, his pale hazel eyes were misted over. "Thanks." He raised his hand. "For this. For Frenchie. There aren't many people like you. And Sophie."

He turned and started to walk away.

Jack was speechless for a moment. "Hey! Wait."

Jeremy stopped and turned back. He shook his head. "No. I don't want to pet her. I don't want to hold her. It would kill me. Understand? She's okay now. She has you. I'm good with that."

Jeremy started jogging, putting distance between himself and Jack.

Jack watched after him, feeling pity. Understanding Sophie in a new way.

CHAPTER TWENTY

JACK HELD FRENCHIE in his lap at one of Indian Lake Deli's sidewalk tables. She licked his hand. He couldn't imagine life without her.

The café umbrella blocked the noon sun, though Frenchie's jeweled collar still glittered in the light, casting beams that apparently fascinated Frenchie enough for her to try to catch them with her paws. She patted the tabletop, tapped Jack's chest and clutched at his forearm.

"Hey, Jack! Who's your new friend?" Nate Barzonni called as he approached, arm in arm with Maddie. Nate was wearing his lab coat, suggesting they'd walked over from the hospital.

Jack lifted the dog in his right hand. "Guys, I'm in love. Meet Frenchie."

Maddie sat down next to Jack and scooped Frenchie into her arms. "She's precious! I didn't know you had a dog."

"That's a dog?" Nate joked. "I had a cat bigger than that."

Jack put his hands over Frenchie's ears. "Don't

listen to him. He's just jealous he doesn't have a pretty girl like you."

Maddie smiled at her husband. "I want one. Where'd you get her?"

"I sorta rescued her."

"From the Indian Lake Animal Shelter?" she asked, kissing the top of Frenchie's head. Maddie had such a possessive hold on Frenchie, Jack nearly feared he wouldn't get his dog back.

"No, uh, Sophie found her for me."

"Really?" Nate asked. "Now she's rescuing dogs? The woman is relentlessly—"

"Helpful?" Jack interjected.

"Precisely. She's always volunteering to save the world."

Maddie rolled her eyes. "Like you're not? Donating free time to the clinic up in Michigan?"

"That's different," Nate argued.

Jack shook his head. "No, it's not. Two peas in a pod." He hadn't thought about it that way before, but as soon as the words were out he realized he was right. Nate was as dedicated as Sophie. They were two people with their thumbs holding back the dam.

With the possibility of the hospital being acquired or a new one being built, Jack wondered if there would be money for more personnel. Would Emory continue his cost cutting? Or would there be even broader changes? Generous, talented people like Nate and Sophie were assets to the hospital, but would a big corporation see them that way? Would Emory? Their volunteer work was pulling them in several directions, and that could put their jobs at risk.

The future of Indian Lake Hospital was never far from Jack's mind these days, and he found himself slipping into his own thoughts. Regardless of what Emory planned, there was the chance he'd be forced into early retirement if the merger happened. And if Jack was seen as too closely tied to the former president, he'd never get a meeting with the new hospital board or leadership. He'd be dead in the water before he so much as dove in.

Jack had never had to strategize this much on a deal. The stakes were the highest he'd ever encountered.

Maddie handed Frenchie back to him. "You better take her back, or I'll walk off with her." She smiled and linked her arm through Nate's. "By the way, you live in the condos on the other side of the Lodges, right? We aren't that far from each other, you know. You should come over for dinner sometime. I have more in my repertoire than cupcakes, I swear."

"Dinner?" Jack was slightly rattled. Since he'd moved to town, the only dinners he'd been to had been functions with boring speakers, where he hoped to connect with prospective clients. Leathery chicken, frozen vegetables and limp salad were the norm. Dinner was a means to an end, a way to build his business so he could pay salaries and keep the lights on.

Nate smirked at him. "You remember the concept, right, Jack? Food, wine, friends. Maybe listen to some music?"

Maddie rolled her eyes. "Nate's suddenly into country-western. I have no idea what's going on."

"I got tired of Hopi wind flutes," he joked as Maddie pushed his shoulder.

Jack stroked Frenchie's head. "Can I bring Frenchie? She's got separation anxiety."

"Of course!" Maddie replied brightly, eyeing the dog a tad too possessively. "Though something tells me *you're* the one with the separation issues. I'd love for her to visit anytime. I'll call you and we'll set something up."

Maddie and Nate rose together and walked away with their arms still around each other. Jack couldn't tell where Maddie ended and Nate began, they were so close.

How did they do that?

Staring after them, Jack felt an odd twang in his stomach and realized it was jealousy. Jack had put his personal life on hold for years. But lately, work just wasn't enough. He wasn't fulfilled.

He needed to take action, otherwise he'd always be the odd man out. It was one thing to blame his predicament on business, the move to Indian Lake and the lack of time he had for personal issues. It was another to get lazy. Jack had never been lazy.

He looked at Frenchie's upturned face as an idea took shape. He ruffled her ears and kissed her snout. "Frenchie, I should take you for a stroll. Four blocks ought to do it."

ACTING ON A whim had never been Jack's strong point, and as he approached Mrs. Beabots's, passing Sarah and Luke Bosworth's large Italian stucco house with the massive front porch on the way, Jack felt his resolve melt like sugar in the rain.

"Maybe this wasn't such a good idea," he said, tucking Frenchie under his right arm.

He'd no more thought about turning around and heading back to his office when Frenchie started barking.

"Hey!"

She squirmed, pawed at his wrist and leaped out of his arms. He caught her midflight before she hit the sidewalk and hurt herself.

"What are you doing? Frenchie!"

Then he heard another dog barking. It was the deep, massive, thunderous bark of a large dog.

"Beau!" Jack heard a child's voice yell from Mrs. Beabots's front porch. Apparently, the kid had no authority over the dog because the dog kept barking.

So did Frenchie, though she'd stopped trying to escape Jack's grasp.

"Beau! Stop that!" another child shouted.

The front door opened. "Annie? Timmy? What's going on?" Sophie rushed onto the porch and put her arms around a red-haired girl and wide-eyed little boy. She gathered the two children to her waist.

Jack was awestruck. She was dressed in her surgical scrubs and sneakers, her dark hair pulled back in a French braid. But it wasn't her unassuming beauty that stopped him in his tracks. It was her affectionate gestures, the caring in her eyes and concern in her voice for these two children. He felt his heart opening on the spot.

She scanned the street. "Jack?"

"Hey," he said, setting Frenchie on the ground and holding the ridiculous rhinestone leash in his hand. Sophie was so stunning, he'd forgotten about the dog.

Frenchie lunged forward and snapped the leash right out of Jack's grasp. She bolted up the front steps and over to the enormous, movie-star handsome golden retriever, skidding to a stop at Beau's feet.

Frenchie tipped her nose at Beau, who leaned down and touched his nose to hers.

"Oh, wow!" the girl exclaimed, dropping to her knees. "How adorable!"

"Cool!" her brother agreed. He squatted next to Beau, putting his arm around the dog's neck.

Jack sauntered along the sidewalk, never taking his eyes off Sophie. He noticed that she barely glanced at the dogs or the kids. She was watching him. Warily. But still, he'd take that.

"I think they're entranced," Sophie said.

So am I.

"Yeah. It happens," Jack said.

Sophie ruffled the boy's hair, smiled and walked down the steps toward Jack. She gestured behind her. "Frenchie likes Beau. Cute, huh? I'm, uh, babysitting the kids till their mom gets back. Annie and Timmy, by the way. They're Sarah's and Luke's."

"But it's your lunch hour." He shoved his hands in his pockets. "I mean, I just saw Nate at the deli. I figured since he was taking a break—"

"That I might be home?" she finished for him with a glimmer in her eye.

"I wanted to thank you for giving her to me. Thinking of me. I mean, er, to be her dad." *Good grief!* He was bungling this. Since when did Jack Carter get tongue-tied?

Her face filled with pleasure. "I guess I just knew you'd be a natural."

She seemed overjoyed, as if he'd just handed her a diamond ring.

Odd. He had no idea where that visual had come

from. Why would he be thinking about diamond rings and Sophie? It didn't make sense. Did it?

"I don't think anybody should be alone, especially helpless animals. She's so darling, Jack. The kids love her already. You'll have to bring her by again."

Jack felt something zing through his heart. Okay. That had never happened before. At least not that he could remember. Maybe in high school with Mary Beth Peterson, who was in his algebra class and always let him copy off her tests. But Jack hadn't actually had a crush on Mary Beth. She was just a good friend. No, this feeling was new.

"You were right that I'd need to bring Frenchie to work with me. She likes it. She greets my clients." He nodded. "Yep, a real asset to the firm. Oh, and Owen has really taken a liking to her."

"Sounds like she's made a difference in your life, Jack."

"Actually, it's you who made the difference."

"Me?"

He put his hand on her shoulder and gave it a slight squeeze. "A few days ago, I met Jeremy."

"You what?"

"It was totally random. I still can't quite believe it, frankly. It was at the gas station. He was ahead of me in line and after he walked out, he recognized Frenchie in the car. When he said her name, she knew him."

A lump of emotion cut off his words. For the first time, he understood the empathy that Sophie had for the addicts she worked with.

"I just wanted to say thanks, and that I admire you, Sophie. For who you are. What you do."

"Jack…"

He felt a burning in his chest where a new awareness of others was growing.

At that moment, it was all he could do to fight the impulse to reach out, pull her to him and kiss her.

He didn't care that the kids were watching them from the porch. He didn't care that any passing car could contain his clients or people who would gossip to them.

"You're amazing," he whispered then leaned over and kissed her cheek. "Don't ever stop being you."

She stared at him. Speechless.

"Jack?"

He shifted his weight awkwardly. "I gotta go. I'll just get Frenchie."

He went up the steps, said goodbye to the kids and petted Beau. "See you two around."

"Bring Frenchie back anytime," Annie said.

Jack stroked his dog's head. "Thanks for the in-vitation. I think we'll be walking by quite often."

Jack went back to Sophie, who was still frozen in place. The afternoon sun filtered through the canopy of maple leaves overhead, dappling her shoulders. A slight breeze swept down the driveway and across the front yard. Sophie tucked a stray tendril of long hair behind her ear.

"Jack," she said, reaching out as he passed. Instead of petting Frenchie, which he'd expected, she touched his forearm. "Thanks."

"Well, I didn't mean to barge in on your afternoon gig." He tilted his head toward the kids. They raced down the steps and to the backyard, Beau leading the way.

"Not just for stopping by, but for, well, understanding."

Pursing his lips contritely, he leaned closer. "I'm trying to do more of that."

She stood on her tiptoes and pressed her lips against his.

She felt warm, soft and tender. It was a kiss out of a dream. Jack felt the combustion all the way down to his toes. When she pulled back, he felt an odd sense of longing, as if he'd been abandoned. He didn't know how that was possible, but it gave him renewed empathy for Frenchie.

Jack was tempted to set the dog down, pull Sophie into his arms and hold her close. He needed at least a dozen more kisses to make certain that what he'd just felt was real.

"I gotta go, too," she said before he could give in. She hurried back up the steps, called for the kids and Beau, then went inside.

It was Jack's turn to freeze. He wasn't sure his legs would ever move again. Just then, Frenchie licked his hand. "Sorry, girl." He stroked her head. "Guess I got carried away."

Jack turned toward town. He needed to get back to work.

He glanced back at Mrs. Beabots's house. He needed to do a lot of things.

But all he wanted to do was sit on that front porch with Sophie and spend the rest of the afternoon with her. If he did, would she kiss him again? Or was that just a one-time thing? Spur of the moment?

Frenchie cocked her head and shot him an "are you kidding me?" look.

Jack whistled all the way back to his office.

CHAPTER TWENTY-ONE

SOPHIE INTRODUCED JEREMY to Mrs. Beabots, who stood ready for action with garden gloves, pruning shears and a pair of newly sharpened hedge clippers.

"Jeremy, my garden is a source of delight and aggravation to me," Mrs. Beabots explained as they walked past the boxwood hedges.

"Why's that, ma'am?"

"Time was when both my husband and I kept these boxwoods and Japanese yews clipped in formal shapes. I've always loved the gardens in Paris. Have you ever been to Paris, Jeremy?" Mrs. Beabots asked as she bent over to yank a tall thistle weed away from her Princess Diana rosebush.

"No, ma'am. I never thought about it," Jeremy answered.

"Well, you should, young man. You have all the world to see at your age," Mrs. Beabots continued to ramble as they headed farther into the yard.

Jeremy pointed at the thistle. "We had a lot of these in Phoenix. Considering my painful encounters with cactus spines and thorny mesquite trees, I think cleaning out your gardens won't be such a chore."

"That's good, Jeremy. I admire a person who jumps right into their job."

"I'll need a tall ladder to trim that Mandeville. It looks like it's taking over your garage. It's bad for the siding, you know."

"That's what Luke Bosworth told me," she concurred. "But it's not a garage, Jeremy. It's a carriage house. This house, Jeremy, is one of the oldest on Maple Boulevard. It was built in the late 1800s and the carriage house originally served as a stable and housing for carriages."

"Did your family live here?" he asked.

"No. My husband and I chose this town because we fell in love with the lake."

"Yeah. It's nice."

"Is your family native to Arizona?"

"No. They're originally from New York. They hated the winters and moved to Phoenix."

"How interesting. I adore New York. When I was young, in the early sixties, it truly was the city that didn't sleep. Come, let me show you the rest of my rose garden that needs weeding and spraying. You know, Jeremy, when I was in New York, I used to walk in Central Park all the time. Did you ever go there?"

Sophie listened as Mrs. Beabots reminisced about her travels. This job, small as it was, could give Jeremy purpose. She hoped it would ease his depression and cut the number of phone calls he made to her. Mrs. Beabots continued talking, soliciting Jeremy's thoughts and opinions.

Sophie smiled to herself. The elderly woman was wily indeed. Sophie had voiced her concern about Jeremy's depression and his inability to stay straight. Mrs. Beabots didn't know much about counseling, but she clearly knew about giving hope and shoving life and all its joys under Jeremy's chin.

By the time they reached the gazebo, Mrs. Beabots had finished showing Jeremy what needed to be trimmed and weeded. They paused and went up the steps. There on an antique wicker table sat a pitcher of lemonade and three tall glasses with melting ice cubes.

"I thought we should stop for refreshments," Mrs. Beabots said.

"But, ma'am. I haven't done any work for you yet," Jeremy countered.

Mrs. Beabots chuckled and sat in a deeply cushioned wicker chair. "Of course you have, Jeremy. You and Sophie have kept me company." She grinned as widely as a Cheshire cat and put a sprig of mint in each glass.

AMID SOPHIE'S GRANDMOTHER'S acres of amber, rust and lemon yellow sunflowers, Sophie surgically clipped the best blossoms for Katia's wedding arrangements. Katia needed a large amount of flowers and ivy vines for the thick garlands she planned to tie up along the banisters of the massive circular staircase in the mansion. Olivia and Julia had given Sophie the final list that morning, and she was rather surprised to see that Katia had asked for twelve large crystal vase arrangements for the living room mantel, library tables and hunt boards and the dining room table. She needed flowers for four outdoor table centerpieces and smaller bouquets for the bar, bathrooms and lighted front hall art niches. The guest list was small, less than thirty people, so Sophie figured Katia was going luxe for her "day."

The florist had already prepared all the bases in Austin's mother's antique crystal and silver vases. Sophie was more than a little interested to see what she believed would be a spectacular result.

"Nipotina," Sophia Mattuchi called to her granddaughter affectionately.

"La mia bella," Sophie answered, walking over to the full plant of low-growing sunflowers her grandmother was working on. "I planted this one myself years ago. It's done very well. These will be perfect for the mantel."

Sophie started clipping the blooms, while her grandmother pointed out the dark burgundy Moulin Rouge and the shorter stemmed Early Russian for variety amongst all the golden, butter and sun-colored blooms. Sophie had filled six plastic buckets with water and put them in an old garden wagon for transport. She carefully arranged her chosen stems in the buckets according to size, the shorter stems in front and the taller stems in the back, while her nonna assessed the flowers, pointing to her choices with a sharp snap of her arm, like the unquestionable authoritarian she knew she was. At ninety, her brain was sharp and her attitude even sharper.

Sophie smiled to herself. There was so much about the Old World ways still embodied in her grandmother. Sophia, whom Sophie was named after, had never learned much English, though Sophie believed her grandmother understood a lot more than she let on. She walked a little slower these days, but she still did so without a cane. Once she was among her flowers, Sophia came to life. She titlted her face to the sun and hummed to the flowers as she caressed the petals and faces.

"Bambino." Sophia sighed heavily. Then she turned and touched Sophie's cheek. *"Io ti amo."*

"I love you, too, Nonna." Sophie placed her hand over her grandmother's. "Thank you for sharing your precious ones with Katia. She's becoming a good friend."

"Ah! *Bella sposa!*" Sophia nodded and then jammed a finger into Sophie's sternum. She narrowed her eyes and frowned in that accusatory way that Sophie used to call "Grandma's stink-eye." *"Tu sei la bella sposa."*

Sophie grabbed her grandmother's hand and kissed it. "No. No. It's not my time to be a bride."

Her grandmother shrugged and went back to her clipping, but the words had no sooner escaped Sophie's mouth when the sun slid out from behind a cloud, nearly blinding her. She blinked, the memory of Jack's lips pressed against hers completely erasing the present.

She'd seen Jack at Mrs. Beabots's two days ago, yet her surprise had not abated. She still didn't understand what he'd been doing there. It was as if he'd appeared out of nowhere. He'd said he'd seen Nate on his lunch break and figured she'd be off, too. Jack had come to see her. On purpose.

And then he'd kissed her on the cheek, which she could chalk up to impulse or a friendly gesture. But he'd lingered too long and she sensed that there was something more behind it.

She'd been quite purposeful when she'd kissed him.

Kissing Jack was not like kissing any other guy. And Sophie had kissed plenty. None of them had ever haunted her thoughts two days later. In fact, often she could barely remember what they looked like. She'd always had a serious case of disconnect when it came to men.

For a long time she thought she was noncommittal. Possibly scared of the whole relationship thing.

But the truth was, she simply wasn't interested. No one had lit that fire inside her that made her want to reach out. Touch and grab hold. With Jack, something was very, very different.

But what was this absorbing, consuming, magnetic attraction she was feeling for Jack?

Strangest of all, when she'd kissed Jack, it wasn't like any other kiss she'd given any other man. Instead, it was the sweetest, most endearing kiss she'd ever experienced, and it seared an indelible brand on her heart. She'd never forget it.

But why would this happen with Jack, of all men? Their viewpoints were not just diametrically opposed, but they also carried guilt and resentment about that one tragic night.

And there was another problem. Jack was a forever kind of guy. An insurance man would be all about calculating risks. He'd look long and hard before he leaped into love, but once he did, there'd be no going back.

And that was absolutely the wrong kind of man for Sophie.

Always had been.

Sophie turned away from her grandmother and placed the armful of lush flowers in one of the buckets. "Nonna, I'm finished," she called, straightening up. Her grandmother turned toward her with a wide smile.

Sophie had spent her entire life surrounded by her parents and grandmother and immersed in her nursing work. She'd never explored the borders of her comfort zone, never broken down the gate and sprinted over to the other side of life. Never made many changes.

Until this year.

Now she was trudging through several uncharted territories simultaneously. She was astounded at how good she felt about her explorations…including these unfamiliar, somewhat frightening feelings for Jack.

She just hoped they didn't blow up in her face.

WHEN SOPHIE ENTERED the McCreary mansion on the day of Katia and Austin's wedding, she was awestruck by the magic the florist had created with her grandmother's flowers. The sunflower, ivy and yellow rose garland on the bannister was massive and tied with wide ivory satin bows at the newel posts.

Sophie wore a cream lace sheath over a strapless crepe underdress she'd bought at Judee's Dress Shop, along with gold high-heeled sandals and a matching clutch purse. Though she'd fretted over how to wear her hair—up, down, half up, braided— she finally gave up and simply brushed out her long dark hair, swirling it over her shoulders and clipping it behind her right ear with one of her grandmother's antique rhinestone-studded combs. She wasn't sure she'd see Jack at the wedding, though she assumed that because he worked so closely with Katia, he'd be there. Just the thought of Jack caused her fingers to tremble as she fastened long gold-and-rhinestone bars into her pierced ears.

In an alcove in the front hall sat a man playing a Spanish guitar and a woman violinist. Sophie recognized Debussy's "Clair de Lune."

Before Sophie had a chance to inspect the other florals, she was bombarded with greetings and hugs from Sarah, Maddie, Olivia and even Annie and Timmy.

"Isn't it gorgeous?" Maddie exclaimed, squeezing Sophie quickly and then backing away so Sarah could do the same. "Katia has such great taste."

"Oh, like you don't." Sarah grimaced affectionately, giving Maddie a slight hip bump.

"Look who's talking, design diva," Liz said coming up from the hallway that led to the kitchen.

Liz wore a long, yellow-gold satin gown that tied under the bodice with a huge bow in back. The folds of the skirt billowed around her as she walked, and though she was eight months pregnant, she glowed with health. With her honey-blond hair streaming down her back and her matching antique Art Deco earrings and neck-lace, Liz was a vision of an elegant Madonna.

"Liz," Sophie gushed, "you're absolutely radi-ant."

"Thanks, Sophie." Liz beamed at her then bent in closer. "Wait till you see the bride. She's stun-ning."

"She always has been," Sophie added, and the women smiled in agreement.

"I've got to go back upstairs to see Katia," Liz said with obvious delight. "It won't be long now."

Sophie glanced up the stairs.

No Jack.

Maddie took Sophie's hand. "C'mon. You sit with Nate and me. Since Rafe is the best man, Olivia will sit with us, too."

Sophie looked at Maddie quizzically. "Olivia and Rafe?"

Maddie winked at her. "They've practically been inseparable since she moved back from Lou-isville after the Kentucky Derby."

"I didn't know. He's really a nice guy."

"I couldn't ask for a better brother-in-law. Ex-cept for Gabe and Mica, of course."

"It's a big family, isn't it?" Sophie observed.

"And with Liz's baby, the first grandchild, it's getting bigger by the week!"

They reached the entrance to the living room and Sophie halted, amazed. The space had been transformed into a mini-chapel. The furniture had been removed, the drapes were tied back and silk trees decorated with tiny crystal lights lined the room. The mantel was overflowing with Sophie's grandmother's sunflowers and ivy. Five short rows of satin-covered chairs with gold netting tied in big bows in the back had been set up for the twenty-odd guests.

Sophie marveled at the attention to detail and the care Katia had taken to make her day memorable, not just for her and Austin, but for her guests, as well.

Nate was already seated in a chair and talking to his brothers, Gabe and Mica. In the row behind them was Gina, their mother, and Sam Crenshaw, Liz's father. Sam had his hand on the back of Gina's chair and Gina was hanging on to his every word. If Sophie didn't know better, she would swear she saw a twinkle in Gina's eyes as she gazed up at Sam. Then, as Gina laughed at something Sam said, Sam's hand easily and quite naturally cupped Gina's shoulder. He squeezed it affectionately.

Sophie had the oddest sensation that she'd stepped into a parallel universe, where love and affection drove every individual. It was as if an invisible elixir suffused the air and, once inhaled, humans were addicted.

Love. The ultimate drug.

"Oh, Sophie, dear." Mrs. Beabots waved to

her with a white-gloved hand. She was wearing a beige-and-gold braid-trimmed vintage Chanel suit, a white straw hat with a black ribbon and a black quilted purse with gold chain strap. As always on formal occasions, she was the epitome of 1960s chic. Sophie had heard it rumored that Mrs. Beabots had actually met Audrey Hepburn in Paris, but Sophie didn't believe it. Stories like that grew in small towns like moss on the north side of a tree. Neither had deep roots. But she couldn't deny that Mrs. Beabots had style.

Sophie couldn't help scanning the guests once again for Jack. She felt a lump in her throat. Maybe he wasn't coming.

Sophie turned to Maddie apologetically. "I should go sit with Mrs. Beabots."

Sophie wasn't sure, but she thought she saw disappointment flit across Maddie's face. "Sure, Sophie. You go ahead. We'll save a place for you at our table for supper. Don't worry—Mrs. Beabots will be sitting with us, too."

"Thanks," Sophie replied, and as she turned away, she felt a distinct warmth blanket her, as if she were cocooned in love. It was the same feeling of unconditional acceptance she got from her family. Was it possible these people all truly felt that way about her? Or was this feeling just part of the celebratory atmosphere? After the wedding, would it fade like twilight in the evening?

Sophie refused to think the disturbing thoughts that had defined her life for too long. She'd always found it difficult to accept gestures of friendship. In the past she'd been afraid of rejection. Maybe she still was—a little.

Sophie eased her way past an enormous white bird of paradise in a Chinese urn, then slid into the row where Mrs. Beabots sat, settling into the chair next to her. Mrs. Beabots patted her knee.

"You look scrumptious." The older woman practically giggled. "Oh, I just love weddings. People are so happy." Her eyes roamed across the room. "And they're so well dressed!"

Sophie couldn't help but laugh as she followed Mrs. Beabots's gaze. She saw handsome Mica Barzonni move away from his brothers and talk to Isabelle Hawks, Charmaine Chalmers and Scott Abbot. Just past them she recognized Cate Sullivan, Louise Railton and Julia Melton, Olivia's mother. Nearly all the guests had caught her eye and had given her a sign of recognition. Sophie smiled back and realized that none of them seemed surprised by her presence.

This was all Katia's doing.

Katia had told the others that she accepted Sophie as a friend, and she'd done many things to include Sophie as one of the group. Sophie glanced at Mrs. Beabots's smiling face.

No doubt Mrs. Beabots had a hand in it, as well.

Sophie berated herself for being suspicious, for believing she wasn't worthy of friendship, and for being a self-sabotaging idiot. Maybe part of her transformation had to be learning to take people at face value. Maybe if she did that, she wouldn't be quite so serious and uptight all the time.

The music swelled and the standing guests scurried to find their seats. A tall, handsome, gray-haired man dressed in formal judges' robes entered the room and took his place in front of the fireplace.

"That's Judge Lantz. Do you know him?" Mrs. Beabots asked Sophie.

"No, I don't."

"Handsome man. His wife died four years ago. Cancer. Poor thing. I liked her a lot. He loves to travel but now has no one to go with him. I was thinking he'd get a kick out of Louise."

Sophie's mouth fell open. "Are you trying to set her up?"

Mrs. Beabots smoothed her bobbed platinum hair with her palm. "I'm just helping. Louise is always going down to Florida in the winter. She takes those cruises to the Caymans and the West Indies. She has a niece in Paris, you know. Maybe the judge and Louise should go to Paris and check on her." She winked.

The music rose in volume and all conversations stopped.

Austin and Rafe entered the room and stood next to each other at the mantel, facing the guests as the music continued to play. Sophie recognized the piece; it was from Puccini's *La Bohème*, one of Sophie's favorite operas. This was Musetta's waltz, "Quando me'n vo." The Italian music, her grandmother's flowers, the romantic atmosphere—all of it was making Sophie sentimental, nostalgic. Astonishingly, her eyes misted up. She'd never cried at a wedding—until now.

She wiped away her tears as Austin's face exploded into a megawatt smile. The music swelled again to announce the bride's entrance. Everyone turned toward the staircase.

Liz descended the steps first. Mrs. Beabots put her hands on Sophie's shoulders and whispered, "I predict the baby will be a girl and look just like Liz."

"If it's a boy, I hope he looks like his father," Sophie replied quietly. She couldn't imagine a man being any more handsome than one of the Barzonni brothers. Except... Her thoughts trailed off as Jack Carter, dressed in a black tux, snowy white shirt and bow tie appeared on the staircase escorting a resplendent Katia toward the living room.

Katia's strapless ivory satin gown was simple and elegant. There wasn't a scrap of lace, a crystal or pearl in sight. The bodice was nipped in at the waist with a satin wide tie that formed an enormous bow at the back then trailed down the voluminous skirt. Katia wore her auburn hair up in a shower of tendrils that were sprinkled with rhinestones. On her ears were Victorian-style chandelier diamond earrings that Sophie had no doubt were real.

Jack walked Katia to the front of the room, kissed her cheek and gave her hand to Austin, who stepped forward and linked her arm in his.

Sophie thought she'd never seen two people so in love in all her life. Except for Liz and Gabe, who were blowing each other kisses across the room. And except for Maddie and Nate, who sat with their arms entwined, nearly cuddling in the row in front of Sophie. Or even Sarah and Luke, who sat across the aisle with Timmy and Annie. Luke kept winking at Sarah and each time he did, Sarah smiled and blushed.

Sophie had just torn her eyes off Sarah and Luke when she realized Jack had come to sit down in the seat next to hers. She felt a *whoosh*, as if his presence had filled a vacuum she hadn't realized existed. His familiar, spicy scent enveloped her.

He briefly glanced her way. Sophie felt her heart melt, turn to flame and then explode. She smiled. "Hi."

Without shifting his gaze from the bride and

groom as the judge began the ceremony, Jack whispered, "You're stunning."

"So are you."

Jack turned to Sophie and held her gaze.

Sophie knew she'd gone into A-fib.

CHAPTER TWENTY-TWO

As soon as Judge Lantz said, "You may kiss your bride," pandemonium struck.

The gorgeous sunset Katia had dreamed of for her wedding had disappeared beneath ebony skies. The light filtering through the windows vanished and the room turned dark.

Just as Austin took Katia in his arms and kissed her, a huge bolt of lightning split the horizon, followed by another and another. Thunder rolled and shook the windows.

Sophie cringed. Katia had planned to serve the dinner outside on the terrace.

Everything would be ruined.

The guests shuddered and groaned.

Katia pulled away from Austin, her eyes wide, and then she started laughing. Austin let out a huge guffaw.

"What's so funny?" Sophie asked Jack.

Jack was stifling a chuckle of his own. "Austin proposed in the middle of a tornado. If there was going to be a summer storm anywhere within the three state area, it would be right here, right now."

"What kind of bad luck is that?" Sophie asked.

Jack grinned mischievously. "The dramatic kind, I'd say." He grabbed her hand. "Come on. Let's save the day."

Sophie followed Jack out of the living room as the guests rose and leaped into action. As Sophie and Jack raced down the hallway, Sophie heard Katia giving directions about how to move the dining tables, bar, flowers and hors d'oeuvres into the house.

In the kitchen, Olivia and Julia were already rearranging serving dishes. Daisy, the housekeeper, dressed in an ice-blue silk suit, was tying her apron on.

"I knew I should never have agreed to be just a guest. It's all hands on deck!" Daisy groaned as she started clearing the island of dishes. "What a mess this is going to be."

Sophie smiled compassionately at Daisy as Jack opened the door. "Nonsense. It's the most beautiful wedding I've ever been to, and this is just a glitch."

Daisy waved a wooden spoon at Sophie. "I like your attitude. Now go!"

"First, can I have some of those dish towels?"

Olivia handed Sophie a stack, and she rushed through the door. The wind whipped through the trees and ripped leaves off the branches. Already, the small tent with the pretty hanging baskets of yellow begonias looked as if it would be yanked off its stakes. Under the tent were four round tables draped with white cloths, which were fluttering wildly. The gold-rimmed china glinted as the next bolt of lightning lit the sky.

"Hurry!" Sophie shouted as Jack gathered plates and she scooped the cutlery into the kitchen towels.

"Can you get the wineglasses?" Jack yelled above the mounting thunder. Then he took off carrying a huge stack of dinner plates to the house.

Sophie left the bundles of silverware on the tables for a second trip and crammed a half dozen glasses in the crook of her left arm instead. Another gust of wind lifted the table skirt high enough to disrupt the floral centerpiece and flip it over. She ran to the house and deposited the glasses on the kitchen table.

Katia was helping Daisy, Julia and Olivia with the food.

"What are you going to do?" Sophie asked.

"We'll eat in the dining room instead of having the buffet in there. People will just have to serve themselves from the stove and island. My mother and I set that table for twenty-two when she worked for the McCrearys. We can do it again. The kids will just have to scoot together on the ends. We'll be fine."

"It'll be fun!" Sophie interjected. "Just like a big Italian family meal."

Katia beamed. "Exactly."

Jack handed off the plates to Luke, who took them to the dining room. "We'll get the rest in before the rain hits."

Timmy ran into the kitchen, an iPhone in his hand and held high for Katia to see. "My mom got the Doppler up. It says tornado warnings!"

Katia started laughing again. "Go show that to Austin. This is just too hysterical."

Timmy shook his head. "Brides are crazy." He ran away, calling for Austin.

Sophie and Jack shot out the back door and were halfway to the tent when they felt the first fat raindrops. They had just made it under the canvas when sheets of rain began to sweep across the clay tennis courts, the terrace and the pool, nearly cutting off the view of the house.

"Was a storm even predicted?" Sophie asked, slightly out of breath as she peered at the downpour.

"It was supposed to go way north of us. That's why Katia turned her nose up at the forecast. She said it couldn't possibly storm on her wedding."

Sophie grinned. "Hmm. Is that misplaced faith?"

Jack gathered up the remaining wineglasses that the wind threatened to smash. "These look precious."

Sophie nodded. "Antiques. I bet they were Austin's grandmother's. Here, I'll take them."

Sophie heard a banging that was different from the thunder and the sound of wind rushing through the trees. "What's that?"

Jack looked around. The banging continued.

"It's coming from the house," Sophie said. Then she spotted Katia standing at a window on the second floor, holding something black in her arms. "What in the world?"

Sophie whirled toward Jack. "You brought Frenchie to the wedding?"

He scrunched his shoulders, holding his palms up guiltily. "She was invited. What could I say to her? She saw me getting all dressed up in my tux."

"You're saying the dog was jealous?"

"She's French."

"You don't know that for a fact." Sophie was enjoying their humorous banter. "Still—" she glanced back at the window "—I think Katia's trying to tell us there's a problem. I'm going to bet Frenchie is afraid of thunder."

"Thunder?" Jack repeated. "I hadn't thought of that. She's probably terrified. And I'm not there."

Sophie nodded. "Right, she's got separation anxiety."

"Uh-huh." Jack seemed to be doing some mental calculations. "I'll put the dinnerware in my pockets. Good idea about the towels, by the way." He whipped one of the tablecloths off the table and held it over his head. "We can't hold the party up. So, here's my plan. This tablecloth will be our umbrella." He pointed at her gold sandals. "You need to take those off. Once we start running, it'll be slippery. You could trip."

Sophie chuckled. "Afraid I might break the glasses?"

"I don't want you to get hurt." He smiled impishly. "*And* I want to protect the glasses."

His smile went straight to Sophie's heart. She believed him. Was that a bad thing, like Katia ignoring the dire weather predictions?

She bent down and peeled the sandals off.

"Here. I'll carry your shoes," he offered. "You take the glasses. I'll hold the cloth over both of us. And we run."

Sophie positioned the glasses in her arm as she had before then slipped her fingers around the stems of four more. "I'm ready."

Within three strides, the pounding rain had soaked through the cloth and Sophie felt her hair getting wet. Two more strides and they were halfway to the house. She heard Jack muttering under his breath. By the time they reached the terrace, she realized they were carrying a massive amount of water on their backs. Her dress was damp. They scooted under the awning by the back door, and Jack whirled the tablecloth away from Sophie. In the process, he dumped water all over himself.

"You're drenched!"

"And you're not exactly dry!" he chortled as they went inside.

Sophie put the glasses down on the table next to the others she'd brought in. "Let's check on Frenchie."

Jack took Sophie's hand and just as they started toward the hallway, Sophie slipped on her wet feet. She hit the floor hip first, still holding on to Jack.

"Sophie! Are you all right?" He bent down to help her up, but then he slipped, though he didn't fall.

"Jack, be careful!" she said, helping him regain his balance as she rose off the floor. She took hold of his upper arms and remembered all too well the toned biceps she'd seen when he'd passed her on a run. He was rock solid. Just like his personality.

She stood, took her sandals from him and said, "If I'd been wearing these I probably would have broken my ankle."

"Don't even think it," he groaned as he gripped her around the waist. "Too painful. A sprain is bad enough."

"You're really wet," she commented as another clap of thunder rumbled through the house.

Jack's eyes widened. "That was close. This storm isn't moving on as fast as I'd thought it would." He marched toward the staircase. "Let's go see about my pup."

Katia was waiting at the door to the master bedroom, holding a shivering Frenchie. "Jack, she's absolutely terrified. I didn't want to leave her, but I have to help out downstairs. Austin's been calling me on his cell. He can't find the silverware."

"Shoot!" Jack patted his jacket. "It's all here. In my pockets." He withdrew the bundles that Sophie had made up.

Katia handed Frenchie to Sophie while taking the silverware from Jack. "Great. I'll figure out supper. I put out towels and a hair dryer for you both to clean up. Thanks for saving the day, Jack." Katia kissed him quickly on the cheek, then breezed past them, her satin skirt filling the staircase as she descended.

Sophie speared Jack with a quelling look. "She says that to you all the time, doesn't she? Saving the day and all. That's not a Jack-ism, is it?"

Frenchie licked Sophie's chin. She barely noticed and stroked Frenchie's head unconsciously.

"Guilty as charged," he replied, moving into the master bedroom and taking off his sopping jacket.

Sophie followed him in and glanced at the massive iron four-poster French bed covered in a beige-and-gold duvet and a pile of matching pillows. In the middle of the bed was a pink doggie blanket and the teddy bear they'd bought Frenchie at the pet store that first day. Sophie felt her heart melt another fraction. Frenchie sprang out of Sophie's arms and directly onto the pink blanket. She cuddled around the teddy bear, still shivering, though measurably less now that Jack was in sight.

Jack continued into the bathroom and picked up a towel to dry off his face, shirt and shoes.

"The teddy bear," Sophie said, pointing at Frenchie. "She seems attached to it."

"She is. We picked it out together, as I remember." He came to the doorway, still scrubbing his hair with the towel. "You and I, that is."

Sophie eased around Jack and found the hair dryer, then turned it on full blast. "Come here," she ordered.

"My hair's dry enough," he said, but he moved closer, anyway. "I could dry yours for you, though."

Sophie dropped to her knees to hide her blush and started drying his pants' legs. "If you let the water set, there will be a permanent stain around the edges. As soon as you can on Monday, take the tux to the cleaners and ask them to work on these water stains. Maybe you can save the suit." She was rambling.

"The jacket is probably toast, but it was worth it."

Sophie continued drying his pants' legs, pretending she hadn't heard what he'd just said. She was thankful she was on the floor because being this close to Jack, in this intimate setting, had turned her bones to jelly.

Jack reached down and gently pulled Sophie to her feet. He took the hair dryer from her and turned it off. Suddenly, the room seemed as quiet as a church at midnight.

"You can't help it, can you?"

"What?"

"It's just in you to always help," he explained. "The broken, the wounded, dogs, anyone in pain. Me included. Do you ever put yourself first?" He didn't wait for an answer. "If you do, I certainly haven't seen it."

He put his palm on her cheek and stroked her temple with his thumb. His eyes roamed her face slowly, as if memorizing it. "You didn't dry your own hair, which is quite wet. Still beautiful. But wet. You didn't towel off your dress, which probably needs to go to the cleaners just as much as my tux. Maybe more. My tux is a decade old. And that's new, isn't it?"

"Uh-huh," she murmured with only a tip of her

head. She couldn't take her eyes off his. Something monumental was happening to her and for the first time in her life she didn't want to stop it, slow it down or change course. She wanted to meet it head on. Fling herself over the waterfall and see if she survived.

Her gaze dropped to his lips. She felt hers trembling. She wasn't afraid of the thunder like Frenchie, but the storm inside her heart terrified her.

She'd kissed him before.

But now, things were different. She was different. What if Jack wasn't feeling the spark she felt? What if he chose his own guilt, his prejudices, over her?

And if he did, could she live with that? What would she do? Her grandmother always told her that once she'd tasted paradise, she'd never be satisfied with life on earth. Now Sophie knew exactly what she meant. Jack held the key to heaven for her. She felt it. Knew it in her heart and soul.

She put her hand over his. "Jack, we should go downstairs."

"We should do a lot of things. But we won't."

His kiss was more explosive than the thunder outside. Sophie had felt safety and gentleness the first time their lips had touched, but this… this was powerful and meant to be shattering. He slipped one hand to the nape of her neck while the other clung to the back of her dress, pressing her closer to him.

Sophie allowed the kiss to take her to another world where there was no party downstairs, no obligations to anyone. Just the sea of longing and desire she was floating on. This universe had been built solely for Jack and Sophie. She'd never explored it before. She sensed, but couldn't be certain, that he hadn't, either.

Sophie's muscles had dissolved to molten lava and her bones barely held her upright. She sagged against Jack and when she did, his strong arms reeled her to his hard chest. She held his arms for the longest time, but as the kiss lingered, she wrapped her arms around his neck and surrendered to his embrace.

Sophie, who had spent her life cherishing her family, who only felt comfortable living in the town where she'd been raised, realized her definition of "home" had been lacking.

Kissing Jack and feeling his arms around her showed her that there were many places where the heart could dwell. Jack was offering her a home unlike any she'd experienced before.

When Jack finally broke the kiss, he pressed his forehead to hers. She admired his long lashes, which she'd forgotten about. She hadn't studied his face so closely since she nursed him in the hospital.

"I've wanted to do that for a long time," he whispered.

"You have?"

"Yes. Since the first night I saw you. I thought…" He stopped himself and tilted his head back. "Well, it doesn't matter what I thought. I was pretty out of it."

"You were."

With a gleam in his eye, he smiled. "I also wanted to show you I could kiss better than you."

"Oh, you did, did you?" Was that a challenge? "Well, it wasn't a fair competition, then. When I kissed you, it was on impulse."

He loosened his hold on her, his expression still mischievous. "Oh, and this was premeditated?"

"It sure sounds like it," she countered.

His dark eyebrows knitted together. "I suppose I drummed up that rainstorm all on my own. Made sure we were both soaking wet and then finagled a way to get you up here all alone."

"That's not what I meant."

"Then what did you mean?"

"That you thought a lot about kissing me ever since the other day at Mrs. Beabots's house."

He put his hands on his hips. "Of course I did! Didn't you?"

She started to shake her head. He put both hands on either side of her face.

"Be honest."

She bit her lip. There were some things in life that were good to deny. Ice cream was one. But to deny Jack right now might be the biggest mistake of her life. She still didn't know his true feelings. He could be playing games with her, much like she'd played with men all her life. Karmic payback was never pretty.

She looked into his eyes and made her decision. "I thought about it."

"Good answer. My next question is the kicker," he said with a distinct crack in his voice.

Was he nervous?

"Go ahead and ask," she taunted him. "Nothing has ever held you back from speaking your mind before."

His dark gaze pulled her in as surely as if he was the lighthouse and she was a ship headed to rocky shores. "Would you kiss me again?"

Her breath froze in her lungs. Her heart stopped. She felt as if he were asking her to commit for the rest of her life. She knew he wasn't. All he'd asked was if she would consent to a kiss.

But she felt that cosmic train rushing past her and knew that if she didn't flag it down, demand to get on, that the rest of her life would pass her by and all she'd have to show for her days on earth was regret.

Sophie didn't give Jack an answer.

All she did was pull him close and kiss him like he was the last man on earth.

CHAPTER TWENTY-THREE

SOPHIE DROVE ALONG Maple Boulevard on her way to the Salvation Army shelter. Eleanor had instructed her to make unannounced visits to check on Jeremy, and she hoped to see him today. When they were living on the street or in shelters, addicts had few people to whom they owed any responsibility. That allowed them to convince themselves that no one cared if they used. No one would ever know. Sophie's presence in his life, both scheduled and unscheduled, was much like normal family relationships, especially to a person like Jeremy who had started using so young that his emotional and social development had been affected. Jeremy reacted to people and situations like a child in many ways.

She glanced at Austin and Katia's house as she drove by, and her thoughts of Jeremy faded.

She'd never be able to pass that house again without remembering that it was the place where she'd had the first heart-stopping, mind-blowing kiss of her life.

Since Katia's wedding, Jack had called her three

times and had started texting her regularly with silly comments about work, his runs or adorable Frenchie. She saved one selfie of Jack and Frenchie to her albums.

In her previous relationships—no, flings—with men, she'd seldom talked about ordinary things. She'd never shared her feelings about her family or disclosed her guilty pleasures like ice cream or extra foam on Maddie's cappuccinos. But she felt like she could talk about anything with Jack. And she wanted to. They compared their personal running styles. He asked her to be his tennis partner against Katia and Austin after they returned from their honeymoon. Sophie didn't play tennis, so Jack offered to teach her. What she didn't tell him was that her mother had always warned her about taking any kind of lessons from a man she was in love with.

And that's when it had hit her. Sophie had realized she was falling in love with Jack.

She'd tried to tell herself that though kisses like the one they'd shared were unique, they didn't always mean love.

But the more they talked, the more common ground they discovered, the more certain she became that it wasn't just the kiss making her feel this way.

At the end of each of their calls, Jack had mentioned Katia's wedding and being caught in the rain together. He'd told her he liked kissing her and hoped they could try it again soon.

It had only been three days since their kiss and Sophie found her lips missing his more than she liked to admit.

Sophie parked near the shelter and went inside to the reception desk, where a slender young man wearing a sleeveless shirt, obviously to display his extensive tattoos, greeted her. Though he couldn't have been more than twenty-five, his head was bald in that way that suggested chemotherapy rather than a preferred style.

"Hi, I'm here to see Jeremy Hawthorne."

"Sure," he replied with a closed-mouth smile. He consulted his computer screen. After a moment, he said, "Jeremy isn't a resident anymore."

Sophie didn't do well hiding her surprise. She felt ambushed. And betrayed. "When did he move out? Does it say?"

"Uh, two days ago."

"Did he leave a forwarding address?" she asked, desperation in her voice.

He shook his head and said knowingly, "They never do."

"Gotcha. Thanks, anyway."

Sophie turned and went back to her car, feeling a growing emptiness inside her. It had only been a little over a month since she'd brought him here. She'd bought him nicer clothes so he would feel better about himself. She'd called him on her breaks to let him know she was thinking about him, even though most times she'd had to leave a message. Jeremy didn't have a cell phone and her only connection to him was at the shelter. Each of the residents had a phone in their rooms and three times she'd caught him there and had a pleasant conversation.

Naively, she'd been encouraged by what she saw as progress.

She pounded the steering wheel and dropped her head into her arms. She'd barely begun working with Jeremy and she was failing already. Eleanor's warnings raced through her mind. She'd been told not to blame herself when there was a setback.

Sophie couldn't help it.

Eleanor told her to strike "betrayal" from her vocabulary.

Sophie didn't know how.

All she could think was that she had to find him. But she had no idea where to begin.

She started the engine and pointed the car toward town. Jeremy could have walked to Michigan by now. If he was ignoring her, there was nothing to keep him in Indian Lake. Was there?

He'd left his home and family in Phoenix. He'd left every other town and city he'd stopped in before coming here. Why wouldn't he continue that pattern?

Obviously, Jeremy hadn't cared or trusted her enough to tell her about his plans to move. Maybe she was wrong to have spent so much energy and emotion on him. She thought they were building a rapport and didn't understand why he'd leave without a word. But she knew addicts didn't think like she did.

She was just as Jeremy had said: she was normal.

She gripped the steering wheel as she braked at the light at Main and Maple. The corner of Jack's office building.

Jack. She needed his advice, reassurance and comfort. They'd been exploring a new side of their relationship since their kiss, and she hadn't wanted to broach the subject of addicts and drugs in case it brought them back to Aleah. But now she wished he could be there for her.

What she wouldn't give for a moon roof. She could look up and see the windows. See if he felt her presence. See if he knew she was close.

She turned the corner and pulled up outside the Alliance. She needed to tell Eleanor that Jeremy was gone, but she also needed her counsel.

A group session had just broken up and the clients were standing around chatting. Eleanor was pouring coffee into a Styrofoam cup in the back.

"Sophie, hi." Confusion crossed her face. "Did we have an appointment? I misplaced my calen-

dar over the weekend and I'm lost without it."
She chuckled.

"No, but do you have a few minutes?" Sophie
asked. "I need your help."

Eleanor's expression became concerned. "It's
Jeremy, isn't it?"

"Yes. He left the shelter and didn't tell anyone
where he was going. He didn't tell me."

"I expected this."

"You did?" Sophie asked with a jolt of surprise. "Because I'm shocked. I thought he and I
had bonded. That I was getting through to him."

"He let you think he trusted you."

Sophie nodded.

Eleanor turned. "Let's go into my office."

Sophie followed her into the cubbyhole of a
room that served as her office. Someday, Sophie
hoped there would be money for a build-out,
maybe even a larger facility. But that was down
the road. Way down the road.

Sophie listened attentively as Eleanor reiterated
much of what she'd told Sophie in the beginning.
"You must remember, Sophie, that this is all on
Jeremy. He has to want recovery. In my talks with
him, he hasn't even come close to surrendering
to a higher power. In fact, he's quite resistant."

"Maybe I should have set a specific meeting
with him each week. Maybe once a week isn't
enough."

"Remember, he has to reach out to you. You can't do the work for him. Once he's made the overture, then you can guide him."

"I understand. Well, I guess I have to wait for him to show up again. If he's even in town."

Eleanor smiled knowingly. "I'll bet he's around."

"Why do you say that?"

"He's been in town over a month. That's enough time for him to get the lay of the land. He knows we have food here. There are several soup kitchens and two churches in town offer free dinners. He can go back to the shelter anytime."

"But if that's true, why would he leave?"

Frowning, Eleanor replied, "He found somebody. Either a girlfriend who's taken him in or a buddy he's bunking with. What we have to hope is that they aren't into drugs, that they'll help him stay clean."

Sophie peered into Eleanor's wise and experienced eyes. "But you're not optimistic."

"I do try to have hope. But no, I'm not optimistic. Sorry. I've been there too many times."

Sophie's eyes stung and though she tried, she couldn't stop her tears.

What was going on with her? Sophie had never cried easily. Not that she didn't cry at all, it was just that with years of nursing behind her, she'd learned to deal with disappointment. Lately, just about every new experience was touching her emotionally. Jack. Jeremy. Even Frenchie.

Sophie rose. "Thanks for your help, Eleanor. I guess I have to wait."

"If I hear anything, Sophie—anything—I'll let you know immediately."

Sophie let herself out and returned to her car. She was just about to get in when she heard her name.

"Sophie! Sophie!" Eleanor called, vigorously waving her arm. "Come back!"

Sophie locked the car and sprinted back to Eleanor. "What is it?"

"He's on the phone! Jeremy. I told him you were here. He sounds really down, but he asked for you."

"Thank God." Sophie rushed toward her, overcome with relief.

Back in Eleanor's office, Sophie picked up the phone. "Jeremy? How are you?"

"Okay. Not good. Bad. Real bad."

"Talk to me."

There was a long pause. "You're a cool dude, Sophie. I know you wanted to help, but I couldn't stay at that shelter. Too many do-gooders. Not in a good way."

"How do you mean?" she asked.

"Sophie, I have a lot of problems. I'm a heroin

addict. I'm also bipolar, and for a long time I took medicine for that. It didn't help, so I stopped."

"It's not good to drop your medication without supervision. I could take you to the county clinic and a doctor—"

He cut her off. "Look, Sophie. You don't want to help me. Nobody does. I'm not worth it. See? That's the thing. I'm just going to use again and you'd get stuck in my black hole. It's like being a ghost. You don't go anywhere. No up or down. No escape. And you're too nice of a person. You need to spend your time with someone who's good for you. Someone like Jack—and Frenchie."

"Jeremy…"

"That's a good idea. You and Jack would make good parents for Frenchie. Yeah. I like that."

Sophie shivered. He was trying to tell her something and she didn't like any of it. "Jeremy, where are you right now?"

"I'm in a phone booth."

Sophie ran through the phone booths she knew of in town. Mini-markets. Grocery stores. And Jack had said he'd met Jeremy at a gas station. "Where exactly? I'll come get you."

"No, Sophie. I have to do this myself."

"Do what?"

"You know. Go out…in a blaze of glory."

Terror struck her. "No, Jeremy, you're not alone. I'm coming there." In the background, she heard the clanging bells of a railroad gate being lowered. Then she heard a train whistle. He was on the other side of downtown at one of the two gas stations along Indian Lake Drive. "You stay where you are. I'm coming."

"Really? You know where I am?"

"Jeremy, I'm here for you. I'll find you. Always."

Sophie dashed out of Eleanor's office and shouted, "I'll call you!"

"Good luck!" Eleanor offered as the door banged behind Sophie.

SOPHIE FOUND JEREMY right where she'd guessed he'd be, sitting on the concrete directly beneath the phone booth with his knees to his chest, his arms wrapped around his skinny legs and his head resting on top of them. He didn't get up as she approached, though he did raise his head.

He had a hollow look in his eyes. She could only guess at how much heroin he'd done that morning.

She got out and opened the passenger car door. "Come on."

Slowly, he rose with the creaks and stiffness of a seventy-year-old. "Where are we going?"

"You tell me. You left the shelter. Where do you live now?"

He eased himself into the seat while she held the door. "With Buddy."

"I'll just bet he is," she growled angrily.

Jeremy gave her directions to a run-down section of commercial buildings that were now used as body shops, machine repair shops and storage facilities. Or places where addicts could crash.

On the north side of the street from the commercial buildings was a row of dilapidated houses, which looked like they hadn't been painted or repaired in decades. Jeremy pointed to a house with peeling gray paint and disintegrating front steps. "You left the shelter for this?"

He avoided her gaze by opening the door. "Yeah. Brilliant of me, huh?"

"What exactly does this Buddy do?"

"He's got friends. He helps people like me. Like you do."

"Buddy's not normal, is he? He's a dealer."

Jeremy got out of the car and slammed the door with surprising force. He leaned over the roof as she got out and faced him.

"Look. You did your job today. You saved me."

"Jeremy, you are not my job or my mission. You are not a project. You are a person. A human in trouble. I want to help, but not if you don't want me to."

He lowered his eyes.

She realized he was crying.

"I did today."

"Then that's enough," she said, compassion filling her voice and her heart.

He opened his eyes. "You're about the most wonderful person I've ever met, Sophie. And I'm trying to be better. I am."

"Then let me take you back to the shelter. I don't feel right leaving you here."

"I'll be fine. I promise. Tomorrow will be better."

Sophie felt hope spark inside her. That was one of the key phrases Eleanor had told her to watch out for. If an addict talked about hope, if anyone who was depressed spoke of hope, then there was hope.

"I'll hold you to that."

She leaned into the car and pulled out her purse, digging around till she found a scrap of paper and a pen. "Jeremy. You call me on my cell. Okay? I have it with me all the time, except when I'm in surgery. Anytime you feel… Whenever you need me, you call me. It was pure luck that I was at the Alliance today and was able to talk to you."

"Yeah," he said, stuffing his fists in his pockets. It was eighty degrees outside and he was wearing the sweatpants she'd bought him at the Goodwill.

Concern and compassion exploded in Sophie. She couldn't help putting her arms around his scrawny frame and giving him a hug. "I want you to be well, Jeremy. That's all."

"I know, Sophie. Thanks."

He broke away from her and shuffled into the house. The rickety steps barely moved under his weight.

Her heart melted all over again and what little hope had sprung to life inside her froze.

CHAPTER TWENTY-FOUR

JACK SLID HIS car into the parking space two blocks from his office, directly across from the county library and around the corner from Maddie's café and Grandy's Groomers. He turned off the engine and punched out Sophie's phone number.

The call went to voice mail. Again.

"Hi, it's Jack. Just wanted to say good morning. It's a beautiful day and I was wondering if you'd be up for a run tonight around the lake. No rain predicted. That's a plus. Call me back. 'Kay?" He hung up and looked at Frenchie, who was staring at him from her doggie seat on the passenger's side of the car.

Jack shrugged. "So, she's busy. It's early. Not even seven thirty. I bet she's got an early surgery today."

Frenchie didn't blink.

She recognized excuses when she heard them.

"You're too smart. Okay. Come here," he said, gathering the dog, her leash and a new tote with her treats in his arms.

"I need a latte. Then we'll tackle the world."

When he entered the café, Chloe Knowland greeted him with her usual pert smile.

"Hey, Jack! Hi, Frenchie." Chloe reached out to pet the Yorkie-Poo.

"She's a cutie, isn't she?"

"Yep. Adorable. You want the regular?"

"Sure do. To go."

Chloe began making a latte and then turned to the cupcake display case, pulled out a yellow cupcake and squirted vanilla bean whipped cream icing on top.

A voice behind him said, "Lucky dog."

He turned slowly. Sophie. She gave him a smile so warm and powerful it could crack through a glacier. It certainly caused the earth to quake under his feet.

He managed to smile back.

"I'm just guessing that vanilla cupcake Chloe is wrapping up will find its way into Frenchie's mouth."

"Sweets are bad for dogs," he countered, with a mischievous gleam in his eye.

"But you don't abide by those rules, do you, Jack?"

He reached into his back pocket for his wallet. "Well, some rules are meant for breaking." He chuckled and handed Chloe his money.

Sophie's grin was filled with self-satisfaction. "I was hoping you'd say that."

"Is that right?"

She nodded and petted Frenchie. "Sorry I missed your call, but I was sitting by the window and saw you coming in. I thought I'd walk back with you to your office. I don't have a surgery till eight thirty. I got a little reprieve this morning."

Jack took the latte and handed the cupcake box to Sophie. "Could you hold this till we're outside? I'll let Frenchie walk to the office."

They left the café and Jack put Frenchie on the sidewalk.

Sophie looked at Jack. "I wanted to talk to you—but not on the phone."

His breath caught. "This doesn't sound good."

"It's private. So I wanted to talk to you, er, privately."

Jack watched Frenchie as they walked. "Is this about our kiss? Because that's why I was calling you so much."

"Actually, yes." She nodded, but kept her gaze ahead. He wasn't sure how to read that.

Jack pulled up short, took her arm and turned her toward him. He needed to see her eyes. See if he'd been mistaken. A smile crept onto her lips, lighting the fire in her eyes that he'd seen during the storm. "And what did you want to tell me about that kiss?"

She hesitated. "I, uh—"

He cut her off. "Because I wanted to say that I

hoped it was the first of many." *Hundreds. Thousands.* He rushed on, "You weren't going to give me that, 'Oh, it was all a mistake speech' were you?" He swallowed a burning lump in his throat. When had Sophie come to mean so much to him?

"No, Jack," she said earnestly, touching his arm and not letting go. "I wasn't going to say anything like that at all. I wanted to apologize. I've been so busy for the past couple days that I've barely had time to text you back. I didn't want you to think I was avoiding you."

"Really?" He felt his heart flip over. Joy? Was that what this feeling was? "Because I was worrying… I mean, wondering if you, well—"

Sophie rose up on her toes and kissed him. Brazenly. And right as Helen Knowland, the town's most active gossip, passed them on the sidewalk. Jack shut his eyes. Shut out the world. He didn't want to miss the taste of Sophie's lips on his. He wanted to hear the sound of her breathing. He wanted the kiss to go on forever. He wrapped his arm around her waist and pulled her close. His emotions overwhelmed him. Frightened him a little in their power.

Sophie's kisses were like raindrops: gentle, endearing. Unforgettable.

Jack didn't want the reverie to end. Ever.

But she pulled away and he opened his eyes. Her eyes held endless caring. But was it love?

Love?

Did he just think that?

Jack Carter did not ponder the concept of romantic love. At least, he hadn't before Sophie. She'd made him think about a lot of things that had never been part of his consciousness. His was a world of business and investments. Security. Retirement planning. Graphs. Statistics. Premiums. Now he was aware of people's needs in a different way. The organizations he'd joined to find clients suddenly represented the children in the community who needed breakfasts where there were none. Playgrounds and parks where not enough existed. Educational programs and sports events that helped disabled children and adults feel productive and valued.

Sophie cared about so many people, yet somewhere in that enormous field of altruism, she held a special place for him. He almost felt he could bask in it. But maybe she was just taking pity on him.

Nah. Not after *that* kiss.

It was filled with wanting and eagerness.

"Jack," she whispered against his lips. "Sorry about that. It was a test. I confess to using you as my guinea pig."

"So, I'm just research?"

She grinned and put her arms around his neck. "No way. I was afraid that what I felt, what happened between us, came from getting caught up in the romance of Katia's wedding. I had to be sure."

"And what's the diagnosis?"

"Positive. With only one cure."

"What's that?"

"We need to see each other a lot more."

"I like this," he replied quickly, before she could change her mind. "How about tonight? We could run together. Supposed to be a pretty sunset."

She smiled sweetly and all he could think about was taking her away—maybe in a little boat on the lake—for hours.

"I could make dinner, if you went shopping for us," she suggested. "I have surgeries all day. I won't have time to break away."

"Sure. What can I get?"

"Start with garlic." She laughed. "I'll text you a list. Any dietary restrictions?"

"None," he replied, releasing his hand from her back. "I've been known to grill a mean steak."

"I was thinking about chicken, angel-hair pasta and homemade pesto."

"Sounds incredible."

"Oh, believe me. It is." She looked off toward the courthouse clock tower and the hospital. "I have to run. Literally. Or I'll be late. Where shall I meet you?"

"My place? Six?"

"Six thirty. I have my running shoes in my car." She gave him another quick kiss. "See you." Then she turned and broke into a sprint as she raced toward the light at Main and Maple.

The entire block seemed empty without Sophie, as if oxygen had just left the air.

JACK FINISHED HIS phone call with Katia, who was checking in for her daily report from Venice. A moment later, Melanie tapped on his door.

"I have to leave early tonight. My son's baseball game."

"Oh, right. How're they doing?"

"Still winning. If this keeps up, his team could be city champs. Next summer we're hoping to send him to baseball camp, but it's expensive."

Jack rubbed his chin. "But he's got real pitching talent. Let's talk about it. I want to help him, er, you, in any way I can."

"Jack." Melanie's voice hitched as her hand flew to her heart. "That would mean so much."

Jack smiled. "It would mean more to me. I have plans tonight, but when is the next game?"

"Saturday morning. City Park."

"I'll be there."

She gave him a thumbs-up. "Great. I'll tell him. Well, I'm going to head out. Owen is still with his client."

"'Kay," Jack replied. Frenchie jumped into his

lap, which was her signal that he'd given enough attention to someone else. Now it was her turn.

Jack finished a couple emails then stepped into the reception area, Frenchie right on his heels.

He went over to the windows and glanced out at the clock tower. Nearly closing time. He'd be seeing Sophie very soon.

He reached into his pocket for his cell phone and checked his texts. Nothing. She hadn't sent him the grocery list she'd promised. He figured she must be stuck in surgery.

Suddenly, out of the corner of his eye, he spotted her. Coming out of the Recovery Alliance. She was with a guy. Jeremy?

He went closer to the window for a better view.

Sophie never took her eyes from Jeremy's face. Even from half a block away, Jack could see she was imploring him with her words and gestures. Whatever point she was trying to make, she was doing it with a great deal of gravity and sincerity.

Jeremy walked away from her, but Sophie went after him and ushered him toward her parked car.

Jeremy pounded the roof of the car. She shouted something to him and he flung the door open and got in.

Sophie got in the driver's seat, then they drove away.

Clearly, Sophie's work as Jeremy's sponsor was difficult and stressful. It required not only her time but a great deal of her attention. He knew it was early in their relationship, but Jack couldn't help wondering: with all the commitments, people and priorities in Sophie's life, would she have time or even energy for him?

Jack had started to lose his heart to her. But what about Sophie? She'd said this morning that she wanted to spend more time with him. Was she being truthful? Or just kind, the way she was to Jeremy. As far as Jack could see, Sophie couldn't help but help others. If she perceived a need, she tried to fill it.

And Jack's need was to be loved by her.

But could she love him?

Would he see her tonight, after all? He glanced at his phone. No emails. No text. No grocery list. The depth of his disappointment surprised him.

He glanced back down Main Street. There was no sign of Sophie's car.

What road had her bleeding heart taken her down this time?

Jack shoved his hands in his pockets. Perhaps it was better if he didn't travel it with her.

CHAPTER TWENTY-FIVE

SOPHIE STOOD ON Jack's doorstep with three cloth bags filled with groceries, a bottle of Liz Crenshaw's Cabernet Sauvignon and a stuffed toy for Frenchie. She rang the doorbell and almost immediately heard footsteps before the door was jerked wide open.

Jack was in his running clothes, one sneaker on his right foot, one in his hand. He put his other hand on his hip and glared at her. "You were supposed to text me."

"I did." She matched his frown with one of her own. "You didn't get it?"

"Obviously not."

Frenchie came to the door and barked at Jack.

"She doesn't like you arguing with me," Sophie said with an amused smile.

"I'm not arguing," he retorted.

Sophie felt terrible. After their last surgery, which had blessedly taken an hour less than planned, she'd found a message from Jeremy on her phone. He was deeply depressed and struggling. She'd left the hospital hurriedly to meet with him and calm him down, while simultaneously boosting his spirits. She'd texted Jack that she would be later than she'd planned and that, to make amends, she would do the shopping.

Sophie's feelings for Jack compounded her worry about Jeremy. In some ways, she felt as if they'd been brought together by cosmic forces. To an onlooker, nurse and patient meeting in the ER wasn't all that unusual. But in Sophie's mind, meeting anyone who made her feel as if her life had been completely disassembled and then put back together in an entirely new configuration was an utter impossibility. Sophie had never planned on falling in love.

Love didn't happen to her.

Yet here she was.

At the moment, though, based on Jack's stormy expression, he was anything but a man in love.

Something had happened to change him from the man she'd kissed on Maple Boulevard this morning to this guy who looked ready to take on the next MMA world champion.

Sophie knew it was best she meet his anger head on. "I can explain," she said, pushing past him into the condo.

"Fine," he replied, tossing his shoe into the corner. "I take it we're not going running."

"I'm game if you are. I brought my stuff."

"No," he spat out. "I'd rather run alone." He

took off his other shoe and threw it down with the other sneaker.

Sophie put the bags down on the granite countertop. "Okay. Out with it. What's got you so riled up?"

"I saw you today." He pointed his finger at her. "On the sidewalk in front of the Alliance with Jeremy. I know you feel responsible for him. A sense of duty. But I feel a bit lost here, Sophie. I don't know what to think. One minute you were kissing me and telling me you want to spend time with me and the next minute, you were standing me up."

"It was a tech glitch, Jack. That's all. I did try to text you."

He slashed the air with his hands. "Stop! Fine. I will give you that. But the real issue here is that I don't understand you."

"Sorry?"

"You have to know that your dedication to the Alliance could cost you your job. I know Emory Wills. He's a control freak about his 'rules,' both written and unwritten. If Emory finds out about you sponsoring Jeremy, he could easily fire you. But the bottom line is that with all your concerns, I just don't think you have room in your life for me."

Sophie felt deflated. She sank onto a bar stool. "That's not true, Jack. I want there to be time for us. And I wish I could stop myself from over-scheduling. Rationally, I agree with what you're saying. I can't keep this up forever. But Jeremy needs me. He's so desperate. He's in so much pain."

"I can only imagine."

"Yes." The night of the accident flashed through her mind then that image was replaced by Jeremy's tortured face. She remembered his fear-filled voice on the phone. "I don't have the answers, Jack. Sometimes, I feel like my efforts are a pinprick in the sky. Yet, on the other end of the line is a person asking for a kind word. A moment of my time to tell him he matters."

"But it's dangerous for you."

"I know it must be hard to understand my need to help Jeremy, but I feel that what I'm doing could make a difference."

"How? Do you honestly believe he can be cured?"

"Eventually, that *is* what I'm hoping for, Jack."

"Is that possible?"

Sophie took a deep breath. "In my world, just about anything is possible. I've held a human heart in my hand and watched it beat. I've held a preemie infant weighing less than two pounds and watched her not just live, but grow and thrive. I've seen patients beat every odd in modern cardiac medicine and live years longer than they should."

"So this is a new challenge for you?"

She was thoughtful for a long minute. "It is."

He folded his arms over his chest. "From what I see, he's the type of person who chooses to use drugs and then goes out into the world and hurts innocent people."

"Jeremy has a disease. It's no different than leukemia," she countered.

"Sure it is, Sophie. It involves choice."

"Jack…" Sophie took a deep breath, hoping to gain some courage. "Aleah is the elephant in the room. I can't help thinking that every time you get upset about something with me, it's really about that night. About Aleah. Will you ever forgive me for what you think I did or didn't do?"

Jack's eyes filled with pain, and he took a long moment before he answered her. "Truthfully? I don't know."

"Great." Sophie's blood turned to ice. She hadn't expected that. She'd thought they'd gotten past that night.

She started to rise.

He reached out and touched her arm. "Please, Sophie. I understand that Greg Fulton killed Aleah. Not you. Not all the other addicts and diseased people struggling with addictions like you tell me. And are showing me. It's taken a lot for me to get there. It was Greg on that one particular night. Logic and fact tell me you did all you could for Aleah."

"But…" she interrupted. Ever since their kiss, Sophie had been picturing a future with Jack. Now that vision was dashed. They were back at the beginning. "You can't forgive yourself."

He lowered his eyes and Sophie felt the weight of his emotions as acutely as she did that of Jeremy's and every other patient she'd known. Her grandmother told her she empathized with other people so deeply that she took on their troubles. It was a curse, not a blessing.

Sophie placed her hand on Jack's shoulder. He covered her hand with his, but still didn't look at her.

"They say that the shadow of a person's death fades in time."

"They do say that."

"I wish it would," he replied, meeting her gaze. His face was filled with questions and doubt.

Sophie's heart sank. "But we might never get past this. You won't let it go, will you, Jack?"

He ground his jaw, his eyes stern and unrelenting. Sophie thought she heard her heart break.

"I don't know how," he croaked.

He hadn't said he loved her, yet that tiny clutch of emotion told her she still had a chance with him—if she fought for it.

For them.

And for the first time ever, Sophie wanted that chance. She wanted this man to believe in her.

To support her. To be on her side. With a jolt, she realized that she needed Jack to be there for her. She had to convince him.

"Jack," she said softly. "Jeremy is a danger only to himself. He doesn't drive a car. He doesn't even ride a bike. He uses drugs and alcohol to self-medicate. He comes from a good family in Phoenix, but he is so ashamed about what he's done to himself that he refuses to even call home. So he's not getting love and support." The next words were so painful, they scratched her throat on their way out. "Jack, he's threatened to kill himself. I've done all I can think of to give him hope... something to hang on to..." Her eyes filled with tears. "But I don't know if it's making a difference."

Jack slipped his fingers under her chin and lifted her face to his. "I'm sorry, Sophie. So sorry. What you're doing is noble, and I'm being arrogant."

Jack slipped off the stool and put his arms around her shoulders. "I think I understand a bit better," he said, kissing her forehead. "But will you listen to what I have to say now?"

"Yes," she replied, liking the warmth of his arms around her and the safe feeling of her cheek against his chest. It was comfortable here, in his embrace. There were no lost souls or broken bodies for her to tend and mend. There was only this man and this moment with him. And it was enough.

"I think you've let this one assignment—and that's what Jeremy is—become your world. I've done a little research on my own about sponsors. Apparently, they have to learn to balance their own lives with their work. To be able to detach, get some distance. Jeremy is part of your work world. You forgot about our plans for tonight. You were late. You texted me, but did you pick up the phone and call when you didn't hear back from me? You took it upon yourself to go the grocery store, when I said I'd be happy to do that for us."

He paused for a moment, rubbing her back and shoulders. "I'm not trying to sound petty, but I guess what I'm saying is that I want to be as important to you as this sponsorship and your other projects. I want a place in your life."

She looked up into his compelling eyes. "You mean a great deal to me, Jack."

"Sophie, you're the kind of woman I want to lasso the moon for. I want to be there for you. But I also want you there for me."

"Jack, I can't tell you how much this means to me. Aside from my family, I've never had anyone, well, on my side."

He held her at arm's length and peered at her quizzically. "Never? Not once?"

"Nope." Then she sighed. "Not that I ever gave anyone a chance."

"And why was that?" he asked, mirth dancing on his lips.

She let herself respond coyly. "Maybe I didn't see potential in any of them."

"Hmm. So that's it? I have potential?"

"And you're a challenge." She chuckled, sliding her fingertips under her eyes to wipe away the last tear. "You're the first garlic-free household I've ever visited."

"Aw, c'mon," he groaned as she rose off the stool and slid her arms around his waist again.

"See, you need my help," she said. "I'll open new worlds to you once I'm let loose in this kitchen."

Sophie knew they hadn't worked everything out yet, but for now she was content that they were making progress.

As Jack unloaded the groceries onto the counter, Sophie took out two wineglasses. Jack got the corkscrew and opened the bottle. Then he poured the wine while showing her where he kept a mismatched assortment of pots and pans.

She kidded him about proper cooking tools.

He picked up her hand and kissed it.

When she mashed the pine nuts in his blender, Jack grimaced, as if she'd defiled sacred territory.

Jack found a bottle of olive oil in his pantry. Unopened, of course.

As Sophie sautéed garlic, filling the kitchen with a heavenly aroma, she gave Jack directions for getting the pasta ready.

The rest of the evening passed sweetly. Sophie complimented Jack on his sous-chef skills and Jack told Sophie her cooking was the most delicious he'd ever tasted. Not once during dinner or at any time while sitting on Jack's deck with a glass of sauterne, gazing at the full moon and talking about their childhoods, did the thought of Jeremy or Aleah cross Sophie's mind.

When she returned home and dressed for bed, brushed her teeth and slathered lotion on her legs, all she could think about was Jack.

Nothing about her growing feelings for Jack was intoxicating or dramatic, like it had been with other guys. This was nothing like those flash-fire attractions that lasted for a few days or weeks before dying away.

And why was that?

For one thing, Jack seemed to be looking deeper than her heart-shaped face and flirty nature. He was seeing the real Sophie, the Sophie who intimidated most men once they got to know her. Sophie had rock-solid goals and intentions. She didn't need a man to pay her bills, be her social life or help her find a football team to root for. She'd created a life for herself on her own terms.

Still, she realized that getting Jack to support

her beliefs and efforts in everything she did, including her work with Eleanor and Jeremy, was of great importance to her.

Whether Jack was up to that kind of challenge, only time would tell.

She hoped he would be.

She could almost feel her heart wince at how much she wanted Jack. She didn't need him, but she wanted him. The more time she spent with him, the more she liked about him.

Sophie had been making significant changes for months now. She'd pinned and repinned, nipped and clipped the pattern of her life, creating a new tapestry. She wanted it to be everlasting and glorious. And she wanted—oh, how she wanted—Jack sewn into it.

CHAPTER TWENTY-SIX

SOPHIE ASSISTED NATE with back-to-back ablation procedures that were as textbook as expected. Both patients were in recovery, each with two nurses pressing on the femoral artery for the prescribed ninety minutes to avoid a bleed-out. Initial reports were that there were no complications in either case.

Sophie finished the last of her notes and set up the equipment for the next operation. She then disposed of her surgical gown, mask and gloves, left the ablation room and went to her locker at the back of the break room. She was pleased with her work today. Because she'd wisely cut back on her hours at the Alliance, her nursing career was back on track. Perhaps even improving. She was proud of her accomplishments at the ablation center.

Though it was early Friday evening, she wasn't heading home; she only had about an hour before her shift in the ER. She'd have most of Saturday to rest, and on Sunday she intended to spend the day with her parents. She might even tell them about Jack. She wasn't quite sure what she would call her relationship with him, but she considered their dinner the other night a date. The attraction and emotion were there. But things were complicated. He'd said he wanted to try to understand her. Support her in all that she did. But he couldn't guarantee it.

Still, Sophie thought about him all the time. When the last ablation was wrapping up, she found herself looking forward to this moment—returning to her locker and checking her phone. Had he texted her a selfie or one of his funny pictures of Frenchie? She had never, ever been a "wait by the phone" woman. She was the one who made men wait.

Until now.

Sophie unzipped her purse and pulled out her phone. No texts, but she had one missed call and a voice mail from an unfamiliar local number. That had to be Jeremy—he tended to call her from pay phones or wherever he could entice someone to let him make a call.

Still, it was odd. He never left messages for her.

She tapped the play button.

"You're not there. I, er, was hoping you would be. But you're not. No one ever is. At least not for me. That's okay. I get it. Guess I was dumb to think anything would change. That's the thing. Nothing is going to change—not for me. Not ever."

Sophie's fingers shook as she tried to play the message back again. Jeremy's voice was filled with desperation. She'd never heard him this low.

She redialed the number he'd used, but it rang incessantly. *Pay phone.*

She dropped her chin to her chest, trying to think of where he might be.

"Sophie? Are you in here?" Monica, one of the receptionists, called from the door to the break room.

"Yeah. I'm here," Sophie replied, coming around the corner from the locker area.

"You're scheduled to work in the ER tonight, right?"

"Yes, I am," Sophie said, glancing down at her cell. She needed to find Jeremy to make sure he was all right. Her instincts went Code Red. She didn't have much time before her shift. "Why do you ask?"

"They need you now. I just got a call from Dr. Caldwell. He wants you stat."

"Let him know I'm on my way."

Sophie reluctantly slid her phone back into her purse and closed her locker. Jeremy would have to wait.

SOPHIE SHOVED HER hands into a pair of nitrile gloves as she swung into Bay 8 in the ER. It had been a quiet week, but all that had changed when an unattended campfire ignited not one, but two houses north of town, burning both to the ground. Monica had filled Sophie in as they raced to the elevator.

Two children and one adult had been badly burned. The children were being treated for smoke inhalation. Dr. Caldwell was trying to save the adult grandfather.

"What do you need, Doctor?" Sophie asked as she looked down at the elderly man, who was clearly not breathing through the oxygen mask.

"V-fib. Get the cart. We're three nurses down here. The rest of the staff is helping the kids."

Ventricular fibrillation was life threatening. The lower chambers of the heart quivered and the heart could not pump any blood, causing cardiac arrest. Dr. Caldwell asked her to get the defibrillator machine.

"Got it." Sophie shot down the hall to get the equipment.

As Sophie returned to Bay 8, she heard the sound of an approaching ambulance. The doors banged open and EMTs were shouting at hospital staff.

"We got a possible DOA here!"

A gurney rattled across the floor.

Sophie couldn't let the commotion distract her. She didn't have time to waste. A man's life was on the line. Every second counted.

Dr. Caldwell grabbed the paddles from her and she turned on the machine, waiting for the beep.

"Clear!" Dr. Caldwell called as the electrical shock jolted through the elderly man's body, causing his back to arch.

Sophie took his pulse and shook her head. "Nothing."

At that exact moment, a young nurse, who couldn't have been more than twenty, rushed into the bay.

"Dr. Caldwell!" she said anxiously. "We need you in the next bay. It's a drug overdose or suicide. He's not breathing."

Dr. Caldwell placed the paddles on the elderly man's chest once again. "I'm saving someone now."

"Yes, Doctor, but I don't know what to do."

"CPR till I get there," he ground out. "Now back away. Clear!"

Sophie hit the defibrillator button again. The patient's body arched even more intensely this time.

She and Dr. Caldwell both took their stethoscopes and listened to the man's heart.

It was faint, no more than the whisper of a dragonfly's wing, but it was there. The beat of life.

Dr. Caldwell looked at Sophie. "You get the epinephrine ready. He may need it. He's barely alive. If he reacts to the pain from the burns we could lose him all over again."

"Yes, Doctor." Her eyes slid to the frantic face of the young nurse who had just appeared in the doorway again. She was practically wringing her hands. Sophie remembered being that new to the job. Fresh out of nursing school. There was no terror greater than a critically ill patient.

Still wasn't.

"Doctor. They said they need you. Stat," the young woman said.

He continued listening to the old man's heart. "Give me the particulars on your patient. How old?"

The nurse's voice hitched with anxiety. "He's twenty-four. We found an ID. Jeremy—"

"Hawthorne?" Sophie could barely get the name out before a tidal wave of anguish ripped through her.

Dr. Caldwell looked up. "A friend of yours?"

"I'm his sponsor," Sophie replied without thinking. A split-second later she realized what she'd just admitted to.

"His what?"

She shook her head to wave off his questions.

"We'll talk later," Dr. Caldwell said.

Sophie turned back to her patient. One part of her wanted to rush to Jeremy and do all she could to save him. Yet as she watched the older man fight for each breath and heartbeat, she was glued to the spot. She made her decision.

"Doctor, go. I've got this," she assured him as he threw her a questioning look.

"Code Blue. Bay 9. Code Blue." The alarm in the hall sounded.

Sophie struggled to focus, to stop herself from racing to Jeremy's side. She'd been here before. With Aleah.

Why was fate testing her again like this? Paths of decision. Forks in the road with life-or-death stakes. She'd known that becoming a nurse would mean facing mortality. She just didn't think it would be like this.

Suddenly, her patient stopped breathing again. She began CPR and pressed the Code Blue alarm.

She had to stop feeling sorry for herself. If she'd learned one thing from Aleah's death, it was that no matter what she did for her patient or for Jeremy—all the eventualities were in the hands of God.

"Come on, sweetheart. Don't you die on me," she whispered to the man she'd met only a few minutes ago. His chart said he was seventy-eight. Old. But not that old. Was he the only world those two kids had? If he died, was there another family member who would be responsible for them, or would they end up in Child Protective Services? Orphans. Wounded physically from the fire. Mentally and spiritually from the loss of their grandfather, whose life Sophie held in her hands.

She had to save him. Locking her elbows, she bent into her work. She counted the depressions.

The man inhaled deeply as if sucking in a breath after being underwater. A drowning man breaking through the surface.

Tears filled Sophie's eyes. She felt the sob ratchet through her lungs and happiness radiate through her like dawn. "There you are!"

She didn't know this man from Adam, but in that moment she felt as if she could read his heart and mind.

His eyes flew open, and he stared at her with intense clarity.

"You're going to be all right," she assured him, while gently placing her hand on his forehead. "Everything is going to be all right."

He winced and then closed his eyes. He tried to speak, but the words came slowly. "My grand— children."

"They're here with us. The doctors are helping them."

"Alive?"

"Yes, they're alive."

"Then I saved them." His head rolled on the gurney. "Fire. Everywhere. Gretchen was burned."

He clamped on to her forearm and with strength she would not have expected, he asked, "How bad is it?"

"I'll find out for you, but you have to promise

me that you'll rest. Your heart can't take much more. At least, not tonight."

Sophie patted his hand with the same gentle, caring touch she gave all her patients as she listened to his heartbeat once again.

Dr. Caldwell entered the bay and stood at the end of the gurney watching Sophie. "I couldn't get back any sooner. Sorry. But apparently you didn't need me, after all. He's doing well?"

"Yes." She flipped her stethoscope around the back of her neck as she turned to him. "And… Jeremy?" Sophie didn't have to ask. She sensed from Dr. Caldwell's drooping shoulders and the shadows in his eyes that the news wasn't good.

"No response. He didn't make it." He put his hands on his hips, never taking his eyes off the elderly man. "I'll never understand it. These kids have everything to live for and they throw it all away." He snapped his fingers. "Poof. Gone. Outta here. Like life was nothing to them."

Sophie was numb. "So, you think it was a suicide, not just an OD?"

"I believe so."

Sophie was numb. She stepped past Dr. Caldwell, but he kept talking. "You want to tell me about your, er, relationship with Jeremy?"

The truth could get her fired, but she didn't see any way around it. Dr. Caldwell was her superior. He'd warned her about working too hard. He knew about her missteps in surgery with Dr. Barzonni. He would report what he knew to Emory Wills.

"I was his sponsor. He'd call me from time to time. I saw him on my time off to counsel him. The usual things." Sophie's voice cracked, but she didn't feel the tears she expected. She was in shock. Empty. Devoid of emotion.

She gazed at the old man resting peacefully. She knew in the marrow of her bones, no matter what, she wouldn't have left her patient.

Sophie flashed back to the night with Aleah. Both then and now, she had made a choice. It didn't matter who was an addict or not, who had a family, whether the patient was a stranger or someone she knew intimately. She'd made her decision based on who she thought she could save. But had she done the right thing? Had she chosen correctly?

Was she even fit to be nursing these critical patients?

Self-doubt swung a mighty blow.

"I'm sorry, Sophie," Dr. Caldwell said again, his tone sincere. "You did great here. Really great." He jerked his head toward the doorway, signaling that she should follow him.

"Take some advice, Sophie. For your own good and that of your career, drop this sponsorship thing you're doing. You belong here in this hospital with me and Dr. Barzonni, saving lives like you did tonight." He ducked his head so that she could see his piercing, stern expression. "I'm serious, Sophie."

"Yes, sir," she replied. He was absolutely right.

THE TECHS HAD covered Jeremy up with a sheet and were about to wheel him downstairs to the basement morgue. She was the closest person he had to a friend in Indian Lake and she didn't even know his parents' names or how to phone them. The Alliance might have some information. Either way, she would find a way to contact them. It was the least she could do.

As per protocol, the hospital had undoubtedly already notified the police. Eventually someone would question her. Probably Detective Trent Davis, the cop she'd met the night Aleah died. She'd have to tell him about Jeremy's "friend" Buddy. There might or might not be some arrests. That wasn't her purview.

She stopped the young male orderly with the shock of red hair and an enormous rhinestone stud in his ear who was pushing the gurney out into the hall. "Can I have a minute?"

"He a friend of yours?"

She nodded. She believed she'd been a friend to him, even if he hadn't always wanted her friendship.

Sophie pulled back the sheet just enough to see him one last time. Shockingly, he looked absolutely normal, though at peace, with a slight curve to his lips that told her his last minutes were good ones. For all the pain he'd gone through in his life, in the end, he'd found some kind of solace. She stroked his forehead and felt tears in her eyes. The emotion in her throat carved a path as deep as a mountain gorge. She couldn't speak. All she could do was talk to him with her heart. She told him she was sorry she had failed him. She told him she was sorry she hadn't forced him to reconcile with his parents.

"Ma'am, I have to take him now," the orderly whispered.

"I know. I…know," Sophie answered, feeling a finality like she'd never experienced before.

There probably wouldn't be a memorial in Indian Lake for Jeremy. Other than herself, Eleanor, Jack and Mrs. Beabots, she wasn't sure who Jeremy had bonded with. His roommate, Buddy? But did he care about Jeremy the way she did? Did anyone?

Once again, guilt clanged inside her head. If only. If only. If only she'd answered her phone thirty minutes sooner and taken Jeremy's last call. If only she'd thought to reach out to his parents days ago. Weeks ago. Maybe his suicide could have been avoided.

She made her way to the nurses' station, her heart heavy.

Maybe.

CHAPTER TWENTY-SEVEN

SOPHIE CONSIDERED THE cold microwave dinner in front of her, stuck her fork in the tasteless diet ravioli and left it there. She pushed away from her kitchen table and went to the refrigerator. She stared at the array of condiments and ingredients that, when properly sautéed and blended with garden vegetables and choice cheeses, would become superb Italian dishes.

She slammed the door closed. She'd never felt less like cooking or eating in her life. She didn't feel like running, either. She didn't feel like working, talking to friends or joking with coworkers. Not even thoughts of Jack brought a smile to her face.

Was this how Jeremy had felt? This massive, yawning tunnel to a frightening future?

Sophie went back to her laptop to continue her search for Jeremy's parents. Eleanor had no record of Jeremy's Phoenix address, so Sophie had run searches on the internet and found six Hawthornes in the Greater Phoenix area. She called them all; four were dead ends, and she left voice mails with her contact information with two others. The next day she received an email that read, *I'm Jeremy's mother. Call me.*

Sophie instantly picked up the phone. "Hello. Is this Elizabeth Hawthorne?"

"Yes. Yes! You're the one who helped Jeremy?"

"I am," Sophie replied, and before she could say another word, Elizabeth cut her off.

"The police called us and told us he was dead." Elizabeth's voice was ragged.

"I'm so sorry."

"They warned us at rehab that it might end this way, whether he stayed with us or not." Elizabeth blew her nose and paused for a long moment. "We hadn't heard from him in over two years. Frankly, I assumed he was already dead. He was so angry when he left. We'd found an enormous stash of heroin and plastic bags of used needles, and he'd managed to steal over five thousand dollars from what we thought was a secret bank account. He'd found the password… It doesn't matter. He just couldn't stop. Jeremy told me he never wanted to get straight. He liked his world out of this world."

"Mrs. Hawthorne, I have to ask. Was Jeremy ever diagnosed as manic-depressive?"

"Oh, yes. One doctor told us he was bipolar. He was prescribed several medications through-out middle school and high school. He was bullied by the older kids. I moved him to a private school and that was just as bad." She sighed. "He was my only child. And I thank you, Miss Mattuchi, for giving him kindness and attention in his last weeks on earth. If I'd known where he was, I would have come to get him." Elizabeth's voice caught, and she paused as she wrestled with her emotions. "My husband and I will take care of having Jeremy's remains brought home."

Sophie gave Elizabeth the number at the hospital to make those arrangements. "I'll never forget Jeremy, Mrs. Hawthorne. Though his life was tragic in the end, he was a good person."

"Thank you for seeing that in him, Miss Mattuchi."

Sophie had hung up the phone knowing she'd done her duty, done the right thing. But still, she felt as if her own spirit had fled her.

All of her training commanded that she remain as neutral in these situations as possible. As empathetic as she was, she was usually able to put up emotional barriers when patients died. Death was part of her job, especially in cardiac care.

Yet with Jeremy, she couldn't hold back her grief. Maybe that's what had tripped her up. Maybe she was guilty of letting her guard down, taking off her psychological armor when she walked out of the hospital and joined the ranks as a volunteer at the Recovery Alliance.

She should have realized what she was doing.

Sophie hadn't known Jeremy all that well or all that long. Yet his death hit her like a bullet. If she didn't snap out of it, her emotions could crush her.

She plopped down on her sofa and turned on the television. She'd scrolled through over three hundred channels before she realized she hadn't read the title of a single show. She turned it off.

She'd just risen to see if there was any ice cream in the freezer when she heard a knock on the door.

Only one person ever came to visit Sophie. Her landlady.

Sure enough, Mrs. Beabots stood on the other side of the door, holding up two articles of clothing, both encased in clear, zippered garment bags. "Which one?"

Sophie peered at the long swirls of bright colors that resembled a shawl in one bag, and then at the black lace top in the other. "What are they?"

"Beach cover-ups. For this afternoon's picnic."

"You'll look stylish in either one," Sophie said diplomatically.

"Goodness, you don't think these are for *me*, do you?" Mrs. Beabots laughed, then grew serious. "I think you need the splash of color, frankly, even though your mood suits the mourning black."

Sophie stared at her landlady. "Who told you?"

"Who do you think? Maddie, of course. Dr. Caldwell told Nate. Why on earth would you think you could keep the truth from me for more than a day?"

Sophie shook her head. "Dumb, I guess." She stepped back to allow Mrs. Beabots to enter. "I suppose you know everything."

"I know the most important thing. Your heart is breaking and you're not allowing your friends to help you," she replied with just enough accusation to stiffen Sophie's spine.

Then she softened. Mrs. Beabots must have endured plenty of deaths and heartbreaks, including the loss of her husband, over the years. She'd lived through love, loss and pain, yet she'd found a way to make life bright for others and keep on going. She knew something that Sophie apparently needed at this moment. Sophie decided to listen.

"Maddie tells me she's called you half a dozen times and you haven't answered once."

"True."

Mrs. Beabots's finely penciled eyebrow arched. "Katia called me from Venice and said she was concerned she hadn't heard from you in a few days." She cleared her voice. "Jack Carter told her he hasn't been in touch with you, either…" Her eyes narrowed into discerning slits.

Sophie whisked her hand through the air dismissively. "Not important."

"I see." Mrs. Beabots turned back to the cover-ups. "Maybe the black one, after all. It's chic. I wore it on the Italian Rivieria."

"You're kidding."

Mrs. Beabots grinned mischievously. "You don't think I was old all my life, do you? Now, you do have a bathing suit, right? All I have are old bikinis that, sadly, have virtually disintegrated."

Sophie nearly smiled. Nearly. "I have a suit. It's black, actually."

"Hmm. Why did I know that?" Mrs. Beabots shoved the cover-up at Sophie. "We'll leave at one. Can you help me take the lemonade and sandwiches?"

"Uh. Yes. You want me to drive?"

"Of course! I thought that was obvious. Sarah's car is full with the kids and Beau. And I have all this food, beach towels, my tote…" Mrs. Beabots placed her hand on Sophie's cheek. "You need this, my dear. Laughter is the best medicine."

She started to walk away and then turned back. "However, it's best to look good when you're mending a broken heart. Wear those gold hoop earrings you've got. Very smashing. Very Sophia Loren."

She left, closing the door softly behind her.

Sophie chuckled and realized she actually did feel slightly uplifted. Was that possible?

She peered at the label through the heavy clear

plastic. "Yves Saint Laurent." Her eyes flew to the closed door. "Hey, this isn't real couture, is it?"

JACK CARRIED FRENCHIE out to his deck and put her down next to the railing, where he'd finally installed a fine screen so that Frenchie couldn't fall through.

It was a crystal clear day—no humidity and a gentle breeze. The lake was filled with end-of-summer water-skiers, speedboats, fishing boats and swimmers. The picnic tables down at Cove Beach were filled with families grilling hot dogs and hamburgers while kids raced around with plastic shovels, pails and beach balls. Motorboats dragged people clinging to blow-up toys in the shape of dragons, Disney characters, fish and porpoises.

"They're all having fun, Frenchie," Jack mused as he popped the top on a power drink.

Frenchie looked up at him. She didn't bark or blink. Just stared accusingly.

Jack took out his cell phone and checked his texts. Not a word from Sophie for two days. He knew from Katia that Jeremy had overdosed. He wondered if any of them would ever know if it was an accident or suicide. Like his uncle Marty. He couldn't imagine the pain Sophie was going through, but he wanted to be there for her. Jack scooped up Frenchie and remembered the day he'd met Jeremy. Frenchie had loved him and he'd cared about Frenchie. Jack felt a tug on his heart in the same place where grief over Aleah had come to live. Now there was a place for Jeremy, too.

Jack had tried contacting Sophie in just about every way he could, but she was MIA. He wanted to console her, but deep down, he had to admit it hurt that she was shutting him out.

"She acts like I'm nothing to her!" he shouted.

Frenchie barked.

"Sorry, girl," Jack apologized. "But she's not giving me a chance to help her." He stared out at the people at Cove Beach.

Jack leaned over the rail. "Wait a minute."

He dashed into the living room, retrieved his Bushnell binoculars, scrambled back to the deck and focused on the stretch of sand.

"Holy cow!" he said, half to Frenchie and half to himself. "Everyone's there! Nate and Maddie. Sara. Luke. Your favorite, Beau. The kids. Oh, and there's Rafe. He's holding Olivia's hand. Hmm. What's up with that? Mica. Gina. Sam. Even Gabe and Liz."

He swung the binoculars to the left and almost dropped them.

"Sophie."

He understood she was in mourning. He was

trying to give her space. But had she cut him out of her life without telling him?

After two full days of torturous silence, he knew he loved her. Jack hadn't realized he could feel this alone. This isolated. It was as if she'd been his anchor and now he was adrift.

"Jack, you are such an idiot. You're in love with her. And you haven't told her."

Frenchie barked.

He smiled. "I think we should go visit Beau."

Frenchie barked again and ran to the kitchen, where Jack had hung her leash on the hook by the door.

SOPHIE SAT ON an American flag beach towel wearing her black halter one-piece and the cover-up that Mrs. Beabots had loaned her. In her ears were large gold hoops that glistened in the sun. Mrs. Beabots sat nearby in a striped canvas fold-up chair. She handed Sophie a tube of Italian sunscreen.

"Use this, dear. It's the best."

"My mother uses this," Sophie said, squirting out a dab and rubbing it into her arms. As she handed the tube back to Mrs. Beabots, she spotted Jack heading directly toward them.

Maddie spotted him, too. "Hey, Jack! Come join us!"

Beau jumped up from Sarah's side and bounded

toward Frenchie. Jack laughed. "You don't mind if we crash?" He held up a large bag. "I brought veggie sticks."

Luke smiled. "There's another towel next to Sophie."

Sophie held her hand over her eyes, pretending to block out the sun, but she was actually trying to hide her frown. Jack was the last person she wanted to see. He'd called her. Texted. Emailed. She'd successfully avoided him for two days. She didn't want to see him, yet his smile lightened her spirit instantly.

She leaned over to Mrs. Beabots. "Why do I feel like this is a setup?"

Mrs. Beabots didn't take her eyes from the lake. "This is what friends are for, dear. Giving fate a little push."

Jack let Frenchie off her leash and immediately the little dog raced over to Sophie and jumped into her arms.

Jack sat down and pulled his knees to his chest. He looked at Sophie. "Is it okay if I sit here?"

"Sure," she replied, unable to stop her smile as Frenchie licked her.

Jack leaned closer. "I've been trying to talk to you for days. I wanted to tell you how sorry I am about Jeremy."

Sophie stroked Frenchie's head. "You heard?"

He nodded and gently touched her arm, letting

his hand linger for a long moment. "I'm here for you, Sophie. If you need someone to talk to."

His tone and expression were sincere. She believed him. At least at the moment. But what about weeks from now? Months or years? Was it possible for either of them to get past their grief? About Aleah, about Jeremy…?

"Jack…thanks. I—" A loud bang brought all conversations to a stop.

Rafe was standing in front of them, hitting a cast-iron skillet with a metal barbecue fork.

Mrs. Beabots winked and whispered, "Here it comes."

It?

"May I have your attention?" Rafe spread his arms wide, his red-and-white Hawaiian shirt flapping in the breeze.

"What's going on?" Jack asked Sophie.

She replied with a shrug.

"With my mother, my brothers, my sisters-in-law, Sam, and all my good and dear friends present…" Rafe continued. Then he reached out and pulled Olivia to her feet.

Olivia gasped, noticing something behind them. Sophie turned to see Olivia's mother, Julia, walking toward them carrying a multi-tiered cake.

"Right on cue, Julia!" Rafe laughed.

Mrs. Beabots beamed widely. "Cat's out of this

bag!" She clapped her hands together and then placed them over her mouth.

Sophie reached over and put her hand on her knee. Mrs. Beabots was crying.

"What are you doing, Rafe?" Olivia asked.

Rafe dropped to his knee and held Olivia's hands.

"For real?" Olivia's eyes filled with tears. "Rafe?"

"In front of all our friends and family, including your mother, Olivia will you be my wife? Marry me?"

Olivia sank to the sand, flung her arms around Rafe's neck and shouted loud enough for the swimmers in the lake to hear, "Yes! A million times, yes!"

Mrs. Beabots continued crying. Sophie applauded and smiled as everyone whooped, hollered and jumped up to congratulate the couple.

Sophie was surprised at her own joy. Mrs. Beabots squeezed her hand so tightly, she fleetingly wondered if she'd be left with a bruise or two.

"Isn't it wonderful?" Sophie gushed, and then turned to see Jack's sour expression. "What's wrong with you?"

"Me? Uh, nothing."

"Yes, there is. We just witnessed one of life's most exciting moments and you look like you just watched a bad movie."

He sighed. "Can we go for a walk?"

Sophie had the feeling that being alone with Jack probably wasn't a good idea. She was heartsick and grieving over Jeremy and she was on the verge of believing that it would be best if she and Jack went their separate ways.

Frenchie had jumped out of Sophie's arms and was carrying on a tête-à-tête with Beau. She wished she could be as trusting and as carefree as the two dogs.

"Okay, let's walk."

Jack hooked the leash to Frenchie's collar and they moved away from their friends. Sophie noticed that Jack's face softened. "So are you going to tell me what upset you about Rafe and Olivia?"

He scoffed. "I just thought Rafe's proposal was too, well, stagy. It was just as you said, I felt like I was watching a play."

"Well, I thought it was sweet. It was all for his family and close friends. Obviously, Olivia didn't have a clue, so no one outed him beforehand. Even her mother was in on it." Sophie remembered seeing yellowed photographs of her parents' engagement party. There had been a big dinner at the farm. Her aunt and uncle had been alive at the time. And her grandfather. The table was piled with food, flowers and wine bottles. "To be honest, it made me think of my parents."

"Oh? That's how people in your family would propose?"

She nodded. "Yes, Jack. That's exactly how my family would have done it." She glanced at him.

He had a serious expression on his face, but he stayed quiet.

"Not your family's way, is it?" she offered.

"I just think there should be some romance, you know? And spontaneity. I'd just do it differently, if it was me, I mean."

"Olivia was happy…" Sophie paused, wondering if Jack was trying to say something without saying it. Why was he suddenly so interested in how people proposed?

If he was thinking they had a future together, it was going to make what she had to say to him even tougher. Maybe impossible.

Sophie's insides felt as if they'd been ripped apart. Why should talking to Jack be so difficult? This morning she'd convinced herself they were simply not right for each other. There was too much between them. Jack stopped and took her arm. "Sophie, I'm so deeply sorry about Jeremy."

Sophie had to snap her thoughts back to the present. He was trying to be empathetic. She nodded. "I know, Jack. I believe you. And I've thought a lot about, well, everything over the past few days. Especially about you and me."

Jack moved closer and lowered his head to hers. "What have you thought?"

Sophie choked back the burning emotion in

her throat. She wrung her sweating hands and then stuck them behind her back. Her mouth had gone dry.

"Jack, it's going to take me a minute to get this out, but please, bear with me."

"Okay…" he replied hesitantly. She could hear a measure of fear slipping into his voice.

She wanted to cry, but prayed the tears wouldn't come. "You and I will never agree about certain things. We were brought together by an accident and I don't believe we can get past what happened. We've both tried, but I believe that deep down you still think I could have handled things differently." He opened his mouth to speak, but she held up her hand. "Let me say this, please."

"Okay."

"I've realized I'm more than just a little invested in this fight against drugs. Jeremy's death proved that to me. I'm going to do more to help addicts in the future, not less. And I know I can do it. I have the education and the energy and, most importantly, I'll be dedicated to it." She swept her arm toward their friends still sitting on the beach. "I look over there at Timmy and Annie Bosworth and I know that in a few years, older kids or drug dealers are going to approach them. I want to prepare kids like them. I want them to know how to resist. How to fight back. What to do."

Tears streamed down Sophie's cheeks as she continued. "Jack, all my life I've only wanted one thing from a man, and I never got it."

"What's that?"

"Support. A man who's all in. That's what I need. Looking back on my life, I see now that I wasn't just having fun flirting or seeing how many different guys I could date. The reason I never settled on anyone was that I sniffed out their interests in seconds. Frankly, I was too serious for most of them. I only thought I had a chance with Nate Barzonni because he was a doctor. That was as close as I ever came to finding someone who would support *my* earnest intentions."

Jack pursed his lips. "And I don't measure up, do I?"

Sophie felt the last shreds of her heart rip into pieces. She could be making the worst mistake of her life. Or she could be staunching a wound before it bled out. She and Jack could have a fling, a summer romance, but a year from now, they'd still be at odds. Whenever she brought up the Alliance, or an addict she was working with, she'd be hurting him all over again.

"Jack, we've danced around your guilt about Aleah. Until you address it and deal with it, you'll always blame me. Each time, I'd risk losing you."

Jack looked stricken, then his expression hardened. "I have nothing to say to that. And nothing more to say to you."

"Fine."

Sophie stood on the sand and watched Jack walk away with Frenchie, her rhinestone leash and collar glinting in the sun. She couldn't stop the sobs. They erupted in aching peals that she suffocated by shoving her hands over her mouth. Her tears seared her cheeks. She'd just sent away the man she loved, and in her heart she knew she'd never meet another man like Jack again.

CHAPTER TWENTY-EIGHT

SOPHIE RETURNED TO the beach, where she expected to find everyone gathered around Olivia and Rafe still congratulating them. Instead, she felt she'd walked into the middle of a cyclone.

Blankets and towels were being whisked into the air, twirling sand spirals in their wake. Beau barked at Annie and Timmy, who were picking up their pails and toys, while Sarah put away the food. Nate raced across the sand toward the parking lot, while Liz leaned against Gabe. Was he holding her upright?

Mrs. Beabots, normally the most sane person in a crisis, was handing Liz a towel.

"Liz?" Sophie asked. "What's going on?"

"My water broke."

"She's having a baby!" Mica shouted, handing Gina a basket of food. Rafe had grabbed the cooler. "We have to get her to the hospital."

"Not right this second!" Liz grimaced in pain. She dropped the towel and pressed both hands to her stomach. "Oh, Gabe!"

From what Sophie could see, the entire entourage of capable, take-charge Barzonni men were all out of their element.

"We gotta get her to the car!" Gabe yelled.

"Carry her, idiot," Rafe shouted.

Gabe hoisted Liz into his strong arms and shouted to Mica. "Where's your camera? We wanted a video, remember?"

"Be careful with her. She's precious cargo!" Mica exclaimed and started to record on his iPhone.

Mrs. Beabots looked to Sophie. "I've never had children. I haven't the slightest what to do."

"Nobody panic," Sophie said calmly but firmly. "Has the pain passed?" she asked Liz.

Liz nodded as Sarah took her other arm and Maddie brought up a stack of folded towels.

"Now, let's walk to the car," Sophie suggested. "Gabe, check your watch and let's time how far apart the contractions are. If her water just broke, they could start coming quickly."

Nate raced up, one flip-flop in his hand, one on his foot. "Car's running. Let's hurry."

Sophie shook her head, resolving that she'd never have a video when she gave birth. Someday.

Thankfully, Liz made it to the car before the next pain hit.

"We'll see you all at the hospital. Hurry!"

"Oh, my heavens!" Gina slapped her hands against her cheeks and buried her face in Sam's shoulder. "We're going to be grandparents."

"You ride with me. I'll check that we've gotten everything from the beach," Sam offered.

"No!" Mica said, turning off his phone. "Rafe and I will gather it all and put it in my truck. You guys get to the hospital. Help Gabe if he needs it."

Sophie took Mrs. Beabots's arm. "I'll drive you home."

"You'll do no such thing! We're going straight to that hospital and we're not leaving till the baby is born. We're family. And that's what family does."

Sophie didn't argue.

By the time they all traipsed through the ER entrance, Liz had been taken up to Delivery. They crowded into the elevator, with only Luke, who had taken Beau home, missing from their ranks. Sarah held Annie and Timmy's hands.

"This is really cool," Annie said, grinning up at Sarah.

"Yeah, when can we have a baby brother?" Timmy asked.

"Sister," Annie argued.

Sarah stifled a smile.

When the elevator doors opened, Gabe was emerging from Liz's room.

"Rafe! Mica! Mom! Everybody!" he shouted, rushing up to them. "You won't believe this, but Liz says she's been in labor since this morning and didn't tell me because she didn't want to miss Rafe's proposal. She said it was too romantic to miss." His dumbfounded expression said it all, Sophie thought.

"The doctor's in there. I'm going back in." He shot Mica a stern look. "And no, Mica, Liz decided not to film the birth."

Sophie suppressed a chuckle. "I know just where to get some half-decent coffee."

"I'll come with you," Maddie said. "We'll need extra carriers with this group. Sarah, you want juice boxes for the kids?"

"Please," Sarah replied.

Sophie and Maddie went to the cafeteria and ordered coffees, waters, sandwiches for the kids and a fruit plate for everyone to share.

"So, you disappeared with Jack and then he didn't come back." Maddie ventured a guess. "Is everything okay between you two?"

"Between us?"

"Yeah. You know. Like did you have a fight?"

Sophie wasn't sure how to answer. They hadn't fought. They hadn't made up. They'd dissolved.

Maddie pressed further. "Sophie, I'd have to be blind not to see that you've got it bad for Jack. Katia says he's crazy about you, too."

"She does? He's never said a word."

"Yeah. I know a lot of guys like that. I now happen to be related to a bunch of them." She laughed. "The stories I could tell you about Barzonni men…" She waved her hand to shake off the tangent. "So, about Jack. Can you fix it?"

"I don't know." Sophie felt another painful fissure open in her heart that no suture could mend.

SOPHIE HAD FOUND a children's magazine in the family lounge and was reading a story to Annie and Timmy when Gabe flung the door to Liz's room open. "It's a boy! Come on, everybody! Come see my son!"

As they all jumped to their feet, Sophie was struck with the thought that this was joy. For days she'd been mired in grief, but life went on. And with life came blessings and joy. And love.

"What's the baby's name?" Mrs. Beabots asked as they all pushed past Gabe to go inside.

"Angelo Ezekiel. After my dad. Mom was always big on angel names for her sons, too. We thought we'd carry on the tradition."

Mrs. Beabots nodded approvingly. "I like that."

Sophie stood with the magazine in her hand. Slowly, she dropped it and turned to leave.

"Hey!" Gabe said. "Sophie. Where're you going?"

Pointing her thumb over her shoulder she said, "I should head out."

"No way. Come see my boy. You're family now."

Sophie's face crumpled and her tears didn't have a chance to well up. They just fell. Friendship, coming from Gabe. The guy she'd once flirted with so brazenly. Whose brother she'd pursued, as well. "Are you sure? That you want me in there?"

He walked over to her with a smile on his face that could have broken through the darkest night. "I'm sure. So is Liz. We all are." He put his arm around her shoulder. "You're a good friend, Sophie."

"So are you, Gabe."

They walked arm and arm into a room so crowded with love, Sophie knew she was right where she was meant to be.

CHAPTER TWENTY-NINE

JACK CARTER HAD never liked the word *no*. His mother told him that even when he was a toddler, she'd had the battle of the century with him each time she'd used the word. Barry claimed that Jack was a stellar salesman because he never took "no" for an answer. In fact, Jack started his own company because the corporations he'd worked for had tried to pigeonhole him. Tell him "no." He pushed harder and longer for just about everything because he was arrogant enough to defy anyone who tried to stop him from getting what he wanted.

And Jack wanted Sophie.

She wanted support from him and she hadn't seen it. Through Sophie, Jack had come to see things in another light. He'd blamed Sophie and Greg Fulton for Aleah's death for too long. He'd blamed himself and had been tormented by grief. It had to end. Period. Jack wanted a full life...a life that included Sophie.

He started by walking into the Recovery Alliance with a sheaf of papers under his arm. "I'm here to see Eleanor," he said to a teenaged volunteer who was placing brochures on a table.

"She's in her office. I'll show you," she said. "I'm Mindy, by the way."

"Jack Carter," he said, suddenly humble as he noticed a group of people sitting at the far end of the room talking in quiet tones, intent on each other. These were the people who needed help—his help. He felt their compassion for each other and wondered if they were healing. He hoped so.

Jack walked into Eleanor's office and shook her hand as she rose. "Eleanor, I'm Jack Carter. I own Carter and Associates, the insurance agency down the block. I'm very pleased to meet you. Sophie Mattuchi told me you need an umbrella insurance policy for the Alliance."

"Please, sit down. And yes. That's true, but our funds—"

Jack stopped her immediately by placing the folder on the desk. "It's paid for. This year and next. It's my donation to your efforts here. I've come to realize that I've been wrong about a lot of things lately, but what you're doing, Eleanor, is admirable. You and all the volunteers need the backing of the entire town. I'm just one guy right now, but I want to help."

Eleanor threw her hands over her mouth. Her eyes filled with tears. "I don't know what to say! Mr. Carter, thank you. So very much!"

"Call me Jack. I'm here for anything else you need." He reached in his jacket pocket and took out an envelope. "I'm just getting my feet on the ground myself with my business, but as time goes on, I can do better. For now, this should help keep the lights on."

Eleanor didn't open the envelope. Her eyes were glued on Jack. She was speechless.

"I'd also like a couple of those posters to put in my windows. I'm told I have the best visibility in town." He grinned widely.

"You do at that, Jack." Eleanor smiled. "I'll get them for you."

SOPHIE SAT IN Emory Wills's office, wondering if the president's scowl could possibly get any deeper.

She knew why she was here. The fork in her road demanded a decision. She knew her deepest passion was to help addicts recover, but she'd worked too hard and too long for her position at the hospital to let it go without a fight.

Emory folded his hands over his stomach. "I assume you're aware of why I asked for this meeting."

"Sir, I believe it's about Jeremy Hawthorne. I was his sponsor through the Recovery Alliance," she admitted, so he didn't have to accuse her.

Emory raised his eyebrow. "And the coroner is calling it a suicide since his housemate found a note. Did you know that?"

"No, sir."

"We received a report from Trent Davis at the police department. For all intents and purposes, the case is closed. Cut and dry."

Sophie swallowed. "But not for me. Am I being fired?" Better to get it over with.

"Sophie, you have to understand the position you put me and the hospital in. Because you were his sponsor, the expectation is that you would have been able to do something. Counsel him—"

"Save him?"

He shook his head. "No one on staff would think that. But ordinary, nonmedical people believe those things. And those people might try to sue the hospital. That's why I have rules in place that staff members here are not to align themselves with non-hospital-affiliated institutions and groups. This is Indian Lake, Sophie. A small town where people talk. We'll never know if Jeremy would have taken his life under other circumstances, in another town. But do you understand my position?"

"Yes, sir. I do."

"I don't want to fire you, Sophie. Dr. Caldwell and Dr. Barzonni came to me to plead your case. They don't want to lose you. If you can promise me that you will end your work with the Alliance, then I won't fire you."

Sophie had known this day would come from

the first moment she'd agreed to help Eleanor. As much as her passion was to help Eleanor and her clients, Sophie's parents had sacrificed all their lives to give her an expensive education. She couldn't let them down. Nor could she abandon Dr. Caldwell and Nate, who'd come to her defense. Her cardiac and ER patients needed her, too. Perhaps someday she'd find a way to do everything, but today she had to make a choice.

"I'll stay with the hospital, sir."

Emory rose and extended his hand. "You're an asset to this hospital, Sophie. I'm proud of you."

Sophie left the office and closed the door softly. She didn't feel victorious. She was sad. She'd had high expectations for all she could do with the Alliance. She'd wanted so desperately to matter. But in the end, she knew where her expertise lay. And if she wasn't stretched so thin, she'd be an even better nurse for all the people who counted on her.

After stepping off the elevator, she passed the ER, feeling the ghosts of Aleah and Jeremy. It was more than grief that caused her sadness, she realized; it was also the empty place in her heart where Jack had been.

JACK ENTERED EMORY WILLS'S office and found the man pacing in front of the large window. Midday sun streamed across the wood floor, striking dust motes.

"This isn't my day, Jack," Emory said without turning around.

"Sorry?"

"I just went to the Indian Lake Deli for lunch and saw posters for the Recovery Alliance in your windows. I thought we talked about this."

Jack opened his folder. "We did. I'm ignoring you because I think you're wrong." He relished the feeling of taking this stand. He took out the policies he and Katia had painstakingly put together.

Carter and Associates needed Emory's endorsement and recommendation to acquire other Indiana hospitals' insurance business. Jack knew he could be tossing those opportunities away by defying the president. But right was right. Sophie had shown him that. He also wanted to prove to Sophie that he was on her side.

"What?" Emory spun around.

"I've looked into the Alliance and what they're doing, and I don't see where you're coming from with your rules. I'd never be so presumptuous as to tell you how to run your hospital, but they have a valid place in our community and I'm already supporting them. If you considered the bigger picture, you'd see the hospital actually could support them. No laws broken. You could form a partnership. There are all kinds of ways to go about this, if you'd open your mind to it. And I'm willing to help with any liability issues. No extra charge."

Emory's pursed lips were white and his scowl told Jack he'd been shot down. Rejected. "Jack, this meeting is over."

"That's fine, Emory. I've drawn up these policies for you and I assure you my quotes are the best you'll ever see for the coverage I'm offering. I'm saving you a great deal of money. If there's any truth to the rumor that other hospital chains are looking to acquire you, you might want to show them these."

Emory appeared stoic and immovable. The man had dug in his heels. Jack had always relied on his gifts of persuasion to sway clients, but this was more than a sales pitch. It was the right thing to do for everyone involved. Jack deeply believed Sophie would eventually make a difference with her efforts. He wanted to share in that kind of satisfaction. It felt good to help the Alliance and their clients. He knew that now.

"Listen, Emory. There're a lot of needs in this town. You can't do it all. The hospital can't, either. Nor can I alone. But, thanks to a certain employee of yours, Sophie Mattuchi, I've learned that I can do what I can do. Maybe if I'm lucky, I'll have an impact."

Emory stared at the folder and gave his head a slight shake. "I don't see it."

Jack slid the policy closer to Emory. "Listen, you helped me a great deal when I came to town. Many of your employees are my clients. I'm a loyal kind of guy and I like to pay back when I can." Jack held out his hand. "I like doing business with you, Emory. I hope you change your mind."

Emory looked Jack in the eye. "It's not that simple. Right now, I don't think it's likely, Jack."

"Well, I'm sorry about that." Jack shoved his hands in his pockets, still refusing to accept defeat. He'd leave the folder. Jack wanted to believe there was still hope. He turned to go and stopped. "Emory, think over what I said about the Alliance. Please."

"See you at Rotary, Jack."

Jack gave him a crisp nod and left.

THE BACKS OF the silver maple leaves glinted in the setting sun as Sophie pushed herself around the running trail. The west wind whipped across the top of the lake, turning small whitecaps into beckoning waves. The first chill of autumn teased the air and already Sophie mourned the end of summer. With summer's passing, she would have to admit to the end of her romance with Jack.

It had only been a little over a week since she'd sent Jack away, and she'd never felt so empty or so alone. How was it possible that before she'd met Jack, she hadn't minded coming home after a long day and simply curling up with a book? She hadn't minded walks to The Louise House by herself. She hadn't minded that her phone sat dormant except for calls from her mother.

Everything was different now. It was as if the sun had lost half its warmth. Her days were longer—and her nights. The nights were interminable. All she did was think of Jack, and if she actually managed to fall asleep, she dreamed of him.

Sophie blew out the heaviness in her chest. It seemed impossible to miss his silly selfies of Frenchie, but each day that passed without some crazy photo, another hole opened up inside her. Most of all, Sophie missed the way Jack would look at her as if she were the only woman in the world.

Maybe he'd loved her. But not enough to support her the way she needed.

One thing she knew for sure was that despite all her nursing education and experience with cardiac care, she didn't have the first clue how to heal her own heart.

Sophie raced past Jack's condo and peered up through the trees, only to see his empty deck. No one to wave to. No one to notice her passing by.

Sophie reached her car and checked her fitness tracker. Three miles in eighteen minutes and five seconds was still a good run. Not her personal best, but she'd take it.

She unlocked the car and saw a missed call from Mrs. Beabots. She grabbed her phone and called her landlady back.

"Hi, Mrs. Beabots. I saw that you called…No. I'm out at the lake. Is there something you need?… Sure. Sure. I can stop and pick up some ice cream for you…Oh, Louise has it ready? That's nice… Sure. I'll tell her to put it on your bill…Okay. See you in a bit."

Sophie pulled on her black velour zip jacket with silver cords down the sleeves. The nip in the air was just enough to give her a chill. She yanked the clip out of her hair and fluffed her waves, knowing the sweat would dry momentarily.

She used a baby wipe to clean her face and glanced at the cloth. Apparently she hadn't quite cried off all her mascara.

When she reached The Louise House, Sophie was surprised to find the place full, considering the cooler temperatures outside. Then she noticed the chalkboard sign announcing that Louise's pumpkin and gingersnap ice cream was back.

Now Sophie knew why Mrs. Beabots wanted ice cream tonight.

"Hi, Louise," Sophie said with a little wave as she walked up to the counter. "I understand Mrs. Beabots called in an order. I'm here to pick it up."

"Huh?" Louise cocked her head. "She did?"

"Uh, yes. I assumed it was for the pumpkin ice cream. If she forgot to order it, could you scoop up a pint for her?"

"Sure, honey." Louise smiled broadly. "Tell you what. Why don't you have a seat? I have another recipe I'm trying out on my favorite patrons. Would you be willing to taste my gingerbread and brownie ice cream for me?"

"Sure," Sophie replied. "Anything to help."

Louise glanced toward the glassed-in candy shelves. "There's a spot over there. That table."

Sophie followed her gaze and saw Jack standing up, staring at her with an apprehensive smile on his lips.

She started to turn away.

Jack bolted toward her. "Sophie. Don't go," he said loud enough for everyone in the room to hear. "I need—"

He was at her side in two more strides. Long strides. Purposeful ones.

"What, Jack? What do you need?"

"I have to tell you something. It can't wait." He took her elbow, urging her toward his table.

She looked around the room. People were staring at them. "Jack." She shook her head. "I don't think—"

"I love you," he said. Loudly.

"You what?"

"I love you."

Was this happening? She continued shaking her head. "No, Jack. You don't."

"Yes, Sophie. I do. And I'm not afraid or too embarrassed to say it front of everyone here. Complete strangers, by the way."

He put both his hands on her shoulders, pulled her to him and kissed her. It was a lingering kiss, soft and committal. It promised forever. It was the most exciting, endearing and loving kiss she'd ever received in her life. She knew absolutely that she couldn't live through another wrenching breakup with him.

But they would have to part.

They had to.

"Jack." She breathed his name as their lips parted.

"Sophie." He rested his cheek against hers, his breath feathering her ear. "Hear me out. Stay."

The fight had gone out of her. "Okay, Jack."

Jack held her hand as he led the way to his table. He pulled out the antique ice-cream chair for her and when she sat, he kissed the top of her head.

"I thought about what you said to me. And you were right, Sophie. How could you ever trust and respect a man who didn't support you and your beliefs?"

Sophie opened her mouth to respond, but he placed his fingertips over her lips.

"I was a little slow on the uptake, and I blamed you and Greg Fulton for Aleah's death. Then I blamed myself. I was wrong. My guilt got in the way of us. I've forgiven myself, and I know I'm not completely healed, but I'm a work in progress." He took a deep breath. "What I'm trying to say, Sophie, is that I've put a few things into action that I think will help people like Jeremy. I gave Eleanor that policy you asked me for. I also told Eleanor I'll contribute in any way I can."

"You didn't? You did?"

"Did." He smiled and touched her cheek. "I also went to Emory, and he's finally agreed to help underwrite the Recovery Alliance and to do away with his rules. He'll tell you himself, but if you can work the hours out, he'll let you continue volunteering for Eleanor."

"Jack, is this true?"

"Uh-huh."

Sophie had to make an effort to shut her gaping mouth. She was staring at a hero. Her hero.

Sophie rested her cheek in his palm. "This is too much. I mean, you accomplished something that Eleanor has been trying to do for so long. So have others."

Sophie felt her heart open. She savored his touch, the sincerity in his eyes. She'd missed him.

"Jack, you're amazing. I'm stunned. It's going to take me a bit to absorb all of this."

"Don't take too long," he teased. "Sophie…"

"Jack, stop. I need to say something and I'm going to bumble it because I've never felt this way—ever. I love you, Jack. There I said it. Didn't I? Did it come out right?"

"Yes…" he croaked. She could have sworn his eyes misted up.

"I love you," she repeated. "I have for quite some time, actually. I didn't think I'd ever find love. And then came you. Everything changed." She leaned so close, their noses nearly touched. "Am I making any sense at all?"

"Perfect sense," he replied, but before he could finish his thought, Louise came over and placed two sundaes in front of them.

"Try yours first, Sophie. I think you're going to like it." Louise winked at Jack and gave them both spoons.

Jack leaned in even closer. "Promise me that the next time I act like a pompous fool, you won't break up with me? I never want to be without you."

"I promise." She smiled. With all her cardiac training, Sophie knew that a heart could not melt. It was a muscle. Strong. Vibrant. Powerful. But something was happening inside her that science couldn't explain.

In this moment, she felt she understood every love poem she'd ever read. She'd thought those kinds of declarations were silly. Immature. But now she realized she'd been cynical, thinking she was protecting herself. She didn't want to be safe anymore. She wanted to be adventurous, even foolhardy. She wanted to give everything to Jack.

Sophie took his hand and pressed it to her cheek. "Can you forgive me?"

"I already have," he said, kissing her lightly on the lips. "Now, eat your ice cream and let's talk about going apple picking this weekend."

Sophie stuck her spoon into the mound of whipped cream. "Apple picking? That's what you want to do?"

"Sure. Why not? I'll do anything you want. Watch a movie. Go to the city to see a play…"

"How about I make a real Italian dinner for us and we play with Frenchie?" she suggested, bringing the spoon to her mouth.

Suddenly, she stopped. Her spoon felt too heavy for whipped cream.

"What in the world?" Sophie studied the spoon. No doubt about it, there was a foreign object in her whipped cream. "Louise is getting careless. Looks like a pop-top fell in here."

"No way," Jack said, taking the spoon from her. He pushed the whipped cream away with his finger. "Hmm. Nope. Doesn't look like a pop-top. Looks like—"

Sophie's breath caught in her lungs, and for a

second she couldn't speak. "That's...that's a diamond ring."

"Looks like it." Jack grinned, holding the ring out to Sophie. "I couldn't take the chance you'd break up with me again, so I figured I needed insurance. I thought this might do the trick. I love you with all my heart, Sophie Mattuchi. Will you marry me?"

"Yes!" She threw her arms around his neck. When she pressed her lips against his, she felt as if she'd been lifted to a realm filled with more joy than she'd ever thought she had a right to know.

Everyone in the ic-cream parlor broke into thunderous applause. Louise put on her princess hat and danced a jig.

Sophie reluctantly ended the kiss and took in the happy faces all around them.

"I thought you said you'd never do this in front of a crowd."

"I told you. I had to rethink things. I changed my mind. How'd I do?"

"Oh, Jack, it was perfect. The best surprise of my life."

Jack held her face in his hands and kissed her again. "Believe me, Sophie. I have so many surprises in store for you. This is only the beginning."

* * * * *

LARGER-PRINT BOOKS!

**GET 2 FREE
LARGER-PRINT NOVELS
PLUS 2 FREE
MYSTERY GIFTS**

Love Inspired®
SUSPENSE
RIVETING INSPIRATIONAL ROMANCE

Larger-print novels are now available...

YES! Please send me 2 FREE LARGER-PRINT Love Inspired® Suspense novels and my 2 FREE mystery gifts (gifts are worth about $10). After receiving them, if I don't wish to receive any more books, I can return the shipping statement marked "cancel." If I don't cancel, I will receive 4 brand-new novels every month and be billed just $5.49 per book in the U.S. or $5.99 per book in Canada. That's a savings of at least 19% off the cover price. It's quite a bargain! Shipping and handling is just 50¢ per book in the U.S. and 75¢ per book in Canada.* I understand that accepting the 2 free books and gifts places me under no obligation to buy anything. I can always return a shipment and cancel at any time. Even if I never buy another book, the two free books and gifts are mine to keep forever.

110/310 IDN GH6P

Name	(PLEASE PRINT)	
Address		Apt. #
City	State/Prov.	Zip/Postal Code

Signature (if under 18, a parent or guardian must sign)

Mail to the Reader Service:
IN U.S.A.: P.O. Box 1867, Buffalo, NY 14240-1867
IN CANADA: P.O. Box 609, Fort Erie, Ontario L2A 5X3

**Are you a current subscriber to Love Inspired® Suspense books
and want to receive the larger-print edition?
Call 1-800-873-8635 or visit www.ReaderService.com.**

* Terms and prices subject to change without notice. Prices do not include applicable taxes. Sales tax applicable in N.Y. Canadian residents will be charged applicable taxes. Offer not valid in Quebec. This offer is limited to one order per household. Not valid for current subscribers to Love Inspired Suspense larger-print books. All orders subject to credit approval. Credit or debit balances in a customer's account(s) may be offset by any other outstanding balance owed by or to the customer. Please allow 4 to 6 weeks for delivery. Offer available while quantities last.

Your Privacy—The Reader Service is committed to protecting your privacy. Our Privacy Policy is available online at www.ReaderService.com or upon request from the Reader Service.

We make a portion of our mailing list available to reputable third parties that offer products we believe may interest you. If you prefer that we not exchange your name with third parties, or if you wish to clarify or modify your communication preferences, please visit us at www.ReaderService.com/consumerschoice or write to us at Reader Service Preference Service, P.O. Box 9062, Buffalo, NY 14240-9062. Include your complete name and address.

LISLP15

YES! Please send me **The Western Promises Collection** in Larger Print. This collection begins with 3 FREE books and 2 FREE gifts (gifts valued at approx. $14.00 retail) in the first shipment, along with the other first 4 books from the collection! If I do not cancel, I will receive 8 monthly shipments until I have the entire 51-book Western Promises collection. I will receive 2 or 3 FREE books in each shipment and I will pay just $4.99 US/ $5.89 CDN for each of the other four books in each shipment, plus $2.99 for shipping and handling per shipment. *If I decide to keep the entire collection, I'll have paid for only 32 books, because 19 books are FREE! I understand that accepting the 3 free books and gifts places me under no obligation to buy anything. I can always return a shipment and cancel at any time. My free books and gifts are mine to keep no matter what I decide.

272 HCN 3070 472 HCN 3070

Name _____ (PLEASE PRINT)

Address _____ Apt. #

City _____ State/Prov. _____ Zip/Postal Code

Signature (if under 18, a parent or guardian must sign)

Mail to the **Reader Service:**

IN U.S.A.: P.O. Box 1867, Buffalo, NY 14240-1867
IN CANADA: P.O. Box 609, Fort Erie, Ontario L2A 5X3

* Terms and prices subject to change without notice. Prices do not include applicable taxes. Sales tax applicable in N.Y. Canadian residents will be charged applicable taxes. This offer is limited to one order per household. All orders subject to approval. Credit or debit balances in a customer's account(s) may be offset by any other outstanding balance owed by or to the customer. Please allow 4 to 6 weeks for delivery. Offer available while quantities last. Offer not available to Quebec residents.

LARGER-PRINT BOOKS!
GET 2 FREE LARGER-PRINT NOVELS PLUS
2 FREE GIFTS!

HARLEQUIN®

super romance®

More Story...More Romance

YES! Please send me 2 FREE LARGER-PRINT Harlequin® Superromance® novels and my 2 FREE gifts (gifts are worth about $10). After receiving them, if I don't wish to receive any more books, I can return the shipping statement marked "cancel." If I don't cancel, I will receive 4 brand-new novels every month and be billed just $5.94 per book in the U.S. or $6.24 per book in Canada. That's a savings of at least 12% off the cover price! It's quite a bargain! Shipping and handling is just 50¢ per book in the U.S. or 75¢ per book in Canada.* I understand that accepting the 2 free books and gifts places me under no obligation to buy anything. I can always return a shipment and cancel at any time. Even if I never buy another book, the two free books and gifts are mine to keep forever.

132/332 HDN GHVC

Name	(PLEASE PRINT)
Address	Apt. #
City	State/Prov.	Zip/Postal Code

Signature (if under 18, a parent or guardian must sign)

Mail to the **Reader Service:**
IN U.S.A.: P.O. Box 1867, Buffalo, NY 14240-1867
IN CANADA: P.O. Box 609, Fort Erie, Ontario L2A 5X3

Want to try two free books from another line?
Call 1-800-873-8635 today or visit www.ReaderService.com.

* Terms and prices subject to change without notice. Prices do not include applicable taxes. Sales tax applicable in N.Y. Canadian residents will be charged applicable taxes. Offer not valid in Quebec. This offer is limited to one order per household. Not valid for current subscribers to Harlequin Superromance Larger-Print books. All orders subject to credit approval. Credit or debit balances in a customer's account(s) may be offset by any other outstanding balance owed by or to the customer. Please allow 4 to 6 weeks for delivery. Offer available while quantities last.

Your Privacy—The Reader Service is committed to protecting your privacy. Our Privacy Policy is available online at www.ReaderService.com or upon request from the Reader Service.

We make a portion of our mailing list available to reputable third parties that offer products we believe may interest you. If you prefer that we not exchange your name with third parties, or if you wish to clarify or modify your communication preferences, please visit us at www.ReaderService.com/consumerchoice or write to us at Reader Service Preference Service, P.O. Box 9062, Buffalo, NY 14240-9062. Include your complete name and address.